DESPERATE
PASTORS' WIVES

Ginger Kolbaba & Christy Scannell

DESPERATE PASTORS' WIVES

A Novel

HOWARD
Fiction

A DIVISION OF SIMON & SCHUSTER
New York · London · Toronto · Sydney

SECRETS FROM
LULU'S
CAFE
SERIES

Our purpose at Howard Books is to:
- *Increase faith* in the hearts of growing Christians
- *Inspire holiness* in the lives of believers
- *Instill hope* in the hearts of struggling people everywhere

Because He's coming again!

Published by Howard Books, a division of Simon & Schuster, Inc.
1230 Avenue of the Americas, New York, NY 10020
www.howardpublishing.com

Desperate Pastors' Wives © 2007 by Ginger Kolbaba and Christy Scannell

Library of Congress Cataloging-in-Publication Data
Kolbaba, Ginger.
    Desperate pastors' wives / Ginger Kolbaba and Christy Scannell.
        p. cm. — (Secrets from Lulu's Café series)
    10 Digit ISBN: 1-58229-632-4; 13 Digit ISBN: 978-1-58229-632-6
    1. Spouses of clergy—Fiction. 2. Wives—Fiction. 3. Female friendship—Fiction. 4. Coffee shops—Fiction. I. Scannell, Christy, 1967 - II. Title.

PS3611.O5825D47 2007
813'.6—dc22

2006049727

10 9 8 7 6 5 4 3 2 1

HOWARD colophon is a registered trademark of Simon & Schuster, Inc.

Manufactured in the United States of America

For information regarding special discounts for bulk purchases, please contact Simon & Schuster Special Sales at 1-800-456-6798 or business@simonandschuster.com.

Edited by Ramona Cramer Tucker
Interior design by Tennille Paden
Cover design by Kirk DouPonce

Scripture quotations are taken from the *Holy Bible, New International Version®*. NIV®. Copyright© 1973, 1978, 1984 by International Bible Society. Used by permission of Zondervan Publishing House. All rights reserved.

To my mom, Genny McFarland:
You're the best pastor's wife I know.
Thanks for showing me what living authentically before God is all about.
Ginger

To Judy Bradley:
My favorite pastor's wife!
Christy

To all pastors' wives:
Wow, what a calling you have!
May you find God's blessings on your life, your family, and your work.
We are in awe of you.
The Authors

Acknowledgments

To the pastors' wives we interviewed: we were so touched by your vulnerability and candidness. We hope we did you proud with these women's stories, which are inspired by your compelling real-life stories.

To Ramona Cramer Tucker: thanks for helping us get this project off the ground!

To Philis and Denny Boultinghouse: you are two of our favorite people (even if you hadn't contracted for our book). You've been such encouragers—and your compassion, godliness, and sense of humor rock!

To Billie Wilson and the Florida Christian Writers' Conference: it was your annual conference where we met several years ago and developed a friendship, and where we later conceived the idea for this series. (And, yes, you can quote us in the brochure!)

And last, but not least, to our husbands, Scott Kolbaba and Rich Scannell: as they say at the Oscars, "you are our everything." Seriously, you've put up with a lot while we've been tucked away in our offices typing frantically on this novel. We love you . . . and we owe you big-time.

Prologue

"Where we goin', Mommy?" four-year-old Megan Plaisance asked as she and her mother, Mimi, sat at a red light heading out of town.

Mimi sighed. What she really wished she could tell her daughter was that she was escaping for an afternoon of peace. But that wasn't the case now that Megan was in the car. An hour earlier, Mimi had called Gladys, her trusted sixty-seven-year-old babysitter, to confirm her babysitting "date." But Gladys's husband, Wesley, had answered the phone and told Mimi that Gladys was in the throes of a kidney stone. He didn't think she'd be up for watching a feisty four-year-old.

Ever the controlled person, Mimi had simply thanked Wesley, said she hoped Gladys felt better soon, then hung up. Inside, though, she'd wanted to yell, "One stinking afternoon—that's all I ask for! I have to get away!" Instead she had sighed heavily, turned to Megan, and told her to get her coloring books together. They were going on an adventure.

Now Mimi glanced in the rearview mirror at Megan, who was in her

1

car seat. "We're going to have lunch at Lulu's Café," she said finally, trying to sound excited.

At least her other two children were in school, but Megan was underfoot. Constantly. And while Mimi loved Megan dearly—as she loved all her children equally, she was always clear to point out—she really, *really* needed a break. And not just a break from the kids. A break from the house, the church. But mostly a break from Red River, the community where if you took out your garbage, everybody knew it.

And now she had a backseat tagalong on her only sanity outing for the next two weeks. As a Rich Mullins's song played on the radio, Megan looked out the window and belted out the lyrics, *"Our God is an awesome God . . ."*

Mimi bit her lip, wondering what the other women were going to say when they saw Megan.

Nearly a year ago, when Mimi and the other three pastors' wives—PWs, as they called themselves—started getting together for lunch, part of their agreement had been no children. Just the four PWs, away from Red River and every busybody who lived there.

But what was Mimi supposed to do? She couldn't leave Megan with her husband, Mark. He was at the church preparing his Sunday sermon. Gladys was not an option. And Mimi didn't want to call anyone from the church. She was afraid they'd ask her questions about where she was going.

Either Mimi missed this week's outing, or Megan had to come with her. And of everything she was involved in, these every-other-week get-togethers were the one time she felt calm and relaxed. The PWs' lunch seemed to be the only thing keeping her sane nowadays. Mimi was desperate for peace.

Mouthing "lunch appointment" and pointing at the clock, Felicia Lopez-Morrison zipped by her always-on-the-phone secretary—who acknowledged Felicia with a nod as she handed her a folder—and practically jogged to her car.

Okay, lunch with the girls, Felicia thought as she mentally ran through the rest of her day. *Then back to the office to get Jim's contract written, then . . .*

The thought of her new client stopped Felicia as she stuck the key into the door of her cobalt blue BMW Z4. How would she tell her pastor-husband, Dave, that she'd been hired to do PR for a bar owner who was being sued for "overserving" a patron who was now in prison on vehicular manslaughter charges? What kind of pastor's wife would try to improve the image of a bar, for goodness' sake?

"*This* pastor's wife!" Felicia said defiantly as she opened the car door and got in the driver's seat.

She'd always been confident in her career. But now, while she drove, a familiar frustration began to smother that confidence. Was she doing the right thing by taking on this particular client? Although Felicia was savvy at balancing the demands of her career with her home life (she thought so, anyway), the last year of her added role as a pastor's wife had really begun to wear on her. The PWs' forty-mile drive away from Red River for lunch was one symptom of that growing conflict.

Why does the church think they got a two-for-one when they hired Dave? she wondered. *I certainly don't see a First Baptist Church paycheck with my name on it every month. And why doesn't anybody seem to understand that I like having a career?*

Felicia sighed. She'd talk it over at lunch. The girls would understand. They always did.

Maybe they were the only ones who could understand how much she wanted to realize all of her ambitions as a wife, mother, professional, *and* pastor's wife. Felicia was desperate for fulfillment.

Jennifer Shores sat quietly on a bench outside the diner as she waited for the others to arrive. She glanced at her watch.

11:40.

Jennifer had purposely left the church office early so she could have a few minutes to herself before the girls arrived at noon. After listening to Greta Hamlin, a forty-two-year-old mother of two teens, who was now eight months along with her oops-baby, go on and on about her aching back as she helped fold church bulletins, Jennifer was ready for some silence.

She chuckled as she remembered catching the rolling eyes of Sam, her husband and the church's pastor, as he eased his office door shut to put a barrier between him and the chattering Greta.

Jennifer leaned her head back, stretching her neck. She breathed in the clean May air. Every year she had been witness to Ohio's consistent springs that seamlessly moved from rainy and cool to sunny and warm. She found this year's promise of spring even more comforting than normal, perhaps because it was the one thing she knew would not let her down. She couldn't say that about much else in her life these days—except Sam. Yet even that relationship wasn't so rosy after the disappointments they had shared.

Anger rose from deep within. Why was it that she couldn't have the *one thing* she wanted—more than anything else? She blamed God for not answering her prayer, her only prayer, for the last several years.

Fine, she thought. *If God doesn't want to help me, maybe I won't help him either.*

Jennifer pictured Sam in the pulpit, glancing over at her with smiling eyes as he shared yet another bad warmup joke before he launched into his sermon.

How can I possibly tell Sam I don't want to go to church anymore?

Just then Felicia's car pulled into a space near hers. Jennifer erased the worry off her face—a PW skill she had learned early on—smiled, and waved.

Dare she share these dark thoughts with the girls at lunch today? Could they understand what she was going through? That she—a *pastor's wife*—was losing her trust in God?

Jennifer was desperate for faith.

Lisa Barton glanced at her watch and pushed her foot harder against the accelerator. She was going to be late. She hated to be late to anything, but especially to her lunches with the PWs.

She glanced in the rearview mirror at her eyes. *Yep, I knew it.* They were puffy and red. Maybe if she rolled down the window, the brisk wind would ease some of the swelling.

She never thought life would be this way.

Even though this past year with her newfound friends had been the best year she could remember, she still felt uneasy telling them everything about her life. *What would they think of me?* she wondered whenever she imagined telling them her secret. *Would they abandon me too? They'd probably say they understood, but would they . . . really? Or would they secretly judge me—like everyone else in my life?*

No, she had decided each time she had considered telling them the truth. *I can't chance it.*

After all, these PWs were the only women who seemed to like her—to accept her for who she was. At least the "who" she revealed in front of them.

Now, if only Joel would do the same . . .

Lisa's eyes welled again with tears. She was desperate for love.

CHAPTER

1

Lulu's Café

Tuesday, May 2
12:07 p.m.

"Sorry I'm late," Lisa said breathlessly as she rushed to the three women seated in a cozy booth toward the back of Lulu's Café. Lulu's was a small dive in Cheeksville, a quaint four-red-light town in the rolling hills of southwestern Ohio, forty miles from Red River.

She slid in next to Felicia, dressed as usual in a business suit, and across from Jennifer and Mimi.

"Hey, Lisa, we were wondering if you got to praising the Lord and lost track of time," Jennifer said with a laugh.

Lisa grinned. Her husband was pastor of the Red River Assembly of God, known for its drum-thumping, guitar-playing, hand-waving worship services. She plopped her purse under the table, pushing the strap onto her knee. "Well, I'll tell ya, we did go more than two hours Sunday."

Felicia raised her eyebrows. Her dark eyes shone with intensity. "I can't imagine what would happen at our church if Dave wasn't giving the altar

6

call by 11:45. Every Sunday I see people checking their watches when someone goes forward, as if the roasts in their ovens are more important than that person's salvation."

"That's why I use the timer on my oven," Mimi chimed in, tucking her blond, bobbed hair behind one ear. "I set it to turn off at noon, so even if we get held up doing the pastor-and-wife thing after church, I don't have to worry too much."

Lisa noticed Mimi furrow her brows at the word *worry*.

"That reminds me," Mimi said. "I need to call the oven dealer for service. Our oven's been running hot. I discovered it when the Taylors, a family from the church, were over for dinner three nights ago. The turkey Tetrazzini was crusty. I was so embarrassed."

"Don't worry about it." Jennifer laughed. "I've served more than my share of crusty creations."

Lisa attempted to smile and act chipper, in spite of the morning she'd had. She hoped her hazel eyes didn't reveal that she'd been crying.

Then she caught Jennifer's gaze. Jennifer nonchalantly dabbed under her eyes, then looked again at her.

Lisa got the hint. Evidently the strain of the morning was showing on her face. *Thought I caught everything in the rearview mirror.* She began, nonchalantly she hoped, to wipe under her eyes.

Mimi reached across the table to pat Lisa's arm. "Everything okay?"

"Hmm?"

Mimi mimicked Lisa's under-eye action.

"Oh," Lisa said, trying to act casual. "Allergies."

Out of the corner of her eye, Lisa caught the suspicious glances that shot between Jennifer and Felicia.

"MJ suffers from allergies," Mimi said, evidently missing the exchanged looks. "We can't give him anything for it, though, or he acts like

7

a zombie. I think it affects his inner ears or something. Can you take an antihistamine?"

Felicia rolled her eyes just as Gracie, their waitress, walked to the table and nearly collided with Megan, who was running to the booth from across the room.

"Whoa, there, little one!" Gracie patted Megan on the head and turned her toward Mimi.

"Mom!" Megan whined as she held out two pieces of an orange crayon. "My crayon broke."

Mimi took the pieces and reached into her purse for the plastic sandwich bag filled with crayons, colored pencils, and watercolor markers. "That's okay, sweetheart. Mommy has another one for you." She handed Megan another orange crayon.

Megan skipped back to her table, where her coloring books and crayons were scattered.

Lisa glanced questioningly at Mimi.

"Gladys has kidney stones," Mimi explained with a sigh about her usual babysitter. "And her husband said she didn't look so good. So I had to bring Megan or I couldn't come."

Although the four PWs had made a pact a year ago that no children would be allowed on their lunches at Lulu's, they had mentioned that exceptions—and only rare ones—would be permitted. All agreed that a babysitter with kidney stones qualified.

"Okay, PWs, what is it today?" Gracie asked as she pulled a pen from behind her ear. "Felicia, are you still on that Miami Beach diet or whatever it is? The one where you can't have bread or potatoes, but you can eat a warm slice of apple pie à la mode?"

Felicia playfully hid her eyes as the other three women laughed at Gracie's joke. Gracie had been their waitress the first time they visited Lulu's, so when they made their meetings a biweekly event, they decided always to sit in her station. One day Gracie had overheard their discussion and figured out they were all pastors' wives.

"Y'know, church just ain't for me," she told them at the time. "And I figure if it hasn't been for me in sixty-eight years, it's probably not going to be. But you girls, you're the salt of the earth, as they say, and I know those husbands of yours appreciate what you do. And the Lord too."

"Gracie, I thought you said church isn't for you. Yet you believe in God? Why don't you want to go to church?" Any other person asking that question might have received a turned back for an answer, but Mimi's sweet, honest approach made people feel at ease.

"Ah, girlie, don't take this personal or nothing, but churches are for praying and paying. I can pray at home, and I don't got nothing to use for paying. Besides, all I hear about churches is that this one's splitting up or that one has a pastor who's seeing some other woman or who knows what. Now who wants to be part of that?"

All four women had stared down at the napkins in their laps. They couldn't argue with Gracie's point. After all, the reason they'd started meeting forty miles outside of the community where they all lived and worshiped was to avoid running into people from their churches. Later they'd prayed for Gracie as they blessed their food, but her plain-spoken words stayed with them.

"What's the special today, Gracie?" Jennifer asked as Gracie stood at their table, pen poised, ready to take their order.

"Same as every Tuesday," they all chimed together and started to laugh.

Gracie cocked her head toward Lisa. "Girl, what's the matter with you?" she asked bluntly. "You got troubles with that pastor husband of yours?"

Lisa forced a smile. "No—"

"Oh, Gracie," Mimi interrupted, "she has allergies. Do you have any green tea or something that will make her feel better?"

Lisa cringed inwardly. Mimi always saw the best in everyone and wanted to help. But this time Lisa didn't want any help—or any attention.

"Green tea?" Gracie chuckled. "Honey, this is a family restaurant, not some Starbucks."

"Okay, how about chicken noodle soup then?"

"I'm fine," Lisa said. "Really. I don't need anything special." She just wanted the attention off her. "What's everyone getting today?"

"I'll have that apple pie à la mode." Felicia winked.

Gracie played along. "Well, it does have fruit and calcium. Would you like a chicken Caesar salad with that?"

"You know what I like. Dressing on the side. Hold the croutons—and the pie," Felicia added.

"Megan will have the chicken fingers and fries," said Mimi. "And a chocolate milk. And I'm going to have the burger combo. I've been so hungry lately. I can't seem to get enough food into me."

Jennifer looked up from her menu. "It's that 'I could be pregnant' time of the month again, so I can't have my usual shrimp—no shellfish, they say, just in case. So I'll go with the Reuben, and a milk."

"Okay, and what about you, Miss I-Have-Allergies?"

"Go with the chicken soup," Mimi urged helpfully. "I've had it before. It's really good."

"Isn't chicken soup supposed to be good for *colds*?" Jennifer asked.

"Allergies, colds—it's the same difference."

"Well, I'm not really that hungry," Lisa said. "I'll stick with coffee for now."

After Gracie completed their order, she plodded off to her next table.

Lisa felt the other women's eyes on her.

"Lisa, is everything okay?" Jennifer finally asked. "I'm not buying the allergies thing."

Lisa held her hands to her cheeks. Did they look as warm as they felt? "Really, I'm okay," she insisted, even though she felt horrible for lying to these women who had become so dear to her. "I had a late breakfast anyway."

The others didn't seem convinced, but they let it slide.

Megan ran back over to the booth, this time holding a sheet of paper that had multicolored scribbles all over it. "Here!" she said excitedly as she presented it to Jennifer.

"For me?" Jennifer took the sheet and held it to her chest. "Thank you! I'll keep this forever."

"I'm hungry, Mommy." Megan had obviously moved on.

"I just ordered for us, punkin," Mimi said sweetly.

Megan ran back to her spot to grab another piece of paper.

"You don't have to keep that," Mimi whispered to Jennifer. "She makes hundreds of them."

"What is it?" Jennifer whispered back and held out the picture, turning it on all sides.

"Who knows? We've killed more trees for that girl. I wouldn't be surprised if she becomes an artist."

"Well then, of course I'll keep this. It might be worth a fortune someday."

Megan ran back to their table with another picture and handed it to Lisa.

"Thank you, honey," Lisa said.

Megan tugged on her mother's shirt sleeve. "Mommy, why are we so far away from home just to eat lunch? There are places to eat in Red River."

Mimi pursed her lips as the amused others waited for her response.

"Well, Megan, sometimes it's good to get away and see new things. You know, like when we went to Florida last summer and you got to play at the beach and go on all those rides at Disney World."

"Oooh, does Mickey Mouse come see the kids at this restaurant too?" Megan asked with such excitement that she dropped a crayon and had to dive under the table to retrieve it.

Jennifer leaned out of the booth. "Where's Gracie with that water pitcher?" Then she shot back around, looking half-terrified, half-shocked. "Oh, you guys, it's not Mickey Mouse. But it is the woman with the biggest ears in Red River."

Before anyone could ask "who?" she was at their table. Katherine Fleming Katt, more casually referred to as "Kitty," and wife of Norman Katt, the pastor at First Presbyterian, Red River's largest and oldest church. Kitty towered over the table in her lime linen suit, her trademark yellow pumps on her feet. She placed her well-manicured hand on their table and tapped it lightly.

"Well hello, ladies," she said, breaking into a large, toothy, and very fake smile. "Is this a pastors' wives' convention?"

All four laughed. None voluntarily. Lisa could see by her friends' faces that they were all thinking the same thing: they'd been caught. Kitty may have been the best-dressed and most "glamorous" pastor's wife in all of southwestern Ohio, but she was also the most annoying. She never seemed to let an opportunity pass when she didn't remind the other pastors' wives that she was "special." After all, she was the one who hosted each month's Southwest Ohio regional pastors' wives' tea . . . which Lisa, Felicia, Jennifer, and Mimi refused to attend anymore. Lisa wondered how they were going to explain not including Kitty in their own get-togethers.

"Oh, Kitty, you know, we uh . . ." Jennifer couldn't seem to find words to create a story.

"We're here to see new things," said Megan, who was crawling into her mother's lap after having successfully rescued her orange crayon. "Mommy says it's good to get away sometimes."

Mimi shot Megan a hush-up-now look. "Yes, well, we thought it might be good to check out some other restaurants . . . for church functions."

"So, Kitty, what brings you all the way to Lulu's on a Tuesday afternoon?" Felicia asked.

Kitty hesitated, her smile fading. "I had some business to take care of near here, then I thought I'd swing by for one of Lulu's pies to surprise Norman at dinner tonight."

Lisa eyed Kitty more closely. Would the woman's perfectly straight nose start growing? After all, Kitty was renowned for her delicious baking, especially pies. Why would she buy a cheap restaurant pie to "surprise" her husband?

But Kitty's smile was back . . . and bigger than ever. "I hope to see all of you at our next pastors' wives' fellowship. We need each other, you know. Don't think for a minute that just because my husband has a large staff and a big budget that I don't know the heartaches you smaller churches face."

Lisa wanted to exhale in exasperation. Kitty's condescension was subtle, but sharp.

"And, Felicia," Kitty added, "I've heard that Dave is under the gun at First Baptist to keep that church from dying out. Good for him that he's trying to get some new programs going! Of course, there are only so many young families in town, and we've already attracted quite a number of them."

Just as Felicia opened her mouth to respond, Gracie arrived at the table, arms loaded with plates—like the cavalry coming to save the day. "Ma'am, I need to get in there," she said, wedging herself between Kitty and the table.

"All right then I'll leave you ladies to lunch, and I'll be on my way." Kitty turned to leave while fake-smoothing her lacquered hair.

After the women called their good-byes, they looked at each other before saying a prayer over their lunches.

"She's something else, isn't she?" said Lisa.

"She sure is." Felicia removed her plaid suit jacket and folded it neatly over the back of the booth. "I still crack up every time I think of her name."

The women laughed, breaking the tension.

"She couldn't help it that she fell in love with a Katt," Jennifer managed between giggles.

"Okay, but she could have changed her name to Kate or Kathy," Felicia shot back. "Or, even easier, she could have hyphenated, like I do."

"Oh, Felicia." Mimi spread some mayonnaise on the hamburger in front of her. "You have a lot to learn about Miss Kitty."

"Hmm. I think we all do." Jennifer pointed toward the window.

Lisa turned to follow Jennifer's gaze and saw Kitty getting into her car—without a pie.

Mimi

Thursday, May 4
1:25 p.m.

Brrrrinnnnng.

Mimi jumped at the sound, making the icing on the cake she was decorating burp and splatter off the side.

"Oh, shoot," she muttered, not sure if she was more bothered by the icing mishap or the phone intrusion.

She debated letting the answering machine pick up, but figured it might be her husband, Mark. She grabbed the yellow-and-blue-checkered dishtowel by the sink and wiped her hands as she ran toward the phone.

"I'm coming! Hang on," she yelled at the phone, wishing it wasn't interrupting her schedule. The phone had been ringing all morning—first people from church wanting to know about the upcoming progressive dinner and Bible study, then her sister, her next-door neighbor, and three solicitation calls. All the interruptions were making her run behind her perfectly planned schedule.

Little tow-headed Megan chose that instant to want a hug from Mimi. "I love you, Mommy. Can I have some cake?" Megan asked sweetly.

"I love you, too, sweetie. Now let go of Mommy's leg so she can answer the phone. It might be Daddy."

"Daddy, yea!" Megan clapped her hands. "I wanna talk ta Daddy!"

Mimi grabbed the wall phone. "Hello, this is the Plaisance residence."

"Hey, Mimi," Mark said.

"Oh, hi. I just messed up the—"

"I wanna talk ta Daddy!"

"So Megan's up from her nap, huh?" Mark said, a hint of a smile in his voice. He knew Megan hated naps.

"What nap? I tried to put her down an hour ago, and she's been following me around ever since."

Mark chuckled. "Well, maybe she can help you in the kitchen."

"You helped enough with that. The phone ringing made me mess up my decorating. Now it's going to take me twice as long to fix it. The icing went all over the sugar roses I made."

"Oh no!" he mimicked. "Not the sugar roses."

"All right, smart aleck."

"I'm sure you'll fix it beautifully. You always do."

"What's up?" Mimi asked, wanting to get back to the cake. She was known for having the best and most elaborate cakes in town, and today's had to be the best ever. Her position in the PTA demanded it.

"Would you mind going into my office and checking to see if I left the letter from the insurance company there? I'm supposed to bring it to the finance committee meeting today."

"Can this wait?" Mimi asked. "I'm supposed to have this cake done and be at the PTA meeting in less than an hour."

"Well," he hedged, "that's just it. I really need that letter, and I was hoping you'd drop it off on the way."

"Why can't you come get it? You *know* I've got a full plate right now."

"I would, but I've got a counseling session with the Bryans in a few minutes."

"That new couple? I thought they were scheduled for tomorrow."

"They were, but they called to reschedule."

Mimi sighed. Mark was always forgetting things, and she always had to come to the rescue. Usually she didn't mind so much, but today was an important day. Hemmings PTA was holding its board elections, and Mimi was up for PTA president. She wanted to win. She *had* to win. There were so many changes she wanted to suggest to the school and to the board, but she knew she couldn't push them through without being in that position.

"Mark, is there *any way* you can come get it?" she asked, already knowing the answer and starting to walk toward Mark's office.

"Mommy," Megan interrupted, pulling at Mimi's pant leg.

"I know, babe," Mark said. "I wouldn't ask if it weren't important."

"Mommy."

"Megan, you can talk to Daddy later." Mimi moved around her daughter. "It's just that the phone hasn't stopped ringing," she continued to Mark. "Megan hasn't stopped bugging me, and now you're interrupting me."

"Mommy!"

"Megan, I told you—"

All of a sudden, the smoke detector blared. Mimi turned quickly toward the kitchen. A heavy haze was seeping toward her.

"I tried to tell you," Megan said, standing next to Mimi.

"The cupcakes!"

"What's going on?" Mark started.

"Nothing! Gotta run." Mimi disconnected the call and dashed toward the kitchen.

With the leftover cake batter, Mimi had decided to make a batch of cupcakes to drop off at MJ's and Michaela's classrooms while she was at the school. Between the phone and the smothered sugar roses, she'd completely forgotten about the cupcakes.

Mimi plugged her ears and ran into the kitchen, looking for some way to stop the blaring noise. She grabbed the dishtowel that was now on the island next to the cake.

Megan followed her in, standing in the middle of the kitchen with her hands covering her ears. "Maaaaaaahhhhmmmm!"

Holding the towel with one hand, plugging an ear with her other hand, and shrugging her left shoulder to try to plug her other ear, Mimi made a poor attempt to fan the smoke detector.

"Megan," Mimi yelled above her daughter's scream, "go open the back door."

While Megan ran to the door and threw it open, Mimi went to the hall closet and grabbed the stepstool.

"Now do this with the door," Mimi said as she stepped on the stool, making a back-and-forth motion with one hand and continuing to wave the towel back and forth with the other.

Megan started to fan the door. Nothing was working. They needed a stronger fan to blow out the smoke.

"Megan, get me Michaela's notebook—there on the desk," she said loudly, pointing and still trying to fan the detector with the towel.

Megan looked shocked. "But Mom, you told me *never* to touch Michaela's stuff!"

"I know, and I mean that. Just not right now. Megan, please hurry!"

"But Mommy—"

"Megan. Now!" Mimi reached up and poked the detector, hoping some button would make it shut off.

Megan rushed to the kitchen desk across the room, grabbed the pink, flowery notebook that had Girl Power written across the front, ran to Mimi, and handed it to her.

"Thanks, sweetie!"

Mimi threw the towel toward the sink and began frantically waving the notebook as close to the detector as she could get it until, finally, it abruptly stopped screaming, let out a single *chirp,* and fell silent.

"Whew," she breathed, then remembered why the smoke detector went off in the first place. Jumping from the stepstool, she hurried to the oven to turn it off. She was almost afraid to open the oven door. When she turned on the oven light, she saw only smoke and dark blobs protruding from a muffin pan.

Before she opened the door, she reached into a drawer next to the oven and grabbed a potholder. Then she peeked inside.

Out spit dark smoke and the stench of burning cupcake papers.

"Eeew!" Megan scrunched her nose. "That stinks."

Mimi ignored her and pulled out the pan of burnt cupcakes. *Well, there's no saving these*, she thought ruefully. She placed them on the stovetop, closed the oven door, and stood and surveyed her disaster. *I'll just have to make a fresh batch tonight.*

Then she snapped out of her misery. *The cake!*

Mimi glanced at the rooster clock on the wall above the sink. *1:30.* She had thirty minutes to make it to Hemmings.

Okay, I can do this.

She glanced at Megan, who had picked up Michaela's notebook and was looking through it.

"Megan, put down your sister's notebook, and go put on your shoes.

19

And the rule about not touching the notebook is back in action again, got it?"

Megan dragged her feet toward the desk to return the notebook. "It smells in here."

"Yes, I know. Now put on your shoes."

"I mean it *really* smells in here. Michaela won't want to eat those."

"Yes, I know, Megan."

"I bet even Buster won't want to eat those."

Buster, their six-year-old fluffy black cockapoo, who had raced upstairs when the blaring started, would eat anything. Megan knew that because she fed Buster anything.

"Megan!"

"Ethan might eat them, though," Megan said as she stopped to ponder this possibility about her friend Ethan who lived down the street.

"Ethan will not eat them either. Now go put on your shoes."

"Well, I wouldn't eat them—"

"Megan," Mimi said, frustrated, "I have to finish this cake and I have about zero minutes to do it in, so move your little backside to go find your shoes, and don't make me have to tell you again."

Megan walked out of the kitchen in search of her shoes.

Mimi eyed the cake. She still had the icing spill on the sugar roses to deal with. She started to step toward the island where the blotchy cake sat when the phone rang again.

Great. Now what?

"I'll get it," cried Megan excitedly as she raced back toward the kitchen.

"Oh, no, you won't, Megan Marie! Shoes. *Now.*"

Mimi contemplated not answering the phone. She glanced at the clock and ran a mental checklist of what she had to do: *finish decorating cake, get*

Megan and cake secured in car, put on makeup, take insurance letter to Mark, drop off Megan at Gladys's, and drive to school. The drive alone would take at least fifteen minutes. She decided to let the answering machine get the call and grabbed her icing bag to mend the mess.

"Mimi, I know you're there." Mark's voice floated across the room. "Pick up."

So much for making it to the school on time.

She marched to the phone and yanked the receiver from its cradle. "What?"

There was a slight pause. "Are you all right? What happened?"

"The oven overheated again and ruined my cupcakes. Honestly, Mark, do we have to go through the church finance committee to get a decent oven for this place?"

As much as Mimi appreciated living in the parsonage and having a convenient place to live near their church, Trinity United Methodist, it drove her crazy that the church finance committee made all the decisions about anything they wanted to do to the house. Just getting a new washing machine, approved the year before, had nearly caused a church split.

"I know. I'll bring it up again today at the meeting."

"That's not why you called." Mimi tried to bring the conversation back to its point so she could finish it and get back to her cake.

"I called to remind you about that letter, since I figured the high drama may have made you forget."

"Ha, ha," she said. "I didn't forget. I also didn't say I'd drop it off."

"You will, though, you sexy thing."

"Nice try. Okay, can I go now?"

"Yep," Mark said. "See you in a few."

"Okay, okay! Just let me get off this phone. And stop calling!" She hung up and glanced at the clock again. *Twenty-five minutes and counting . . .*

1:58 p.m.

Mimi pulled into the school lot and found the closest space to park. She wasn't sure how, but she had managed to fix the cake, change clothes, put on makeup, leave Megan at the sitter's, drop off Mark's letter, and still make it to the school on time. Of course, most of the makeup was applied at red lights on the way, and she felt as though she barely slowed the car to let off Megan. But she'd made it.

She reached for her purse and dug to the bottom, fishing for her favorite lipstick. As she looked in the mirror to put it on, she noticed Gloria Redkins—her presidential opponent—pulling into the lot. Gloria had been nominated for president every year, and every year she had lost. *She tries too hard*, Mimi had thought after the last election.

Good. I'm not the last one. Mimi stepped from the car and went to the backseat for the white-and-pink rose cake. She'd received the rose-swirled glass cake plate when she hosted a Lovely Living party earlier that year. That party had been the talk of the town—hers always were. Mimi prided herself on hosting the most elaborate, elegant parties, in which everyone *oohed* and *aahed* over her decorations and desserts.

"Mimi," called Gloria, walking briskly to catch her, "hold up."

"Oh, hi, Gloria!" Mimi slowed, as if just seeing Gloria, but didn't stop walking.

"I'm running a little late," Gloria said, holding her own plate of covered goodies. "But I'm surprised to see you late." She smiled as she caught up with Mimi.

"I know," said Mimi sweetly as she tried to peek at what Gloria had on her plate. "So many crazy interruptions today! I feel as though I can never get anything accomplished. I didn't even have time to ice the cupcakes I made for MJ's and Michaela's classes, so I couldn't bring them."

Gloria bit her lip, as if she were regretting she hadn't thought to bring her children any sweets.

"Oh, well," Mimi continued, "it's nice to have someone to walk in with."

"Yes," Gloria said halfheartedly, falling into step with Mimi.

They entered the building and spotted a few other PTA mothers hanging around, chatting before the meeting.

"Hi, Mimi!" said Louise, a chunky, red-haired mother of three. "What delicious thing did you bring us this month?"

"Oh, just a little something I whipped up." Pleased, Mimi walked a little taller. "Hope you like it."

"I'm sure we will," Samantha, another mother, chimed in. "We always do."

Gloria followed Mimi in, holding her plate of cookies close to her.

"Good," said Amanda, when Mimi and Gloria arrived. "Let's get this meeting started." Amanda was the current PTA president. She couldn't run again because her son, Henry, was graduating to Madison Middle School. Amanda was kind but disheveled and devoted entirely to Henry—to the point where she rarely paid much attention to herself, Mimi thought.

The first time Mimi had seen Amanda, she had wanted to give the woman a makeover. *At least a nice outfit or two*, Mimi had thought. But she was also drawn to Amanda. While Amanda's overly devoted mother routine got a bit wearisome for Mimi, she did like the way Amanda had a devil-may-care attitude about others. If someone liked Amanda, Amanda was fine with that. But she didn't go out of her way to impress others. Amanda said what she meant, whether you liked it or not. But she'd give you the shirt off her back if you needed it. She was genuine.

Mimi loved that Amanda didn't really care what people thought of her. There was a tiny part of Mimi that wished she could be that way too.

Sometimes she wanted so much to be able to say whatever she wanted. And what glory to be so free that she could even walk out of her house without makeup and her hair done!

But Mimi wouldn't do those things. Couldn't do those things. She blamed her "bondage" on being a pastor's wife. *I have a reputation to uphold*, she always told herself, as if that were an acceptable excuse. But the reality was that even if Mark weren't a pastor, she'd still be that way. And that was a part of herself that Mimi didn't like—and didn't want to think about. For Mimi, it wasn't so much about being accepted as it was about having all the pieces of her life in perfect order. Reaching her expectations meant achieving serenity. But the problem was, every time she thought she was getting close, some new challenge presented itself, and she moved that much further away from her goal.

The ladies, and Todd, the one dad in the PTA, took their seats, still chattering about any gossip and last night's television lineup.

"All right, ladies. And Todd." Amanda nodded toward the lone male.

Todd smiled and waved. Several moms at his corner of the table clapped.

"Today's a busy day, so let's get started. We need to get a final status report on Spring Fling, discuss the teachers' appreciation luncheon we have planned for next week, and the biggie—elections for next year's cabinet. Then everybody's favorite, desserts and coffee." Several more people clapped at that, and a few winked at Mimi.

Mimi smiled politely as she waited for Amanda to continue. *I'm going to win. I have to win.*

The meeting worked its way through the appointed agenda until, at last, it was time for the elections.

Amanda took one of the ballots in front of her and read the nominations for each office. Then she came to the one Mimi was most interested in.

"And now for president. We have two nominees this year: Gloria Redkins and Mimi Plaisance. That's all the nominees, so if Judy would pass out the ballots, we can vote."

Judy, the secretary, a slender mother of five, passed out the ballots. She was wearing a fitted pink blouse and matching Capris. Stepping over to Mimi, she handed her the sheet of paper.

"You look so good in pink," Mimi said sweetly.

"Thanks!" Judy smiled brightly. "Wal-Mart just got these in." Then she moved to the next person.

Mimi eyed her ballot and marked her choices, until she saw her name, Mimi Plaisance, printed neatly under President. She paused, feeling a twinge of guilt. *I should probably vote for Gloria. She's wanted this forever.*

She sat there with her pen, ready to check Gloria's name. But then another voice started to argue with her. *What am I doing? I can't not vote for myself. Especially when I know I'm going to win. They need me.*

She sighed and marked her name, folded the ballot once, and walked over to hand it to Judy.

"Thanks, Mimi," Judy whispered. "Good luck."

Mimi nodded. But, strangely, all of a sudden she didn't want the job. She was worn out, and she knew this position would only be more of a hassle. *I don't have time to be president. I already have way too much on my plate.*

"Your cake looks awfully good," Judy whispered again. "You make the best desserts. I don't know how you do it. You make things look so easy!"

"Thanks, Judy," Mimi said absently, still thinking about the new position. "You're sweet." She sat down to await the results.

Amanda picked up the ballots from Judy. "Let's start with president, shall we?" She glanced at Mimi and smiled. She counted the ballots. "Well, it looks like Mimi is our next president. Congratulations, Mimi."

Everyone clapped politely, including Gloria, who attempted a smile.

Then Judy got up and hurried to Amanda. She whispered something in Amanda's ear and passed her two pieces of paper.

Amanda glanced down at Judy's hand. "It seems Judy missed two ballots," Amanda said, a bit disgruntled.

"Sorry, everybody," Judy apologized. "I accidentally put them in with the treasurer's ballots."

Amanda opened the ballots. Her eyes widened ever so slightly. "My apologies, Mimi. It appears *Gloria* is our new president."

Gloria's head shot up in surprise. Everyone was silent, then Amanda began to applaud. "Congratulations to Gloria."

Mimi was stunned. She couldn't believe it. Gloria Redkins had won! And she had lost. Mimi was supposed to have this position. It didn't matter that she could admit she didn't want it. She'd lost.

And Mimi Plaisance wasn't used to losing. Especially to somebody like Gloria Redkins.

CHAPTER

3

Felicia

Friday, May 5

8:25 a.m.

Felicia looked up from her computer just in time to see her assistant, Delores, making her way through the outer office door, juggling a large box. Delores smiled and waved as she dropped her tote bag from her shoulder while carefully balancing the box. Then she burst into Felicia's office.

"Sorry I'm late, but you won't believe the deal I found at Sam's Club," she explained breathlessly.

No, what I can't believe is that you're late for the fourth time this week, Felicia thought as Delores waited for her response. Felicia managed a shrug and a wide-eyed head shake.

"It's pantyhose. A whole case! And only a dollar a pair. You can't beat that with a stick, can you?"

Felicia felt the blank look on her face.

"I've noticed you get runs a lot," Delores explained, "so I thought we could have a drawer full of backups in case you have an emergency. We don't want our director of public relations to be walking around with ripped hose, now do we?"

Delores leaned over Felicia's desk, eyed her boss's empty coffee cup, and promptly yanked it off the desk before turning to leave.

"Uh, no, I guess not," Felicia answered after her, not sure if she should take Delores's purchase as kindness or reprimand.

Until Felicia had arrived in Cincinnati a year ago, Delores's boss had been an older man, now retired, who saw Delores's key duties as making coffee and ordering his lunch. Felicia sensed that Delores didn't approve of her twenty-years-younger boss, especially one who was a mother ("young children need the full-time care and nurture of their mother," she once told Felicia in a terse tone) and a pastor's wife ("I thought pastors' wives weren't allowed to work anywhere but the church"). And Felicia wasn't so sure she approved of Delores either.

Chloe, Felicia's assistant at the LA office, had been a young go-getter who arrived every morning before Felicia and stayed late every night. Felicia had even confided in Chloe before marrying Dave that she didn't want to give up Lopez, the maiden name she had used while building her career.

"So hyphenate," Chloe had said in her flip, California-girl way. "Lopez-Morrison sounds good together."

Dave wasn't so sure. "Felicia," he'd said with a heavy sigh, "that's fine for now, but when I get out of seminary and we get our first pastorate, you can't be using a hyphenated last name. People will think you're pulling a Hillary Rodham Clinton on them."

Felicia had rolled her eyes at the time, but she'd continued to use the hyphenated name, even after arriving in Red River last year. Hearing "Lopez" brought her a sense of identity as she sought to be everything to everyone: wife, mother, professional, and pastor's wife. It was a constant in her life, a life that had seen a lot of changes over the last several years.

The office line rang, and Felicia started to answer it, then realized Delores was back at her desk from the coffee cart.

"Yes, Mrs. Morrison is available."

Felicia cringed. She had asked Delores to refer to her as "Ms. Lopez-Morrison" with clients, but the message couldn't seem to get through to her. Or at least Delores pretended it didn't.

Felicia's intercom buzzed. "It's Melinda at the Happy Times Day Care." Pause. "Again."

Felicia shot a glare through the window at Delores, but she was busy off-loading her bargain nylons into a file drawer. Felicia sighed as she picked up the receiver.

"Felicia Lopez-Morrison."

"Oh, I was calling for Mrs. Morrison."

"Yes, this is Felicia Lopez-Morrison."

"Oh, I'm sorry. I didn't know you were remarried. 'Mrs. Lopez,' is it then?"

"No, I'm not remarried. I wanted to keep my maiden name because it was the name I'd had my whole career, but my husband . . . well, it's complicated. Anyway, is Nicholas okay?"

"Well, that's just it, Mrs.—"

"Call me Felicia. Please."

"Okay. That's just it, Felicia. He's been biting again. We can't have a biter in our program. It's scary for the other kids, and we risk getting sued by the parents of the kids he bites."

The day-care worker went on to explain how Dave and Felicia could discipline Nicholas. "Maybe you could try taking away a favorite toy or putting him in time-out. Of course, he probably doesn't bite at home, so that might not work so well for this particular situation. Hmmm. Is he maybe acting out here at the center because of a situation at home?"

Felicia had tuned out the day-care worker and gone back to reading e-mails when she realized there was silence on the other end of the phone. "Okay then. We'll be sure to talk with him about it tonight," she said with a fake cheerful tone, eager to end the "conversation."

"Mrs.—uh, Felicia—we need you to pick him up now. We can't have him in our program until we have some assurance from you that he won't be biting anymore."

Felicia consulted her watch. She had to be across town for a press conference in forty minutes. "But it's only eight-thirty! I have a million things to do today."

"Maybe your husband can come?"

"This is his sermon-writing day." Felicia bit her lip. "One of us will be there within the hour. Thanks for calling."

She glanced at her watch again as she clicked over to another phone line and dialed.

"Good morning, First Baptist Church."

"Hi, Linda, it's Felicia. Is Pastor Dave available?"

"I'm sorry. He's in conference with Nancy Borden. She's leading vacation Bible school this summer, so he's—"

Felicia inhaled as the familiar stress pangs hit her. She knew Dave was as busy as she was and couldn't drop everything to pick up Nicholas either. Plus she didn't want Dave to think she thought his day was any less important than hers. He was already hassling her about not being more involved in church. If she started pulling him away, things could get more difficult.

"Felicia?" Linda said with that you're-not-listening-to-me, are-you tone.

Delores set down a fresh cup of coffee behind her.

Doesn't she know I'm getting ready to leave?

"Sorry I was distracted," Felicia said, uncomfortable that Delores was hearing her personal business. "Linda, I hate to ask this, and I wouldn't if I didn't have a press conference I have to be at, but would you do me a big favor? It's Nicholas. He's over at Happy Times and—"

"Felicia, I'm on my way. Call and let them know to release him to me. I'll keep him occupied until my Lauren comes by after marching-band practice. Then she can take him home and watch him until one of you is free."

"Thanks, Linda. I owe you one."

As Felicia hung up, she expected to feel relief. Instead a huge sense of guilt and failure washed over her. Grabbing her briefcase, she stood to head out for the press conference. But as she turned to leave, she spied a small box next to the steaming coffee mug on her desk. On it was a sticky note from Delores:

Here's one to put in your car, just in case

If only my life were more like pantyhose, Felicia thought, tossing the box in her briefcase. *I could go and go until I hit a snag, then start all over again with a new one.*

6:45 p.m.

The smell of half-burned pizza greeted Felicia as she walked up the driveway—and told her that she had missed dinner again.

"Mommy!" Nicholas yelled as he ran to grab Felicia's legs before she was barely in the door. The thrust of his hug made her briefcase drop from her hand onto a paper plate on the floor that was smeared with half-eaten pizza.

"Hey, Nicholas Nickleby." She cradled his chin and noticed anew what a striking little boy he was with his olive skin, dark hair, and bright blue eyes. And also what a messy boy he was! "Let's go wash off that face. And my briefcase."

Felicia slipped off her heels and felt the cool sting of the tile through her hose. She smiled. *Good thing I had that extra pair.* "Where's Daddy, big guy?"

"He's on the phone with some lady from church," Nicholas called as he skipped down the hall toward the bathroom.

Can't they respect our evenings as family time? She was annoyed that Nicholas was running through the house with greasy hands and a sauce-covered face while Dave was occupied with yet another church call.

"Hi, honey. When did you get in?" Dave said as he rounded the corner from the kitchen to the living room.

She thought again how good looking this former college football player was. When they'd first met, she had been turned off by his stereotypical California tanned-boy looks—so typical of the airhead surfer types at UCLA. But his warmth and sense of humor had won her over.

But now, even his good looks didn't stop the caustic words that poured from her mouth. "You know, if you can't even hear me come in the door, just think of what Nicholas could have been doing."

The welcome-home smile fell from Dave's face as he studied her. "Felicia, he was fine. He had his pizza, and I put in a video for him."

Felicia tossed the mail she was skimming onto a side table and walked toward the bedroom to change.

Dave followed her. "Look, I can't not take calls from the people at church. And you weren't here to—"

Nicholas went running by, dropping a white washcloth stained with sauce in the hallway. Felicia stooped to get it, then kept walking with Dave still behind her. She took off her jacket and skirt and hung them in the closet.

"You weren't here to take over, Felicia. So what was I supposed to do? Tie him to a chair?"

"No!" Nicholas screamed.

Dave and Felicia swiveled to see him standing inside their bedroom doorway with a horrified look.

"Oh, buddy, we're just talking silly." Dave ushered Nicholas out of the room. "Let Mommy and Daddy have a few minutes, then we'll be out to play with you."

"Okay, but you promised we'd play my new Zingers game before bedtime," Nicholas said.

"Yep, Zingers it is, buddy. Now go see what's on the cartoon channel."

By the time Nicholas had galloped off, Felicia was in her comfort wear—sweats and slippers. She'd pulled her dark hair up into a scrunchie.

"Now *that's* the woman I want to see when I get home from work," he said with a laugh.

Felicia narrowed her eyes. "You can laugh all you want, but I think that's secretly how you feel. You'd really like it if I gave up my career and stayed home every day to clean your house, do your laundry, and cook your dinner."

"What?" Dave frowned.

"You heard me," Felicia fired back.

"And what's wrong with that?"

"Nothing's wrong with it, Dave. It's just not where we are. You have a job, and I have a job, and—"

"Oh, I get it. So we're merely equal partners running through life with our jobs and our house and our cars. What about our child, Felicia? And our family life? Have you forgotten about that, or do those things simply get in the way of your oh-so-important ca-REER?"

Felicia sighed. She grabbed Dave's hand and started to lead him to the kitchen. "I'm too tired to argue tonight," she said as they walked. "Let's get something to eat and spend some time with Nicholas. We need to talk to him about this biting thing."

"Yeah, you're right," Dave murmured. There was a wistful expression in his Paul Newman–like eyes. "But we should talk more about this later. It seems like we're too busy even to understand our own lives anymore."

"Okay, call my assistant on Monday for an appointment so we can chat," Felicia said as she stopped to kiss Dave on the cheek.

He stiffened before the realization dawned that she was kidding. Then he broke into a weak grin.

Arriving in the kitchen, Felicia grabbed two plates from the cabinet. That's when she saw the small basket on the counter.

"What's this?" she asked, pulling back the cotton fabric with tiny lavender flowers and Scripture verses on it to reveal two bran muffins.

"Oh, Nancy Borden brought those for our meeting today. She said she made extra for you, and to keep the basket. I think she's going to do a great VBS for us this year. And she really seems to have taken an interest in my well-being too. Two weeks ago she brought by cookies, then last week some banana bread, and now the muffins. No one at church has ever done that for me before."

"How thoughtful," Felicia said as she handed Dave a plate with pizza on it. But as he wandered off to find Nicholas, she wondered what kind of "thoughts" Nancy Borden was actually full of. When Dave was at seminary in LA, Felicia had heard stories from professors' wives—who also had been pastors' wives—about women in the church who throw themselves at pastors as though they are rock stars.

Then, as she was admonishing herself for jumping to bad conclusions, she noticed Dave's open planner by the phone. A note for 12:30 on Monday jumped out at her:

Nancy Borden. Lunch.

"Oh, and honey?" Dave called from the family room. "Rhonda Barber called to invite you to that new ladies' Bible study starting next month. Noon on Thursdays. I know it's right in the middle of the workday, but at least it's during lunch. I think you should go if you can. You really need to get more involved at church."

Mmmm-hmmm, Felicia said to herself. *Just like Nancy Borden.*

Jennifer

Wednesday, May 10
10:47 a.m.

Jennifer was bent over tying her shoes when Dr. O'Boyle tapped on the door and reentered the examination room.

"Well, Miss Jen," he said in a cheerful tone, "I can't find any reason why you're not getting pregnant. Your test results are brilliant."

Even though she knew what he meant, Jennifer wished her Irish doctor's word choice were a little less positive in such a negative situation. Still, his grandfatherly appearance—ruddy-skinned round face topped by a dollop of snow white hair—did comfort her in a Santa Claus sort of way.

"So what do we do now then?" she asked quietly. "At thirty-five I can't keep sitting around, waiting and hoping. And praying."

Jennifer knew that last part wasn't true anymore, but she threw it in anyway.

Dr. O'Boyle handed her a slip of paper. "Here is a prescription for Clomid. You appear to be ovulating on your own, but this medicine virtually assures that you'll ovulate on a monthly basis." He hesitated. "But you need to know that there are side effects for most women. You might feel a bit mad at times while you're taking this."

Jennifer knew his Irish "mad" translated to American "crazy." Her heart skipped a beat as she wondered how much more out of sorts she could get and not jump off a bridge into the Red River. The monthly up and down of trying to get pregnant had taken over her world. She wanted off the roller coaster, but she knew she'd never forgive herself if she didn't try *everything* to have a child. And if that meant months of hope shot down by disappointment, then so be it.

"And this is for your husband," said Dr. O'Boyle as he tucked another piece of paper into her hand. "I want him to stop by the fertility clinic downstairs for a sperm test. We need to make sure his swimmers are in good form."

Jennifer hopped off the exam table and reached for her purse.

Dr. O'Boyle started out of the room, then turned to face her and lightly touched her arm. "Look, Jen, I want you to try to relax about this. I see the stress written all over your face. Just trust the Lord, and he will provide. I don't want to see you lose that lovely sense of humor."

The doctor had been Jennifer's ob/gyn for fifteen years, so he knew she was a pastor's wife, and she knew he was a Christian. What he didn't know was that she was in a crisis even larger than her inability to get pregnant.

"Yes, I know," Jennifer said with a half-baked pastor's-wife smile as she breezed by him. "See you in a few weeks."

Opening the exit door to the waiting room, Jennifer nearly gasped at the sight of so many hugely pregnant women waiting for their appointments. A few had toddlers grabbing on to their legs or crying in their laps.

They have so much, and I can't even have one? she cried inwardly as she hurried toward the door. *What kind of God are you?* She strode toward the elevator and saw yet another pregnant woman waiting there. This one was holding on to one child's hand while she rocked a stroller, trying to soothe a fussy baby.

The woman smiled at her. "So how far along are you?" she asked Jennifer, who instinctively crossed her arms over the baggy shirt she was wearing.

Jennifer internally chastised herself for wearing something that could be misconstrued as maternity clothes, especially in this place. "Oh, I'm just wearing a big shirt to . . . yeah, I'm about four months."

She couldn't believe she'd said it!

The woman chuckled as they got on the elevator. "Well, enjoy it now because your waddling days are coming. Just look at me!"

Jennifer watched from behind as the woman left the elevator and indeed looked like a duck—walking side to side—as she made her way to her car.

"Quack, quack," Jennifer said under her breath. "Like you need another kid."

6:38 p.m.

Jennifer set a chunk of German chocolate cake in front of Sam, then sat down next to him at their dining-room table, cradling a cup of decaf.

"Aren't you having any?" Sam asked as he dove his fork into the confection.

"No, I think I need to cut back. Maybe do some Weight Watchers or something." Jennifer was still stinging from the pregnancy comment at the doctor's office elevator.

Sam reached across the table and clasped her hand. "I think you look just fine. Prettiest pastor's wife at Red River Community Church!"

Jennifer playfully pulled back her hand. "Hey, I am the *only* pastor's wife at our church! Unless you count Lucy, but she and Derek aren't married yet."

Their associate pastor, Derek, had proposed to Lucy on Valentine's Day, and their August wedding was rapidly approaching. Jennifer sensed that Lucy was looking to her as a mentor, which made Jennifer feel even more terrible about her crisis.

"Lucy. Ah, Lucy," Sam said in mock admiration. He held his fisted hand on his heart, then laughed.

Jennifer reached across the table and smacked him lightly. "Okay, I know I have some years on her." Lucy and Derek were just out of college. "But it's the vintage wine that's always the most prized, right?"

"Right!" Sam pushed back his chair and reached for his plate to take to the sink. But before he could walk away, Jennifer grabbed his wrist. "Sam, I need to talk to you about something."

He must have read the seriousness in her eyes, for he sat back down.

"I saw Dr. O'Boyle today."

"And how is the ol' laddie?" Sam loved to use his pretend Irish brogue.

"He's fine, but we're not sure why I'm not getting pregnant."

Sam sighed and got up again. "It takes time, Jen. We just need to keep—"

Jennifer grabbed his arm and pulled him back into his chair. "But we've been actively trying for five years, plus we barely even used birth control for the first five before that. That's plenty of time. Anyway, he gave me this medical order for you." Jennifer reached behind her and took the slip from her purse on the hutch. "He wants you to go for a sperm test."

"A sperm test? What—he thinks this is my problem?" Sam was raising his voice, which brought tears to her eyes.

Jennifer hated confrontation and fighting of any sort. As a child, she'd pretended she was one of those roly-poly bugs—rolled up and insulated against the outside world—when her mother and stepfather fought, which was often. Even as an adult, she caught herself going into "roly-poly mode."

She looked away to try to defuse the situation. "Sam, we just want to make sure we cover our bases, that's all."

"Well, I don't need any stupid sperm test to tell me how to conceive a child. Besides, do you know what they do at those places?"

Jennifer looked back at him and shook her head.

"The rooms are full of pornography—videos, magazines. I counseled a man in our church who said his addiction to pornography started when he went for a sperm test."

Jennifer thought for a moment. She'd seen something about that in the infertility online bulletin board that she read sometimes when she couldn't sleep. "I'm pretty sure you can ask for the room to be cleared of that stuff."

Sam sighed. "But still. Come on, Jen. I don't want to be doing that in some room without you there. It's embarrassing. And I think it's unnecessary."

Jennifer's eyes welled up again. "So you're saying you're confident *I'm* the problem here? You're positive you don't have any role in this?"

Sam stood. "I've got to get back to the church for the trustees meeting." He kissed Jennifer lightly on top of her head. "Don't worry, honey. We'll have our baby. God will provide."

What is this—a broken record of the Dr. O'Boyle Band featuring Sam Shores? Jennifer thought cynically as she watched Sam leave, then buried her head in her hands. *Sure, God provides, and right now he's providing me with a lot of suffering and sadness. I can't wait to see what he provides next!*

Lulu's Café

Tuesday, May 16
12:21 p.m.

Felicia drizzled Caesar dressing from a small ceramic pitcher onto her chicken salad while Mimi expertly shook the ketchup bottle until the liquid was right at the rim.

"I wouldn't worry too much about it," Mimi said to Felicia as she poured a ketchup puddle next to her fries. "Megan went through a biting phase about a year ago. I still don't know what caused her to do it, but we spanked her little behind every time."

Lisa took a sip of iced tea. "It's so difficult to spank them when they're that age. I hated doing it to Ricky and Callie, but it seemed like the only thing that would get their attention at times."

"Did it work?" asked Felicia.

"Well, unfortunately no, it didn't." Mimi wiped around her mouth after taking a bite from her messy barbecued-pork sandwich. "I tell you, Mark and I were really worried after a while that we were raising a little vampire.

Then one day I was at my new ob/gyn—Dr. O'Boyle, the one Jennifer recommended to me—and I mentioned the problem to him. He said he had a daughter who did the same thing when she was about three and that I should try shooting some breath spray in Megan's mouth every time we caught her biting."

"You're kidding!" Felicia dropped her fork into her salad. "Don't tell me that worked!"

Mimi dipped a fry in her ketchup. "I know, I know. It was unbelievable. We bought the foulest tasting spray we could find. You should have seen Mark and me in the store trying them out. The one we got tasted peculiar, like rotten potatoes."

"Like *you've* tasted rotten potatoes?" Jennifer said half under her breath and without her usual comic tone as she examined her turkey on rye.

The three others stopped giggling about the mouth spray and eyed Jennifer.

"Anyway," Mimi went on more cautiously, "he was right. After a few encounters with that nasty spray, Megan stopped biting altogether. Of course, she found other ways to get our attention. And still does."

Felicia reached into her purse, pulled out a notepad, and jotted in large letters,

BREATH SPRAY—NICHOLAS

"So, Jennifer," Mimi started hesitantly, "speaking of Dr. O'Boyle, weren't you going to see him last week? What happened?"

Jennifer placed what remained of her turkey sandwich on the plate in front of her. "Yes, I saw him," she said with a dull tone, "after I managed to wade my way through his waiting room full of crying, snot-nosed brats."

Mimi caught Lisa, who was sitting across from her, nudging Felicia under the table. "And did he have any advice for you?" she asked Jennifer.

Jennifer raised her empty soda glass for passing Gracie to see. "There really is no advice he can give at this point. But he did give me a prescription for Clomid to help me ovulate."

"Mmmm-hmmm, that's why you're such a grouch," Felicia said bluntly.

That was one thing Mimi always liked about Felicia—the fact that she didn't mince words.

"My sister was on that stuff, and she turned into a total . . ." Felicia winced. "Well, not a nice person. But it did work for her. My niece, Estella Felicia, is proof of that."

Jennifer seemed to brighten a bit. "How long was she on it before she got pregnant?" she asked breathlessly. "The doctor said to give it a few months. And by the way, I think you're right about the grouchiness. I've only been on the Clomid for six days, but I feel out of sorts all the time."

"That's okay!" the three others said soothingly and nearly in unison.

Mimi could relate. She hadn't been feeling quite herself lately either.

"Hmmm, let me think," Felicia said with a furrowed brow. "It happened really fast. I want to say she started the medicine one month and found out she was pregnant the next. And then I got pregnant the next month. And my cousin the next. People in my family were wondering what was in the water!"

"Wow!" Jennifer said as she half bounced on the booth bench, causing Mimi to miss her mouth with a ketchuped fry and hit her chin instead. Mimi patted Jennifer on the back with her left hand while she used her right to lift her napkin from her lap and wipe her chin.

"If I got pregnant next month, that would mean a March baby. Sam's birthday is March 11—wouldn't that be a great present?"

Mimi and the others smiled at Jennifer's projectionist joy, but she could tell they were all apprehensive. The past year of tales from Jennifer about herbal remedies, meditation, acupuncture, timed sex, untimed sex, and even a month of everyday sex were growing old. When Jennifer talked about infertility being a monthly roller coaster she couldn't get off, Mimi—and she assumed Felicia and Lisa—felt as though they were being dragged along on the same ups and downs. Even though Mimi cared about her friend, she wanted off the ride. But there was no way she could share that with any of the other PWs—especially Jennifer. After all, they were here to support one another.

So Mimi was glad when Felicia boldly changed the subject. "I have a new account with a bar in downtown Cincinnati that's involved in serving a guy who hit and killed a teenager. It's a really difficult one."

"Oh, I read about that in the paper," said Lisa. "Isn't some drunk-driving group picketing there?"

"Yes, that's the one," Felicia replied. "They hired me to get rid of the protesters so they can get their business back on track. I'm going to meet with the owner next week."

Mimi pushed her empty plate to the end of the table, where Gracie could easily retrieve it. "I don't know how you do some of that stuff," she said to Felicia in a firm but nonjudgmental tone. "I know that bar has a right to its business, but I can't imagine what those parents must be feeling. To lose a child to something as tragic as drunk driving!"

"I know." Felicia nodded. "I've struggled over this one."

"What made you finally take on the bar as a client?" asked Mimi.

"Honestly?" Felicia wiped her mouth with her napkin. "I realized I may be able to show Jesus to that owner in a way nobody else could. Let's face it. If Dave walked in and tried to witness to the guy, how far do you think that would go? But in my position—as a businesswoman, *not* as a pastor's wife—I can do ministry my husband can't."

Mimi nodded. She admired her savvy friend. She knew Felicia was very good at her job.

Lisa slid her round plate on top of Mimi's oval one and rested her cheek on her hand. "I know that's true. But still, those poor parents. I pray for my kids every time they go somewhere without me," she said without a hint of exaggeration. "I'm a firm believer that the Holy Spirit watches over them."

"So what would you say to Sam then?" Jennifer asked, back to her sulky tone. "Emily was killed by a drunk driver, and she was a Christian. Did the Holy Spirit turn his back on her, or what?"

"Who's Emily?" Mimi asked, more intrigued about someone connected to Jennifer's husband than a discussion on the work of the Holy Spirit.

"His first wife," Jennifer said, looking away.

"Sam was married before?" Felicia asked as she laid the dressing pitcher in her half-empty salad bowl.

"Yeah. He and Emily met at college. It was about fifteen years ago—they were a few years into their first pastorate in Indiana when she was killed," Jennifer said quietly. "A drunk driver plowed into her one night on the way back from choir practice. All I know is I was about a year into being the church secretary when Sam came from Evansville to interview for the pastorate. He must have mentioned Emily's death to someone during the interview process, because word traveled fast. Everyone was talking about it—you know how that is. Then when we called him to be our pastor, the head of the search committee gave me specific instructions before Sam arrived not to ask about Emily's death. I guess everyone knows how prone I am to blurting out questions! But even after Sam and I started dating, I'd try to bring it up and he'd change the subject. Eleven years later I don't know much more than I did before he came to Red River."

"That's awful." Lisa shook her head. "I've never met Sam, but I sure do admire him for continuing on in ministry after something like that. And what I said earlier about the Holy Spirit watching over—"

Jennifer interrupted. "I knew what you meant." She cracked a slight smile toward Felicia. "I think this Clomid is making me a not nice person."

"Wow." Felicia dipped the tip of her napkin into her water glass, then took the wet end and cleaned the tips of her fingers. "Thanks for sharing about Sam. We never knew."

"It's not something I like to parade around shouting." Jennifer lifted her head and acted like she was using a megaphone. "Sam was married before! I'm not his first."

"Oh, honey," Lisa consoled her, "I bet that doesn't matter at all to him. He loves *you*."

"I know."

But Jennifer appeared uncomfortable, as if she were having second thoughts about having shared that information. Mimi saw her swallow hard.

"And I love him too," Jennifer continued. "But sometimes I don't like being his second choice. He always assures me, though, that I'm his *next* choice, not his second."

"And you need to believe him on that," Lisa said, squeezing Jennifer's hand. "You're a fantastic woman. Any man would be pleased to have you as his wife. And you'll make a wonderful mother to his children too. You can believe that as truth."

Mimi nodded and said, "Mmmm-hmmm" along with Felicia.

Jennifer exhaled and covered the remnants of her turkey sandwich with her napkin. "I hope you're right. I hope God thinks that way too."

6

Mimi

Wednesday, May 17

3:28 p.m.

Something within Mimi had snapped. She'd never lost to anyone before—especially on something she was so sure she'd win. In the days following the PTA meeting she tried to brush off the election and Gloria's win by telling herself she really didn't have the time or energy for the job. But, deep down, her failure to succeed was eating away at her.

Who doesn't like me? she wondered while she scrubbed her kitchen floor on her hands and knees for the third time that day. She thought best when she was "doing something productive," as she liked to say. So after the kids were off to school, she cleaned out the refrigerator, scrubbed and bleached it; organized and realphabetized the spice rack; and rearranged the china in her mother's old cherry cabinet.

But even after accomplishing so much around the house, she still couldn't shake the loss. So she put her muscle into washing the kitchen floor, hoping that would provide some relief from her accusing thoughts.

Through most of her life, Mimi had succeeded at whatever she'd put her mind to—whether it was as a homemaker, a volunteer, or a third-grade teacher (before her own kids were born). But none of that mattered now. Rejection was all she felt. And then that old, familiar chaos began to bubble up inside her.

I can't even win a PTA election. What's wrong with me? she thought, almost feverishly plunging the scrubber brush into the bucket of sudsy, warm water and letting the water roughly slosh over the sides.

Footsteps on the back porch pulled her back from her thoughts. She was in no mood for visitors—and people from the church were forever popping in unannounced. Bracing herself for whoever was now standing at the door, she glanced around and saw Mark about to enter the kitchen.

"Don't come in here!" she warned. "It isn't dry yet. Go to the front door."

Mark eyed the clean, gleaming floor. "Didn't you just do the floor this morning?"

"Megan spilled some juice," Mimi lied. It was only a tiny white lie, she figured, since Megan was spilling juice all the time. She didn't want Mark to confront her about what was wrong. She couldn't take it.

"Why not just clean that part of the floor then?" Mark asked through the screen door. "Why go over the entire thing?"

"Because it needs cleaning." She found she was holding her breath, wanting him to go away and stop asking questions.

Mark didn't say anything for a moment. Then he crouched down to peer through the lower screen. "Mimi," he asked sympathetically, "what's up?"

Her lie hadn't worked on him.

"Nothing," she said, dipping the brush back into the bucket. Moving away from him, she deliberately turned her back.

"Come on, Mims. You only go into supercleaning mode when something's bothering you."

Mimi didn't say anything, but she was thinking, *Go away. Leave me alone.* She didn't want to admit her feelings about her failure—especially to her husband. He always did things so well, and everybody respected him. She didn't want to add his disappointment to her own.

She overheard him removing his shoes on the porch. And then he eased open the door and tiptoed in.

"Mark!" she started anxiously.

"It's dry here," he said. Then, more softly, he asked, "Is this about not winning the PTA thing?"

"Don't be ridiculous," Mimi said, not even glancing up. "This is about the kitchen floor. Go through the front door, please."

Mark tried to ballerina through the kitchen.

"Ah, ah, don't even think about it," Mimi hissed.

"It's okay to admit you're upset about it," Mark pressed, ignoring her irritability. "So you lost. So what? You really didn't want that position anyway."

"First of all," Mimi said, still scrubbing and not looking up, "I'm not upset, so there's nothing to admit. Second, whether or not I wanted the position isn't the point. Of *course* I didn't want the position. Who does?"

"The point is that you lost, isn't it? And you've never lost anything. And that bugs you."

"Now you're making up things, Mister Armchair Psychologist. And stop walking on the kitchen floor."

"So it's not a problem? It really is just about cleaning the floor?"

"Yes. That's it." She wasn't about to tell him she'd also rearranged the cabinets and pantry.

"Well, if that's not bothering you, then I guess I can tell you that Kitty Katt stopped by my office about an hour ago."

Kitty's name brought Mimi's head up. She knew Kitty had paid her visit to rub in the PTA incident. *That woman doesn't have a kind, decent bone in her body,* Mimi thought bitterly. *She loves to try to make me feel bad.*

Mimi tried to act disinterested and hoped she sounded casual. "Oh? What did she want?"

"Last week at the pastors' breakfast I mentioned I was struggling with my sermon series on humility," Mark responded, "and Norm offered to loan me the tapes of his series from last fall."

Mimi snorted. "The Katts—well, *they're* just the picture of humility."

"So Kitty stopped by to drop off the tapes," he said, ignoring her comment. He tiptoed across the floor and extended an envelope with Mimi's name written on it. Mimi wiped her hands on her jeans and took it. She sat back on her heels and tucked her hair behind her ears before she opened the envelope.

The card had a single daisy on the cover with "So sorry to hear of your loss" dangling over the shining, happy flower. It was obviously homemade from a computer-software greeting-card program. A wave of nausea washed over Mimi. She could imagine Kitty sitting at her computer, laughing, as she picked the perfect daisy and typed those wretchedly mean words across the top.

Inside the card was a handwritten note.

I heard you lost the PTA election to Gloria Redkins. I'm so sorry to hear that—especially since I know you were so intent on winning. Take heart—it just wasn't God's will for you. There will be other opportunities. Know that you are in my thoughts. With God's love and blessings, Kitty

Mimi seethed. "She's hateful!" she spat and flung the card toward Mark.

"I know," Mark said, opening it. "But her husband is—"

"Yes, I know, Mark. Her husband is the pastor of the largest church in town. He knows the governor. The mayor and town council attend his church. They can do anything and everything they want. What pleasure could she possibly receive in belittling me?"

Mark started to respond, when she held up her soapy scrub brush in protest.

"And don't tell me we have to love them as Jesus does," she added sarcastically. "I know the Bible just as well as you do, Mark Plaisance. But I still have to say that I wonder if there are times when even God struggles to love that woman. She's mean. And she covers it up with her fake smile and fake eyelashes and fake manicure and ugly pantsuits. And there are barracuda teeth behind that smile, I'm telling you." Mimi was on a roll. "And why did she drop off the card to you? Why didn't she stop here and deliver it personally?"

Mark swallowed hard, as though he feared he might be the next subject of Mimi's wrath. "She said she didn't want to disturb you since she figured you were upset."

"Ha!" Mimi stood and lifted the brush in triumph.

Mark chose his words carefully. "Don't bite off my head, Mims, but I'm wondering if maybe Kitty's right." He raised his hands as if in self-defense. "I mean," he continued hurriedly, "you said losing wasn't bothering you, but I come home to find you scrubbing the kitchen floor. *Again.* And who knows what else you've done around the house."

"I don't know what—"

"*And* what's this I hear about you volunteering to run the Ladies' Missionary Society tea?"

"They needed help, so I volunteered." Mimi picked up the bucket and headed toward the back door.

"But at the *Lutheran* church?" Mark said, following her outside. "We're Methodists, Mimi."

"Well, we're all Christians, right?" Mimi walked down the porch steps and threw the dirty water into the yard. "We should all work together."

Mark started down the steps behind her. "You know, Mimi, it's okay not to win. Nobody thinks any less of you." He caught Mimi's eye for an instant before he made a path toward the front of the house.

Mimi leaned against the porch railing. *Maybe not. But I do.*

Lisa

Friday, May 19
11:00 p.m.

Lisa and Joel Barton walked silently into the darkened parsonage they called home. Lisa glanced at the glaring yellow 11:00 on the DVD player in the family room. Joel turned on a light in the hallway and headed toward the kitchen in the back of the house.

Lisa yawned and headed up the stairs to check on their two children, Callie and Ricky. She hoped they were asleep, although she knew Callie was probably on the phone with her best friend, Theresa, and Ricky was playing video games.

Sure enough, as she got to the top of the stairs, Lisa saw light peeking out from underneath both kids' bedroom doors. She quietly opened Ricky's door and peered inside. The twelve-year-old was lying on his stomach on his twin bed, facing the TV screen, intently playing The Legend of Zelda. Lisa reached across the wall to the light switch and flipped it on and off several times to get his attention.

"Hi, Mom," Ricky said without looking up from his game.

"Isn't it bedtime?" Lisa asked. She sat beside Ricky and ruffled his dish-water blond hair. Ricky was her younger child, but even as a preteen he was outgrowing everything he owned. Tonight he was wearing blue shorts and his favorite T-shirt—the blue tie-dyed with I'm a Jesus Freak in bold print.

"Where's Dad?" Ricky asked, finally lifting his eyes to Lisa.

"Downstairs in the kitchen, probably checking the answering machine. Have you rescued the princess yet?"

"I got to the fifth level. Right now I'm in the Lost Hills."

"Is that good?"

"It's okay. But Steve Markins already made it to level eight."

"Wow. Well, keep practicing." She ruffled his hair again. "But not to-night. Did you brush your teeth?"

"*Mom.*"

"*Mom,*" Lisa mimicked back. "What's your sister been doing all night?"

"What she does every night."

"Okay." Lisa kissed Ricky's head, then stood. "Finish up, brush your teeth, and hit the sack. Got it? You can rescue the princess tomorrow."

"Got it," Ricky said, refocusing on the television.

Lisa walked across the hallway to Callie's room and knocked on the door. It was covered with signs that read, Keep Out, Callie Avenue, and Girls Rule.

"Come in," called the high-pitched voice from the other side of the door. Lisa entered and pointed at her watch. Callie nodded and waved her away.

"Uh-huh," Callie said into the phone, continuing on with her conversation.

Callie, fourteen, was proving to be a handful. At five-foot-two, she was thin but starting to fill out her surfboard-flat figure. Her straight brown hair partially hid her hazel eyes and pink-rimmed glasses.

"Callie," Lisa said, hands on her hips. "It's eleven. Say good night to Theresa."

Callie put up her finger, motioning for just another minute.

"Now," Lisa emphasized.

Callie sighed dramatically and told Theresa she had to go. "Yeah, I'll talk to you tomorrow. Bye." And she hung up.

"How'd it go tonight?" Lisa asked. What she really wanted to know was, What could you possibly find to talk about for that many hours?

Lisa was continually amazed at the gift of gab her daughter had. Every night it was the same. One girl would call the other, and they'd end up chatting about things that, according to Callie, were of the utmost importance.

"You wouldn't understand," Callie had told Lisa once when she'd had the audacity to ask about their conversations. Lisa had simply chuckled. She probably would have said the same thing to *her* mother, had she ever asked.

"Fine," Callie said as she absently dropped the phone on the dresser between her bottle of raspberry-pear body spray and piles of earrings and necklaces twisted around each other. "Ricky stayed in his room all night playing those stupid video games. The only time he left his room was to go to the bathroom and run to the kitchen for pizza—which he actually wanted *me* to bring up to him. He said he couldn't get away because he was trying to save some Princess Imelda or something." She rolled her eyes. "I'm surprised he didn't ask me to go to the bathroom for him too."

"Thanks for the play-by-play." Lisa tucked Callie's hair behind her ears. "You're such a beautiful girl."

"I know," Callie interjected sarcastically. "I should keep my hair out of my face so everyone can see how pretty I am."

"That's right, baby girl."

Lisa could hear footsteps on the stairs. Joel had apparently finished listening to voice-mail messages and was coming to bed.

"Don't stay up too late." She kissed Callie's forehead. "You need your beauty rest, you know. And you need your strength to ward off all those boys who keep following you around at church."

They smiled at each other. Lisa stepped into the hall.

"Hey," Callie yelled after her. "Close the door."

"Sorry!" Lisa obediently grabbed the knob and shut the door.

Lisa walked toward the master bedroom. It was decorated in a rose-colored Victorian motif. Delicate, feminine lace covered the dresser. The queen-sized bed in the middle of the room was covered with a rose- and lace-patterned comforter.

Joel was in the master bathroom brushing his teeth. She stood for a moment at the doorway and watched him. Joel unceremoniously spit out his toothpaste and rinsed the brush. Even with toothpaste making a ring around his mouth, he was still attractive. Midthirties suited him well. He had a sprinkling of gray hair at his temples, but the rest was still shiny black. He stood well over six feet and was muscular.

"Can you go with me tomorrow morning to help pick out Ricky's birthday present?" she asked.

"You know I can't," he said before he leaned down to rinse out his mouth. "I'm supposed to meet Frank and Andy for coffee in the morning to go over this week's service." Joel, who was senior pastor of Red River Assembly of God, always liked to get together with the worship leaders on Saturday to run through the service order and to discuss any information pertinent to that week's ministry.

"I meant after your coffee meeting with them."

"Can't you get Callie to go with you?"

"No, she's got band practice until two." Callie played the clarinet, and her school, Red River High, was practicing for the final spring concert the following week.

"Well, get the stuff in the afternoon, then, and you can take her."

"I was just thinking it would be nice for you and me to spend a little time together."

"I can't make it tomorrow," Joel said, dismissing Lisa's last comment.

He brushed past her on his way back into the bedroom. She considered pushing the subject, then thought better of it. Once Joel said no, that was it. Discussion ended.

Lisa moved behind the sink and took her turn brushing her teeth. *I don't get him on Sunday. I don't get him on Saturday. I don't get him during the week.* She finished her teeth, put on her floor-length beige nightgown, and ran a brush through her long, thick brown hair.

Joel was already lying in bed when she entered the room. She crawled under the sheets, got settled in on her side, and turned off her bedside lamp. For a moment, she thought about snuggling up next to him. Then she felt Joel turn on his side, away from her.

Lisa stared up at the ceiling, her eyes starting to adjust to the darkness. A sliver of moonlight came from the slightly open window across the room. She could hear the light breeze that wound through their big oak tree. The house began its nightly settling . . . creaking and groaning in the way that only an old parsonage can do.

But Lisa was far from settled.

When was the last time he kissed me good night?

Her mind wandered into the past, trying to remember.

When was the last time he kissed me at all?

Her mind was a blank slate. Nothing. The empty thought disturbed her, yet it was a feeling she'd had before. Quite often lately. But she couldn't pinpoint why there was a problem in her marriage.

When did this happen? How did this happen? And why?

She knew Joel loved her. Or at least she thought she knew. Over the last year, she was no longer so sure. Yet she knew that wasn't true either. It had been longer than a year. It just had seemed more pronounced this past year, more empty and painful. She knew he wasn't having an affair or anything like that. He held himself very accountable in that regard. He was never alone with another woman. Ever. And Lisa knew that in the pastorate there was always plenty of opportunities for that to happen.

No, that wasn't it. They were drifting apart. And there was nothing Lisa could do to stop it. She felt alone and saddened by the thought. She considered the past few years again. Had she changed? Had the problem been something she'd done or caused? She knew Joel had felt a lot more pressure since taking the pastorate in Red River three years ago. But that had been his dream position—he'd always wanted to be a senior pastor. And he was good at his job.

She recalled the evening's events. The Van Johnsons, a family who had started attending the church about six months ago, had invited Joel and Lisa for supper. They spent the evening eating and talking about faith and football. She had been amazed—as she often was—at how easily Joel could fit in and how he made people feel comfortable. Lisa loved watching her husband interact with others. He had such a gift of making them feel at ease and important. And he'd done it again tonight. But it seemed that gift no longer carried over to his own family.

Does he still love me? There was a part of her that didn't want to know the truth. That was afraid of finding out he might not. Then what would she do? She'd tried to talk with him about her concerns and fears before, but he'd always brushed them aside, saying it was all in her mind. Even though she knew it was late and probably not the best time to start a serious con versation, she decided to give it a try anyway.

"Joel?" she whispered.

A light snore answered her. Hot tears threatened. She forced herself to hold them back. *No, I won't cry. He's not staying awake worrying about our marriage. Why should I?*

But she did worry about their marriage. Terribly.

"Good night," she whispered to his back.

The wind, mixed with another snore, was all that responded.

Lisa turned onto her side facing the door. "Jesus, help him love me," she mouthed in silence. Then she closed her eyes and prayed for sleep.

8

Felicia

Tuesday, May 23
10:58 a.m.

The acrid smell of booze and cigarettes wafted down the alley as Felicia approached the back door of the Brew-Ha-Ha Pub. *Five minutes in this place, and I'll have to go home for fresh clothes,* she thought, regretting that she'd worn her new red suit. And the uneven pavement was wreaking havoc on her black pumps with the skinny heels, the ones Dave told her were too *Sex and the City* for a Midwestern pastor's wife. She'd told him he didn't even know what *Sex and the City* was ("I've seen the commercials!" he protested) and that she didn't have time to return them (lack of time was something Dave understood these days, so she knew she'd win with that one).

Wish I'd returned them, she thought as she struggled to stay upright after stepping on yet another piece of loose asphalt.

A homeless man looked her over while he pushed by with his cart.

Felicia clutched her briefcase tighter. She had decided to enter through the back door rather than risk someone from church seeing her go into a bar on this busy city street. But now she was wondering if the safety of the front door might have outweighed the risk of being seen. After all, Red River was fifty miles away—the chances of someone being in Cincinnati and driving by on a Tuesday morning were slim to none. Still, a pastor's wife could not be too careful!

As Felicia reached the door, a rolling bin of bottles came flying out and nearly knocked her down. Her startled yelp was met with a chuckle from behind the bin.

"Sorry 'bout that. We don't usually have women who are all made up coming in the back door—at least not this early anyway!" The man laughed at his own joke. He was tall and thin with graying hair. He wore a Reds polo shirt and khakis.

He looks like he should be on a golf course instead of running a bar.

"You must be Ms. Morrison. I'm Jim Powers. Come on in."

Felicia shook his hand as he backed against the door to let her pass. Entering the bar, she stopped to let her eyes adjust. *A dark place for people who want to hide from their lives,* she thought as she noted a few guys already bellied up to mugs of beer.

A lifelong Baptist, Felicia had never been in a bar. She didn't understand drinking alcohol. Back at UCLA, one of her roommates frequently had "blender parties," where all the guests would toss various liquors and juices into a blender, then force one another to drink their concoctions. Studying in her bedroom, Felicia could hear them getting sillier and sillier as they consumed glass after glass. She couldn't figure out why people would want to drink something that made them out of control.

Jim led her to his small office behind the bar. He moved several boxes of glassware from a chair and motioned for her to sit. "It's a good thing these are cheap," he said as he stacked the boxes. "People steal 'em all the time. I can't believe people go to the trouble of stealing old pint glasses, but they do."

Felicia had felt unsure at first in the bar environment, but Jim put her at ease. She liked the guy.

"So Mr. Powers," Felicia said as she snapped open her briefcase to grab a notepad. She loved getting down to business. "How can we help you?"

"Well, I was hoping you'd have some ideas." Jim pulled up a chair behind the desk. "Ever since that guy killed the kid, MADD has been picketing my place nearly every night. You know, it wasn't our fault that idiot jumped in his car and tried to drive home. We can't watch everyone, especially on a Saturday night. Besides, my bartender swears she served him only one beer."

Felicia thought for a moment. "Didn't I read in the paper that his friend said the guy had been drinking heavily all day before he even got to Brew-Ha-Ha?"

"That's what he said, and I believe him. He's got no reason to lie. But it doesn't matter. MADD's targeting me because this was the last place he was before he got in the accident."

Accident? Felicia jotted some notes.

There wouldn't have been an "accident" if he hadn't been drinking all day. Do I accidentally gain weight when I eat chocolate cake?

"Okay, so I see several things we need to do here," Felicia said. "But first you need to issue a public apology for what happened."

"Aw, come on." Jim buried his head in his hands. "If I start taking the blame for every jerk who comes in here and does something stupid after he drinks, I'll be saying, 'I'm sorry' twenty-four seven."

"Jim," Felicia started hesitantly, "this 'something stupid' was a murder. I'm not trying to force the blame on you, but a teenager was killed. You need to acknowledge"—she flipped through some pages on her notepad—"Nick Fisher's death, and the loss to his parents, before anything good can happen for your business."

"But what am I supposed to do? Call them up? Invite them in for a drink?"

Felicia grimaced at his last suggestion. Maybe she didn't like this Jim so much after all. "I'll come up with something. Meanwhile, the next time MADD is at your door, fill a crate with bottled water and hand out the bottles to the protesters. And be sure *you* do it, not one of your employees."

Jim reluctantly agreed.

As Felicia rose to leave, a man at the bar started yelling. "Did you follow me all the way here? Haven't you caused me enough trouble? I told you I want nothing to do with you anymore. Now get out and leave me alone!"

Jim jumped up, threw open his office door, and darted out to check on the commotion. Felicia followed closely behind, in some strange way eager to see her first bar fight, but mostly afraid to be alone in such a dark place.

"Hey, what's your problem?" Jim asked as he strode up to the man.

That man's problem is that he's drunk, Felicia thought as she strained in the dim light to see the back of a well-dressed lady—the focus of the man's anger—who was already walking toward the pub's front door.

Felicia continued watching the woman walk, wondering why someone like that would be in a place like this. *Two women in suits and heels in one day*, she thought. *Must be a record for this place.*

Then the woman stopped, checked her reflection in the mirror, smoothed a hair back in place, and stepped outside without looking back.

Who would stop to fix her hair when some drunk is screaming at her? Felicia wondered.

Just then the woman passed an open window. Felicia drew in her breath. In the light, she had no trouble identifying the woman.

Wait 'til I see the girls at lunch on Tuesday!

But would they ever believe that she was at a bar with none other than . . . Kitty Katt?

Lulu's Café

Tuesday, May 30
12:03 p.m.

From their usual table, Jennifer called out to Lisa, "Hurry up! Felicia's got something good to tell us, but she won't spill 'til we're all here."

Lisa's face brightened, and she made a silent "Oh!" with her mouth, then rushed to where Jennifer, Felicia, and Mimi were seated. She brushed back her long hair behind her shoulders and dropped her purse on the table. She had barely slid into the seat next to Felicia when Jennifer looked across at Felicia and gave the word: "Okay, we're all here!"

Felicia leaned forward, hands clasped, and eyed each woman in turn as she said, "You won't believe who I saw in a *bar* last week."

The others looked blankly at her.

"*You* were in a bar?" Jennifer asked.

"Remember? She had that meeting with the guy in Cincy who has the protesters," Lisa reminded her.

Jennifer was puzzled for a second, then nodded in recognition.

Mimi frowned in concentration. "Some celebrity or something?" she asked in an I-give-up tone.

"Sorry!" Felicia responded, clearly enjoying the delicious anticipation of sharing whatever the shocking news was with her friends.

"Give us a clue then!" Jennifer asserted.

Felicia put her finger to her mouth. "Let's see if this does it for you: the person's initials are KK."

The other three stared wide-eyed at Felicia, but none spoke.

Lisa sat back and crossed her arms. "No way. I do not believe that Kitty Katt was in a bar. Are you sure you saw her? Did you talk to her?"

Felicia recounted the whole scene, from hearing the man yell, to seeing Kitty prance down the sidewalk outside the bar.

While Felicia was talking, Gracie started toward their table to take their orders. Jennifer motioned for her to wait, not wanting to miss a detail.

"So did you talk to the man then?" Lisa asked skeptically. "I mean, I know she's a Presbyterian, and they drink and all, but who could Kitty possibly know who hangs out in a downtown Cincinnati bar that early on a weekday?"

Fingering her menu, Jennifer considered possible scenarios but came up blank.

"I've thought a lot about it, but I don't have any answers . . . except that maybe he used to go to their church and he's backslidden," Felicia offered.

Jennifer laughed. "Come on. I care about the people at our church, but I don't think it's the pastor's wife's responsibility to pull drunks out of bars and force them back on the right track. None of us would do that! And especially not Kitty Katt. All she cares about is herself."

"But there must be something more to it. Something juicy for Kitty to get involved," Mimi said with a touch of disgust. "I'm convinced that

66

woman thinks everything is her business. Do you know she sent me a card not long after our last lunch here?"

"Inviting you to another one of those horrible pastors' wives' get-togethers?" Jennifer asked with a mock shudder.

Mimi hesitated. "No. It was a sorry-for-your-loss card," she explained cryptically.

Lisa had opened her menu but closed it again after Mimi's words. "Your loss? Who died?"

Pausing for dramatic effect as she pretended to cry, Mimi said, "Yes, I had a loss." Jennifer looked at the others with alarm.

Mimi dropped the act and changed her voice back to normal. "Kidding! Well, I did have a loss, but it was for president of Hemmings PTA. I lost the election."

"That's a bummer," Jennifer said. "But in a weird way I'm glad to hear it. You need to chill out a little, Mimi. You're too busy, and you're going to wear yourself out."

"Like I told Mark, I didn't really want it anyway," Mimi said with what appeared to be a forced smile.

She's faking, Jennifer thought. *I bet that loss is killing her.*

"I mean," Mimi continued, "who wants to deal with that three-day school carnival in the fall and that huge T-shirt sale in the spring?"

"It's a big job, that's for sure," Lisa said as she glanced over the menu.

Mimi looked at her. "Were you on PTA at Hemmings, Lisa?"

"Yeah, I was president back when Callie was in second grade. Before your kids would have been there." Lisa shut her menu and motioned for Gracie to take their order.

Mimi blinked a few times, then buried her head in her menu.

Yep, I was right, Jennifer realized. *Poor Mimi—to hear that she failed at something Lisa had accomplished.*

Jennifer stopped her train of thought abruptly. She could say the same about herself—that she couldn't measure her failure or success by comparing her situation to the three mothers sitting around the table with her. But she didn't want to think about that. She was glad when she spied Gracie approaching.

Gracie sauntered up to the table. She took her pen from behind her ear and licked a finger so she could turn the page on her order pad. "All right, what are you all having today? And we've got that coconut cake you like, Jennifer."

Lisa snapped her menu on the table. "Ugh, hearing about cake reminds me. I've got to tell you guys about Ricky's birthday party. Wha—" Lisa was interrupted by Gracie's clearing her throat.

"If you girls want to have lunch, let's get it ordered." She tapped the pen against her order pad. "Otherwise you're going to need to order dinner soon."

"Yes ma'am!" Felicia said, using a military voice. "I'll go first."

After they ordered, the PWs immediately turned their attention back to Lisa.

"You were going to tell us about Ricky's party," Mimi reminded her.

"Well, Joel has been nothing but a jerk lately," Lisa started. "If someone from church needs something, he's right there. But if it's the kids—or especially me—he has no time for it. And it's been getting worse and worse."

Felicia turned and studied Lisa, who was sitting next to her. "Does this have anything to do with those watery eyes you had a couple of lunches ago? That *wasn't* allergy problems, was it?"

Lisa paused and looked at everyone as if she were deciding whether to say anything more. Then hesitantly she said, "I'm sorry, but it's really hard for me to talk about it, and I wasn't ready at that point. But I do need you to pray for me." She scratched her eyebrow with her ring finger, then pushed her fingers against her forehead. "Joel has become a stranger in our home. And even when he is there, he's not involved with the kids. We haven't been close in . . . a long time."

"I'm so sorry to hear that," Mimi said sincerely.

"Anyway," Lisa continued, as though she didn't want to discuss her marriage, "back to Ricky's birthday. First I asked Joel to come with me to get Ricky's present, a new bike. Not that I couldn't do it on my own, but I thought it would be good to get a guy's perspective. We used to have fun shopping for our kids. But, surprise, surprise, when I asked him to go with me, he said he had a church meeting and couldn't do it. The kicker, though, was two days later."

Lisa paused while Gracie set their drinks on the table.

"Is this regular or decaf?" Jennifer asked when the cup was placed in front of her.

Gracie rolled her eyes. "See that doily under your cup?"

Jennifer nodded.

"That means decaf. You should know that by now, girly. What's the big deal anyway? It's the middle of the day. You can handle a little caffeine."

"Gracie," Felicia interrupted, "Jennifer could be pregnant, and she wants to be healthy for her baby."

Validated, Jennifer gave Felicia an appreciative smile.

Gracie jutted her chin and grunted, then walked away.

Lisa stirred sugar in her tea. "On the morning of Ricky's birthday, I reminded Joel that Ricky was having ten friends over at five o'clock for pizza and video games, then we'd have cake and ice cream later. Since the bakery is right next to our church, I asked Joel if he would pick up the cake and bring it home. He agreed he'd be home no later than four.

"So four o'clock rolls around, then four thirty, then four forty-five. Right before the first kid got there, I called Joel at the church. He said he was just finishing up a meeting, but he'd be home in time for cake. By *eight o'clock*, Joel still wasn't there. I thought about calling him again at the church, but I knew I couldn't take whatever flimsy excuse he'd offer. And since it was a school night and the party needed to end by nine, I couldn't keep the kids waiting for their dessert forever. So I had to make do with ice cream. I put a candle in it and we sang 'Happy Birthday'—like it was a cake."

Jennifer groaned. "Poor kid. Was Ricky upset?"

"Interesting you would ask that," Lisa said. "I fully expected him to get angry, but as I put the ice cream with the candle in front of him, he leaned over to me and whispered in my ear, 'Dad was supposed to get the cake, wasn't he?' In a strange way, I was comforted to know that he recognized that Joel was not pulling his weight. Not that I want my kids to dislike their father, but hopefully they'll see his mistakes and not make them with their own children someday."

Felicia toyed with the straw in her soda. "So what time did jerky Joel finally show up?"

Lisa smirked. "I don't even know. I spent the night in the guest room."

Gracie arrived with their food. As the PWs stopped talking and dove into their lunches, Jennifer realized anew that each one of these women had significant needs. And she silently thanked God they had one another to lean on.

Lisa

Tuesday, June 6
12:19 p.m.

Lisa sat across the table from her mom at the Breaker Hill Pancake House. It was her mother's favorite restaurant, so whenever they met for lunch, it was always at the pancake house.

They'd just finished ordering their usual: Lisa, a tuna-salad sandwich on pumpernickel, with a side of fries and fruit, and her mother, a Denver omelet, well done, with a side of salsa, hash browns, and an English muffin, hold the butter. They both got iced tea—one sugar, no lemon.

"How are things at the church?" Lydia Jenkins asked.

It was always the same question. They always ordered the same meal, then Lydia started the conversation the identical way. It had never bothered Lisa before. In fact, it had been a comfort. The routine was nice, safe, and most of all, known. But for some reason, today it grated on her.

"The church is fine," Lisa said blandly. She picked up her straw, peeled off the paper covering, and shoved it into her tea, swishing it around mindlessly. "How are things with yours?" she politely asked her mother.

Lydia, also a pastor's wife, lived in the neighboring town of Cloverdale. She and Lisa's father, Stanley, pastored the Assembly of God there.

"Good, except Paul just told your father he's feeling called to do short-term missions."

Paul Adkins was the associate pastor and youth leader who had taken Joel's place after he'd left to become senior pastor at Red River.

"Really? But he's only been there a few years."

"I know. But last year . . . you remember he led our youth group on a weeklong mission trip to Haiti? Well, since then God's really got a hold of his heart for the people in Third World countries. He said he and Lizbeth have been praying about it this past year."

"What are you going to do?"

"Well, we can't *not* let them go. Although, selfishly, I wish we could." Lydia smiled and sipped her tea. "Paul asked your father to recommend him to the missions board. They plan on leaving by the end of the year."

"That soon?"

Lydia nodded again, then appeared lost in thought. Her eyes narrowed before she regained her composure. "How'd you say your church was?"

Lisa cringed. She was hoping her one-word answer had gone unnoticed. No such luck.

"It's fine."

Should she tell her mom what she'd been keeping bottled up for more than a year? She gazed at her mother. Everyone always told them how much alike they looked. Lisa had the same sable brown hair and hazel eyes as Lydia. Although, at sixty-three, Lydia's eyes had pronounced crow's feet, and her hair was more salt than pepper.

Lisa decided to take a chance. "Mom," she began hesitantly. "Something's bothering me, and I'm not really sure what to do about it."

She waited for her mother's response—for some sense of compassionate listening. But she only heard the question, "Something with the church?"

"Yes. No. Well, indirectly."

Lydia only nodded. Lisa could tell her mother had moved into "pastor's wife mode," a sort of spiritual self-assuredness she wore like a royal cape. Lisa had grown up watching her father's ministry and her mother standing proudly beside him, doing everything a pastor's wife should. And one of those things was the "pastor's wife mode" that Lydia had perfected and displayed hundreds of times. Lisa had tried to model it when she herself became a pastor's wife.

It was a mode in which Lydia listened politely, thoughtfully, and compassionately. But then, no matter what the situation or story, she responded with a catchall platitude. Lisa had heard them all her life: "Just give it to God." "God works all things together for good." "It just wasn't God's will." "You can't know the mysterious workings of God, but know that he is working for and in you." And the list went on and on . . .

Lisa had them used on her so many times, she could almost spout off which one she thought her mother would use. *Hmmm,* she'd think, *she'll use number 12,* as though she were picking out a special card from a magician's deck. She knew it wasn't that her mother was insincere. It was simply important for her mother to respond to people with compassion and hope. And for Lydia Jenkins, compassion and hope came in the form of a spiritual cliché.

Lisa's mind flickered past the pat Christian responses and desperately hoped that, for once, her mother would give her a genuine, honest-to-goodness, real, practical answer. She looked again at her mother, sitting across from her, with the perfect, straight-backed posture, head cocked slightly to the left, as though ready to listen intently . . .

No, today wouldn't be any different, Lisa decided. So she sipped her tea instead, then gently smiled.

Lydia narrowed her eyes again. "Something's obviously bothering you. You're usually so jubilant and happy. What's wrong? Is somebody causing trouble at the church?"

"No no, it's nothing like that. Everything's going well at the church. Several new families have started coming. And Joel's last sermon series was really good. It was on how to love God with all your heart, soul, mind, and strength."

"Then what is it? Something with Callie? Ricky?"

"No." Lisa picked up the white straw paper and began to fidget with it. "It's just . . . Joel."

"Joel? What's wrong with him?"

"I don't know. That's just it. He's—" Lisa paused to search for the right word. "Distant."

"Distant? What do you mean, distant?"

"From me. From the kids. He never seems to spend time with us anymore."

"Well, Lisa, he's a senior pastor now. He's got a lot of responsibilities."

"I know that, Mom. But it's almost as if he ignores me. Like he *tries* to avoid me."

"Nonsense," Lisa's mother stated matter-of-factly. "He's got a lot on his mind. And he needs you to support him, not question him."

Well, Lisa thought wryly, *at least it wasn't a cliché. Instead it felt like a reprimand.*

"But why does it always seem to come back to what *I* need to do for Joel? It never seems to be what Joel needs to do for me. That apparently isn't an option for a pastor's wife."

Lisa couldn't believe the words had slipped from her mouth. Her stomach did a flip-flop, waiting to see how her mother would respond to her outburst.

When Joel had first entered the pastorate almost a decade ago, Lydia had taken Lisa aside one afternoon and told her, "Your job is not to overshadow your husband. Your job is to support him and make him look good. He'll have enough troubles with the people at church. He won't need them at home too."

Lisa had only nodded and taken her mother's advice to heart. But back then, it hadn't been difficult. She and Joel shared everything. They were best friends and loved each other deeply. Joel shared all his dreams about becoming a pastor and how they'd do ministry together. It was wonderful. Then.

"Mom, how have you and Dad made it in the ministry this long with your marriage still okay?"

"I don't know what you mean," Lydia said in a frosty tone. "Honestly, Lisa, the things you come up with. Now, don't worry about that anymore. Remember, Joel is doing God's work. And your blessings come by supporting him and his ministry. Why don't you make his favorite meal tonight? He works hard, and I bet he'd appreciate your doing something thoughtful for him. And if this thing is still really bothering you, well, just give it to God."

And there ended the conversation. Lydia had fulfilled her listening responsibility, then provided her pat Christian answer. Lisa knew her mother wasn't trying to be mean or disconnected. That was all she knew to do. It just saddened Lisa that the only people she felt she could go to for help—her husband and her mother—turned out to be of no help at all.

Lisa smiled and nodded again. Obviously, she wasn't going to get comfort or sympathy on this day. She decided the best tactic was to keep quiet about it and change the subject. Fortunately their food arrived, giving her time to think of something else to talk about. Something safe . . .

"Did you get the JCPenney sale flyer in the mail? It had some great coupons. I was thinking about driving into Cincinnati to see what I could get for the kids . . ."

1:09 p.m.

On the drive home after lunch with her mother, Lisa thought about her parents' marriage. It wasn't that it was cold and distant. They obviously loved each other. But they weren't overly affectionate—not in public, and not at home. Lisa couldn't remember a time when her parents had quarreled. Yet neither could she remember a time when they'd spoken loving words to each other. Her mother simply "played the game." She was the perfect pastor's wife, never complaining about the multitude of times church members interrupted family time, taking her husband away. She was always pleasant at church—even to the church members who caused trouble—and always took care of her man. It was almost as if they were business partners. The ministry came first, and everything else second.

But I don't want to live that way, Lisa thought harshly. *I want to live with passion. I want to be partners, yes, but I also want to be lovers. What happened to us? We used to be passionate.*

Then her mother's words came back to her: *"He's a senior pastor now. He's got a lot of responsibilities."*

Maybe that was it. Lisa had noticed that the stress of being a senior pastor did take a toll on him.

When Joel had left Lisa's father's church three years ago to take over the senior pastorate at Red River Assembly of God, he'd been so excited and full of ideas for helping the church mature and grow. But instead of taking the church by the reins and leading it, he seemed to be led by the church, which was taking him by the reins and demanding complete servitude. He began to spend more and more time away from home and at the church. Every meeting, every function, Joel was there. He was the first at the church and the last to leave. If somebody called the house needing something, Joel dropped everything to help out, even if it proved inconvenient for him or the family.

But it was their marriage that took the greatest hit. They never did things together anymore. And if they did have a rare "date night," inevitably they'd run into a church member who butted into their evening. Talk about a romance killer! They had to be careful about everything they did—from what movie they went to see (for fear someone would see them, and it would get back to the church) to what restaurant they ate at (for fear someone would see them, and it would get back to the church). Their entire marriage was scrutinized. And she watched helplessly from the sidelines as the church took more control over Joel. The more they pushed, the more her marriage took the backseat in his priorities. It had slowly eroded until she felt miserable—unloved and unlovely. If this was after only three years at the church, how would it be after ten or fifteen or twenty?

She thought again of her mother's advice: *"Why don't you make his favorite meal tonight? He works hard, and I bet he'd appreciate your doing something thoughtful for him."*

Well, it couldn't hurt.

Lisa turned the car east and headed toward the Kroger grocery store.

5:38 p.m.

"What stinks?" Ricky scrunched his nose as he entered the kitchen.

"Pork roast, sauerkraut, and dumplings. And put that pudding away.

You'll ruin your appetite," Lisa said as she watched him open the refrigerator door and grab a chocolate pudding cup.

"Too late."

Joel walked into the kitchen holding the mail.

"I made your favorite," Lisa said brightly.

He began shuffling through the bills and junk mail, acting as though he hadn't heard her.

"It'll be ready in about ten minutes," she prompted.

"I think I'm up for pizza," Ricky interjected. "That's *my* favorite."

"Hmmm?" Joel tore open one of the envelopes.

"Dinner. Ten minutes."

"Oh, sounds good," Joel said. "I need to eat soon, though. I forgot to tell you, I'm meeting with a few other pastors tonight to discuss the July Fourth community service."

"I thought you weren't going to be that involved this year."

"I know, but one of the ministers asked me to help out."

"You haven't had a relaxed meal with your family in a long time. You're always rushing off to do something with the church. Couldn't you get there a little later?"

"I'm not sure pork, sauerkraut, and dumplings would make *me* all that relaxed," Ricky contributed, opening the pudding cup.

"Ricky, go wash up for dinner," Lisa said impatiently. "Joel, your family should be the priority. Surely those other pastors understand the need to spend time eating a nice dinner with their families, and they will wait for you."

"Lisa, this is for the community. It's my chance to get to know my peers better. And it's important for our church. It's great exposure."

For the church, or for you? Lisa opened her mouth to utter another argument, then stopped herself. She knew it wouldn't do any good. She dropped her head and busied herself with finishing dinner preparations.

I don't even like pork, sauerkraut, and dumplings. I probably should order pizza. It'd serve him right.

Lisa opened the fridge and grabbed herself a pudding.

CHAPTER
11

Mimi

Friday, June 9
7:42 a.m.

"There are mocha cappuccino muffins and pecan-pie muffins in the container for your classes," Mimi told MJ and Michaela as they headed out the front door and down the front path. "And make sure you give one to Alice. Have a good day. I love you! Oh, and MJ," she half yelled, half laughed, "try not to get into trouble today!"

MJ and Michaela ran down the sidewalk toward the bus that had just pulled up. The door swung open. As the kids hopped inside, the bus driver leaned out.

Alice Beesom was in her forties and a single mom of three teenagers. She'd come home one day to find her husband in bed with her best friend. After the divorce, Alice took the bus-driving job to help pay bills.

"Hi, Mimi!" she called. "Thanks for the muffin!"

"You look radiant today, Alice."

"Yep. I'm celebrating the last day of school. Finally I'll get a break!" They both laughed.

"Hey, I heard you volunteered to work at the food pantry next month," Alice said. "That's great news. I'll be working with you. Make sure you bring some of your famous coffeecake."

"You bet, Alice," Mimi called back. "Have a good day." The bus filled with noisy children pulled away as Mimi stood in the doorway, smiling and waving. She stepped back into the house and exhaled heavily. *I completely forgot about that. I'm not even sure where the food pantry is. Somewhere downtown Red River, I think.*

Mimi was still lost in her thoughts of the food pantry as she stepped over Buster, who'd plopped down in the middle of the hallway after he'd seen the kids off to school. She wasn't sure why she'd volunteered to work at the food pantry. She'd never even been there before. But when the leaflet came to the church about needing help, Mimi figured she'd do her part.

It all came down to the fact that Mimi liked doing things for other people. While it made her feel good to know something she'd done could help another person—that she was in a sense serving Christ by taking care of people—it also made her feel good to hear people tell her how good her cooking was or what wonderful people skills she had. It wasn't that Mimi was proud or egotistical. It was just that she couldn't rest until she'd accomplished things, and accomplished them *successfully.*

All her life Mimi had tried to be what others needed her to be. In college, when she and Mark started dating and she knew he was going to become a pastor, she took piano lessons to be better prepared. *After all*, she thought, *all pastors' wives I know play the piano or organ.*

Then when Mark took his first pastorates at smaller churches, she did everything except preach—taught Sunday school, played piano for the services, organized and led vacation Bible school, sang in the choir, hosted the young-marrieds class, worked every other Sunday in the nursery, directed the Christmas play, baked a majority of the items for the missionary bake sales, and hosted weekly dinners for members of the congregation.

All that on top of being the best third-grade teacher she could be before her kids came along. She spent hours preparing exciting lessons for her students. When parent-teacher conferences came around, she presented each parent with a homemade photo frame that she'd assembled and painted, with a photo of his or her child inside.

Sure she was exhausted, but it seemed worth it all to hear people compliment her abilities and go-getter spirit. "Your husband is such a fortunate man," they'd say. But she wondered sometimes if Mark felt that way. He never seemed to appreciate everything she did.

When Mimi became pregnant with their first child, Michaela, Mark had encouraged her to quit her job and stay home. "Maybe this will slow you down some," he'd joked. She'd thought being a mother would fill the void she sensed. So she planned out her three pregnancies and went into motherhood with a passion. But even there, peace eluded her.

2:15 p.m.

"Habitat for Humanity?" Mark stared at Mimi, aghast at the latest volunteer announcement she'd nonchalantly made as she was putting his clean, folded socks and T-shirts into their respective drawers. He had come home early that day because he had to go to a men's fellowship barbecue in the evening and wanted to prepare a devotional talk for it. "You don't even know one end of a hammer from the other. You hate getting dirty. What were you thinking?"

Mimi picked up the laundry basket and walked into Michaela's room. "This is about helping people in need," she responded over her shoulder.

"No." Mark cut her off angrily. "This is about some unfulfilled need you have. I let the whole Lutheran ladies' tea thing slide. I let the food pantry thing slide too. And all the stuff you do at church. But this is getting ridiculous. You can't keep this up, Mimi. You're so busy doing for other people that you're letting things slide with your family. With me." He paused for effect.

Mimi finished putting Michaela's clothes away and moved into MJ's room.

"See?" Mark continued, following her and grabbing at the basket. "You can't even have a sane discussion anymore. The only time we talk is when you're busily doing something else. You don't focus on any one thing."

"That's not true! I do everything for you, Mark. I *am* a good wife and mother."

"How do you know? Because everybody says so?"

His words stung, and she clenched her jaw to keep from crying.

Mark softened his tone. "You're overcommitted. I just don't understand this incessant drive you have. You're outta control. As though you're trying to grab at something and it keeps eluding you. What are you trying to prove?"

Mimi refused to answer him.

"That's it?" he asked. "Silence?"

She turned on her heel and put away the towels in the kids' bathroom.

"I don't even deserve a response?" he asked.

Mimi stiffened her back toward him.

"Fine," Mark said, almost resigned. "Fine. You win. Let me just say one thing. You're doing all this so people will like and respect you. You think you're winning, but you're not. You're in a losing battle. Because nothing you do will ever be enough. Nothing. You're chasing after peace as if it's something you can catch."

With those words, Mark walked downstairs and slammed the front door on his way out.

Mimi dropped the basket on the bathroom counter and examined her face in the mirror. The dark circles under her eyes used to be easy to hide under her makeup. But it was taking more and more makeup now to make them disappear.

Mark was right and she knew it. And she hated herself for it.

Jennifer

Sunday, June 11
9:48 a.m.

Jennifer felt a sense of dread as she walked into the church narthex. Her Sunday school class had been interesting—Ralph Witmer always led a compelling discussion—but it had been more like school and less like church. It was the worship services that were becoming less and less meaningful for her. Singing, praising, and praying to a God who wouldn't answer her one important prayer made her miserable.

"Hey there, Jennifer," called Bitsy Underwood from near the nursery. "Have you seen my Jaime's newest?"

Jennifer tried to wave and keep walking, but Bitsy trotted over anyway, cradling a baby in a seafoam green blanket. Jennifer crossed her arms, hoping to avoid what she knew was coming.

It came anyway. "Here, you need some practice." Bitsy pushed the squirming bundle toward Jennifer.

"Oh, Bitsy, I would love to hold her, but I don't think I should," Jennifer said, arms firmly crossed. "I seem to be coming down with a cold. Wouldn't want to pass it on to—"

"Is that Jaime and Matt's new one?" Lana Maxter squealed as she walked up and put a hand on both Jennifer and Bitsy's shoulders, looking down at the baby.

Bitsy nodded. "Konner. Her name is Konner. Isn't that a cute name for a girl? I just love it."

Bitsy and Lana cooed at Konner while Jennifer scouted for an escape.

"So when are you and Pastor going to get your family started?" Bitsy asked, eyes back on Jennifer again. "I'm sure he'd love to have a little one to dote on. You know, Matt is such a great dad—"

"And you would be a wonderful mother!" Lana chimed in. "We could use some little PKs around here, causing trouble."

Bitsy and Lana chuckled while Jennifer glanced around the bustling narthex, still hoping for an out. She spotted a family she didn't recognize. *Oh, thank God.*

"Ladies, I see some new folks I need to greet," she said, smiling, as she inched away. "Beautiful grandbaby, Bitsy. Really."

Jennifer unfolded her arms and walked quickly to the new family, but another couple beat her to them. Not wanting to take a chance on more baby interaction, she decided to go in to the sanctuary and pretend to read her Bible.

Purposefully looking the other way, she strode by Bitsy and Lana, who was now holding Konner. The two women had their heads close together over the baby.

"How sad it must be for Sam not to have a family," she heard Bitsy whisper to Lana.

"I know. Especially since he lost his first wife without getting one," Lana replied.

Hearing the women as she passed, Jennifer stopped short of the sanctuary door and took in a sharp breath. She was accustomed to parishioners getting involved in her personal life—they seemed to claim ownership over Sam and her—but this was salt on a very deep, festering wound. This evidence that others were watching and waiting for her to get pregnant instantly compounded the already enormous pressure she'd placed on herself.

The usher held out his hand with the church bulletin, waiting for her to take it.

"I think I'd better make one more quick stop before worship, if you know what I mean," she told him with a fake smile—her most fake ever—and turned from the sanctuary in the direction of the women's restroom.

But instead of stopping at the restroom, she walked out of the church, got into her car, and drove away. And she didn't stop driving until she got to Cincinnati.

Lulu's Café

Tuesday, June 13
12:14 p.m.

"You walked right out the door while people were walking in?" Felicia asked Jennifer, incredulous. "Didn't anyone see you and inquire where you were going?"

Jennifer smiled slightly as she remembered how free she felt driving away from the church that Sunday morning. "Not one person asked. Not even Reggie McAvoy, when he held open the door for me to leave," she said triumphantly.

"Well, who would expect the pastor's wife to be leaving right before the church service?" Lisa said. "I've thought sometimes that as long as I was back for the Meet and Greet at the end of the service, no one would even miss me!"

"You could probably do a *day's* worth of chores in the time it takes one of your Assembly services to wrap up," Mimi said with a wink.

Lisa moved from left to right, clapping her hands, as if she were hearing music. "Maybe you ought to give it a try sometime, Mimi. You might find that you like rocking out for God."

"Hey, our organist sometimes goes full pedal on a really big hymn," Mimi said, wearing a mock look of offense.

"And Sam didn't know?" Felicia asked about Jennifer's big escape.

"Fortunately we drove separate cars that day because he wanted to get to church early. He told me later that when he looked down from the pulpit and I wasn't there, he assumed I was working in the nursery. But when I wasn't home when he got there, he called my cell. I told him I'd left church a little early to clear my head, but that I'd be home soon."

"So where'd you go?" Felicia asked Jennifer.

"I was afraid someone might see my car in our driveway and think something was wrong. So I just hopped on I-71 and drove into Cincinnati. When I got down there, it was about lunchtime, so I decided to stop at a Skyline and get some chili." Jennifer shook her head and chuckled. "But of course I was standing in line when someone tapped me on the shoulder."

"Uh-oh," Mimi said, her grayish blue eyes widening.

Jennifer laughed. "Yeah, 'uh-oh' is right. I turned around, and it was our new associate pastor's parents. They looked at me like they were seeing a ghost."

"What'd you say?" Lisa asked, squeezing a lemon into her iced tea.

"There wasn't much I could say." Jennifer shrugged, a strand of her strawberry-blond hair falling into her eyes. "I think out of nerves they started chattering immediately about how much Derek was enjoying his ministry and how they were thrilled with Lucy, his fiancée. Then they stopped talking and kind of looked at me weird. I think they expected me to explain why I was at a Skyline Chili all the way down in Cincinnati on a Sunday at 11:30 a.m."

"And you didn't say *anything*?" Felicia asked.

"Not one solitary word," Jennifer said, proud that she hadn't blurted out a lie. "I figured it was none of their business what I was doing. I'm sure they told Derek, but I don't think he'd have the guts to ask me to my face. He and Lucy really look up to Sam and me."

Gracie arrived at the table just in time to hear Jennifer say her husband's name. "Hey, that reminds me," Gracie said as she reached across Lisa to set Felicia's salad in front of her, "when am I going to meet these husbands of yours? I'd like to put some faces to their names."

The PWs connected glances, as if they might be able to form a wall around the secrets they shared if they did so. Although they'd never discussed it, Jennifer instinctively knew none of them planned to bring their husbands to Lulu's. Ever. This was *their* place.

"Oh, our husbands are busy working men," Felicia said nonchalantly. "We're lucky if we can get them out to dinner in Red River, let alone down here."

Jennifer grinned inwardly with relief.

"Red River." Gracie shook her head as she wiped her hands on her apron after setting plates in front of all of them. "I can't believe you girls come all the way from Red River to eat at *this* place."

"It's the *ambiance*," Jennifer said with a straight face, causing Gracie to walk away, shaking her head. Once her back was to them, the PWs let go of the laughs they'd been holding in.

"You know, maybe *someday* we will get together . . . the four couples," Mimi said while she slathered tartar sauce on her fish sandwich. "But not at Lulu's. I'd love to have you all over for dinner and—" Mimi's words trailed off in an uncomfortable silence.

That would never happen, Jennifer knew. At least not for a while.

Lisa broke the momentary silence as she used the edge of her fork to break off a bite of meat loaf. "Jennifer's not the only one who ran into someone recently."

"Do tell," Felicia said quickly.

"Well, I had to go to the post office last Friday because I got one of those slips," Lisa said. "I don't know how the mailman missed me—it seems like I'm always at home—but he did."

"Get to the point!" Jennifer barked.

The others swiveled to stare at her, as if to see if her freckled skin had turned green like the Hulk's.

"Sorry, guys. Must be that medicine," she explained meekly. "It makes me so easily agitated."

Jennifer was glad when Lisa jumped back in. She didn't want this to turn into a fertility discussion again. Her friends always listened intently and kindly to her infertility problems. But she could tell her one-track mind was wearing thin on them, even if they'd never said anything about it.

"So I get in line at the post office, and," Lisa changed to a singsong voice, "guess who's in front of me talking on her cell phone in a hushed voice?"

Mimi squealed with delight. "Did you hear anything? What was she saying? Did she see you?"

"Whoa, hang on," Lisa said, as though she was thoroughly enjoying her chance at being a roving reporter. "I'm not sure who Kitty was talking to, but I did hear her say something about, 'Loving you until the day I die, no matter what you do.'"

Felicia gasped. "I hate to say this . . . well, on second thought, maybe I don't . . . but do you think she's having an affair?"

"I'll say the thought crossed my mind when I saw how she was act-ing and heard her say that about loving the person," Lisa admitted. "And there's more. When a baby started crying behind me in line, Kitty turned to look—but saw me instead. I think she must've suspected that I could have heard some of what she said on her phone. So she pretended like she didn't see me, even though she looked me right in the eye, then she turned and left!"

"She left the building?" Jennifer asked, astonished.

Lisa nodded. "And she was only two people away from the counter too."

"Now why would someone wait in line that long—then turn tail and leave unless she had something to hide?" Mimi leaned forward, in detective mode.

Jennifer could feel the Kitty conspiracy starting.

Lisa nabbed one of Mimi's fries. "Who would have an affair with that woman? I don't even like being in the same room with her."

The others giggled in agreement.

"Isn't it always the great ones who fall?" Jennifer asked. "Jim Bakker, Jimmy Swaggart . . ."

"And Kitty Katt?" Mimi laughed. "I'm not sure she's in *their* league."

Felicia turned serious. "Although I can't stand Kitty, I hope she's not having an affair. I mean, how sad for her husband! I know he can be over-bearing, but that doesn't mean he deserves to lose his wife to another man," she said angrily.

Jennifer noted the slight tremor in her friend's voice. And the way she grew quiet and started to pick at her salad. Why was Felicia so emotional about the idea of *Kitty* having an affair?

Mimi pushed her extra french fries over to Felicia, who waved them off. "I know one thing," Mimi said. "I'm going to keep my eyes and my ears open around Red River a little more. If Kitty Katt *is* having an affair, I want to know about it."

Jennifer snickered. "Know about it? Why? What are you going to do? Confront her?"

Mimi stiffened. "I want to know, that's all. It's like Martha Stewart going to prison—we all feel a little better when we find out that those we thought were the best are just okay like the rest of us." She relaxed enough to pick a piece of lint off her fuchsia shirt.

"What have you done with my Mimi?" Lisa joked. Her warm hazel eyes sparkled with amusement. "Since when are you all right with 'just okay,' Miss Perfection?"

Mimi yanked the napkin from her lap, crumpled it, and tossed it on her plate. "No one can be perfect *all* the time at *every*thing. It's impossible."

What the friends didn't say in response spoke volumes. The truth they had known all their lives seemed to be a new revelation for Mimi: everyone fails.

14

Jennifer

Thursday, June 15

10:58 a.m.

"You're just emotional. Give it a few days, honey," Sam said as Jennifer stood in front of him in his office, blotting her eyes with a tissue. "You know this time of the month can be full of mood swings for you."

Jennifer stopped wiping her eyes and shot Sam a glare. It wasn't her "time of the month." Reaching over, she shut the door that separated his pastoral office from her secretarial one.

"No, I want to quit. I know I do."

"What?"

"You heard me. I'm done. I've been the secretary here for thirteen years, and I'm done. Get someone else."

Sam turned from her and fiddled with the books in the case. "You know if I do that, we will have less money coming in," he said with his back still turned. "You'll need to get a job somewhere else to help out."

"Who cares if we even have money?" Jennifer started sobbing again.

"We . . . have . . . no . . . family . . . to . . . support."

Jennifer fell on the small sofa on the other side of his office and covered her face with her forearm. She knew she was out of control, but she wanted Sam to see how emotionally distraught she was.

Tap. tap, tap.

"That's my eleven o'clock with Ray Ammons," Sam said quietly as he reached out a hand to help Jennifer off the couch. "Let's talk more about this later."

Reluctantly Jennifer got up. She hung her head as she shuffled past Ray so he couldn't see her flushed face. Throwing herself into her desk chair, she stared out the window at the blossoming flowers planted along the church entrance. A disgust for new life flowed through her body.

Is there anything or anyone who is not blooming right now, except me?

Scanning the office, she knew she couldn't stay one minute longer. Bulletins were stacked, ready to be folded, but they looked like mountains to climb. The ringing phone sounded like a death toll.

"Jen? . . . Jen, are you there? Can you bring us some coffee?"

Jennifer ignored Sam buzzing her on the intercom from his office as she put on her sunglasses and grabbed her purse, keys, and travel coffee mug. Desperation was oozing from her pores as she started for the front door. She had to get away. But as she walked by the sanctuary, she stopped. Something deep within her decided to give God one more try.

She opened the large sanctuary doors and almost whimpered her distress. The custodian was vacuuming. Although he looked up and waved, she pretended she didn't see him. Now she couldn't go in to pray.

Well, I guess you don't want your last chance, do you? she told God before she walked out of the church and toward her car.

Just as she was sticking one leg in the driver's side, she noticed, for what seemed like the first time, the Catholic church across the street. She remembered seeing an ad in the paper that said St. Peter's was open for prayer 24/7.

Nice try, but I can't go over there, she argued. *What if someone saw me? A pastor's wife going to pray in a Catholic church?*

That's when she looked in her rearview mirror and saw the box of canned goods she'd bought for the Red River Food Pantry. The local drop-off site just happened to be St. Peter's.

"Okay, okay. You got me," she muttered as she climbed back out of the car and reached into the backseat for the box.

Making her way quickly across the street, she gingerly opened the heavy wooden door to the church. She'd never been in a Catholic church before and wasn't sure what to expect.

The aroma of incense greeted her—she'd always liked incense and burned it at home sometimes while she did her devotions. (Well, back when she did devotions.) The church was cool and dark except for some lit candles that were scattered around.

Jennifer left the box at the entrance—she'd take it over to the pantry later—and walked into the sanctuary. At the front of the sanctuary, Jesus loomed high up on the cross, waiting as if she had a private appointment with him.

Moved at the sight of the dominant crucifix, she slipped into a pew and pulled down the kneeler. *Handy to be able to pray at your seat,* she thought as she remembered times when her church's altar was so full that she was sure some people didn't come forward because of lack of space.

Crouching down, Jennifer rested her elbows on the back of the pew in front of her and clasped her hands. There was an eerie silence in the church.

This must be what it's like to be a monk . . . always living in quiet, cool, dark places.

She raised her eyes again to the cross. Seeing Jesus and thinking about the pain he endured caused her to well up again.

"Oh, Lord, you know how it feels to think God has forgotten you," she whispered, tears trickling down her face. "Help me, Lord. Help me."

"What do you need help with?"

Jennifer jumped straight up, whacking her purse and sending its contents across the pew.

"Behind you," the voice said.

Jennifer turned to see a man in a powder blue nylon running suit sitting in the pew two behind hers. His face held a look of peace, mixed with concern. How did he get in there without her hearing him?

Jennifer settled back in the pew and found her voice. "Oh, I thought—"

"Well, he does speak to us in many ways," the man said through his smile as he stood and walked toward her. "Can I pray with you?"

"Who are—"

"I'm Father Scott, the pastor here."

Jennifer studied his clothes. Didn't Catholic priests wear long, dark robes and white collars? Or had she seen too many movies?

Father Scott must have noted her curiosity, for he gestured toward his jacket. "Oh yes. Sorry about the garb. I had to fit in my run between the grade-school Mass and lunch. I stopped in here to check on a few things on my way back. And that's when I saw you."

Jennifer sniffled and nodded. "I didn't even hear you come in. You were quiet as a—" She stopped as she realized what she was saying.

"Church mouse? Yeah, we learn that in seminary—how to sneak up on parishioners and make them think God is talking to them."

Jennifer raised her eyebrows.

"I'm kidding," Father Scott said, slipping in next to her. "Anyway, I don't recognize you from the parish. Are you new to Red River?"

Anything but, Jennifer thought. She had been born and raised in Red River, and had never left.

"Uh, well, yes," Jennifer stammered. "But I'm not—"

"Don't worry if you've missed a few Masses during your move," said Father Scott as he patted her hand.

Oh, I've missed more than a few Masses, Jennifer thought.

"But you are obviously distressed. Is it the move? Did you leave loved ones behind somewhere?" Father Scott probed.

Jennifer looked the priest in the eye. Could she unleash her soul to this man without revealing who she was? What if he found out the truth? What if Sam discovered she was confiding in a Catholic priest—of all people?

"Or would you like to make a confession? I can run to the office and grab my stole if—"

"No no." Confession? Well, yes, that was what she needed to do, but probably not in the way he meant.

"Okay then. You obviously want to be alone with the Lord, so I'll leave you be," Father Scott said as he got up. "Besides, I think 'pew' probably has more than one meaning for me after that run! You hit the kneeler, and I'll hit the showers. Nice meeting you—"

"Je—" Jennifer hesitated, "Jill. It's Jill." *No, that's the name of the collie you buried five years ago,* she told herself.

"Jill, I'll see you at Mass on Sunday." Father Scott walked across the front of the church, stopping to nod at the front (*Is he nodding to Jesus on the cross?* Jennifer wondered), then headed toward a small room off the side.

"I've lost my faith in God." Her voice rang through the cavernous church as if she had called out through a megaphone.

Father Scott stopped and turned back to Jennifer. "Well, now," he said as he strode back over to her, "I guess I *was* right when I suspected you had left a loved one behind."

Tears began streaming down Jennifer's face again, a combination of embarrassment over her situation—a pastor's wife who has lost her faith in God?—and weariness over the whole thing.

When Father Scott arrived at the pew, she moved over so he could sit by her again. And for the next two hours, that's where they sat, Jesus looking down on them from the rustic wooden cross as Jennifer poured out her pain.

Lisa

Sunday, June 18
8:07 a.m.

"What's going on?" Joel entered the bedroom and looked at Lisa, who was still lying in bed. "Callie said you aren't coming to church."

"No, I have a migraine." Lisa slowly and painfully opened her eyes. She felt as if someone were using a hammer on her head.

"You've been getting a lot of those lately," he said with an edge to his voice. "How can you support the ministry if you're not at church?"

Unbelievable, she thought. *Somehow my migraines turn around to be about you.* "Well, it's not like I'm doing this on purpose."

"I know." His tone softened as he sat on the bed next to her. "I'm sorry. It's just that today's the Sunday I start that series on tithing. And I'm a little nervous. This is the first message I've done on it, and you know how people get when pastors preach on money. I'm hoping by doing it on Father's Day they'll understand a father's sacrificial giving goes hand in hand with the sacrificial tithe. And selfishly I wanted you to be there. It encourages me to see you sitting in the congregation."

Lisa felt bad for her thoughts. He wasn't trying to be nasty, she realized. He just needed her and didn't express it well.

Joel touched her forehead and lightly massaged the top of her head. "Can I get you anything? An Excedrin? Some hot tea?"

She smiled faintly. "Callie already got me some aspirin. But thanks. I'll wait for it to kick in, then try to make it to church in time for the service."

"No." He shook his head. There was a hint of tenderness in his brown eyes. "You rest. It'll be okay."

He started to walk away, then stopped and turned at the door. "We'll say a prayer for you during the service."

Lisa closed her eyes. "Thanks. I'd appreciate that."

Lisa tucked her legs against her chest and grasped her hair, hoping that if she squeezed at the base and pulled, it would alleviate some of the throbbing, stabbing pain.

7:45 p.m.

Lisa slept most of the day. By evening, she felt well enough to leave the bedroom and make a cup of hot tea with honey.

Joel was sitting at the kitchen table, reading the sports section of the *Red River Chronicle*. He barely glanced up when she entered the kitchen.

"How was the service?" she asked, filling the teakettle with water from the faucet.

"It went better than I thought it would. Now we just have to see if it makes any difference."

Two weeks ago there had been an all-church board meeting where the treasurer announced that the church had enough money in reserve to pay the bills for four more months. That was counting the weekly tithes that were coming in. When Joel heard that, he told Lisa he felt personally responsible for the church's not meeting its budget. So he spent several evenings with the treasurer going over the books and looking for ways to cut spending. Otherwise, Lisa knew, the cutting would come from Joel's paycheck. *Ah, ministry*, she thought when he broke the news.

She knew she should be used to that by now. She'd grown up with a pastor father who'd often had to give up his paycheck so the church mortgage and utilities bills could be paid.

"Maybe those families who aren't tithing will start," Lisa suggested, hoping for the best, but knowing from experience that many families came to church, made use of the programs, and contacted the pastor for his "free" services but never felt any obligation to support the church's work financially. Sometimes that really bothered Lisa.

Yes, she had signed on to the ministry when she'd married Joel. And she had known that financial struggles could be part of the deal. It still didn't make it any easier for her to take.

"We'll see," Joel said.

Lisa removed a cup from the cabinet closest to the sink. "Want a cup of tea?"

Joel grunted an "uh-huh."

She picked up another cup and poured hot water into it. "Do you think I should look into getting a part-time job?"

Joel partly dropped the paper and looked at her over it. "Why?"

"Well, if families don't start paying their tithes, then you may have to take a pay cut—or worse, not get paid at all."

"I'm aware of that, Lisa. But you getting a part-time job would only make me feel worse. As though I can't support my own family."

You can't! she thought but decided that may not be the best thing to say. Instead she opted for another approach. "Joel, you're taking this budget thing too personally. You can't force people to pay up. Even God doesn't do that! And anyway, getting a part-time job would get me out of the house and give me something to do."

"No."

Something within her burst. "Joel Barton, you pompous man! Why does everything have to be about you? *Your* pride. *Your* church. *Your* reputation. You never used to be this way. You've changed. And it's not for the better. And what's worse is that you're dragging down your wife and family. Does that mean anything to you? Or are we expendable on your drive up the church ladder?"

"What's that supposed—"

"Stop." Lisa held up her hand to stop his comment. She was angry and didn't want an argument or discussion. She was never good at arguing with Joel. He could think faster, and she needed time to process. After their arguments, *then* she'd think of what she could have, or should have, said. *Not this time*, she told herself. Besides, her head was starting to throb again. She walked her cup to the sink, dropped it in, and strode out of the room.

Felicia

Thursday, June 22
6:12 p.m.

Felicia looked with pride at the dining-room table set for three as the aroma of chicken enchiladas wafted in from the kitchen. Dave had been harping about her late work nights and their lack of a family life, so Felicia had chosen this date a week ago and had Delores clear the late afternoon schedule. Home by four with her tiny sports-car trunk packed with groceries, Felicia had plenty of time to make dinner and clean off the dining-room table—which they used more as a landing spot for junk mail than a place to eat these days—before Dave arrived with Nicholas in tow.

"Mom!" Nicholas burst through the front door and raced to where Felicia was stirring beans on the stove. "I got a Good Kid badge today!" He thrust his chest forward so Felicia could inspect the circle taped there.

"Oh, now that's my sweet boy!" She reached down to hug him.

As Nicholas ran off and Felicia opened the oven door to check on her enchiladas under the broiler, she felt her first inklings of satisfaction since coming to Red River. *Okay, maybe I can handle this*, she thought as she ticked off her accomplishments: Nicholas was behaving, her job was going well, and she was being a good wife and mother by making dinner—which would be ready in just a minute or two.

"Uh, Felicia," Dave said as he walked into the kitchen and glanced around at the pre-dinner mess with a furrowed brow. "You know the VBS committee is meeting here at six thirty tonight, right?"

Felicia heard a sound in her head like a jet screeching to a halt on a runway. "Well, obviously not," she said tersely as she tossed a dishtowel at a pile of dirty bowls and pans on the counter. "I left work early today to make dinner so we could spend the evening together as a family, like you've been telling me—"

She pushed past Dave and stormed into their bedroom. Grabbing a tissue, she sat on the edge of the bed and ripped the tissue into shreds, letting them fall to the floor. Hot, angry tears threatened to overtake her, but she fought them back. Felicia hated crying. It was so . . . weak.

"Honey." Dave was standing sheepishly in the doorway. "I appreciate the effort, but you know VBS is our major outreach this summer. I wanted the planning committee to meet here so we could show them how much we appreciate what they're doing."

He walked over and sat next to Felicia on the bed. "Look, you don't really need to do anything. I'll help you pick up the house. And Nancy Borden is bringing snacks. I told her you probably wouldn't have time to make anything."

"Oh, great," Felicia said. "So not only do *I* know I'm a failure as a pastor's wife, but everyone in the church does too?"

"Not everyone, Felicia. Just Nancy—"

"I'm sick of hearing about Nancy Borden!" Felicia was almost yelling. Dave jutted his head in warning toward Nicholas's bedroom.

Felicia lowered her voice but didn't alter its tone. "Fine. Have your meeting. But don't expect me to be there. I am not on this church's payroll, and I am not going to be taken advantage of. Nicholas and I will enjoy our dinner in the kitchen."

Dinner! Felicia jumped up and ran to the kitchen, but the smell greeted her before she arrived. Her eyes filled again as she threw open the oven door and grabbed a potholder.

Just as she was tossing the casserole dish of burnt enchiladas on the stovetop, she heard the doorbell. *But it's only six fifteen!* she thought with alarm as she peered at the clock. *Maybe it's just somebody selling something.*

But Dave's voice told her otherwise. "Oh, hi, Nancy! Come on in." She could hear him shuffling toys and what she knew were stacks of papers that she had moved off the dining-room table. "Sorry about the mess. Felicia just got home, and we haven't had a chance to clean up yet."

Oh yeah, blame it on me. Felicia's blood boiled. *Why does it take a "we" to clean up anyway? It's your meeting!*

She took a deep breath and began walking toward the living room. *Lord, help me be nice to this woman. It's not her fault that her pastor's wife is a mess.*

"Hi, Felicia," Nancy said energetically as she looked up from the coffee table and her veritable feast of snacks. A quick look at Nancy reminded Felicia how different the two women were. Where Felicia favored tailored suits and Italian leather pumps, Nancy was usually in a seasonally appropriate appliquéd sweater (tonight's was a tribute to July Fourth, with all the stars and stripes a cotton pullover could handle) and crisply pressed khakis. Felicia's hair was sleek, black, and just to her shoulders, while Nancy's brownish hair appeared to be a couple of perms past its prime. And that green shadow—Felicia caught herself staring too long at Nancy's eyes, wondering why anyone, especially someone with fair skin like Nancy's, would choose a moss color for her eye makeup.

"Hello, Nancy," Felicia said through the clenched teeth of her pastor's-wife smile. She shot a glare at Dave as Nancy bent down to pull yet another covered dish from a plastic tub. "Can I help you with that?"

Nancy glanced up and smiled sweetly at her. "Oh, Felicia, why don't you just relax? I'm sure you've had a hard day at work, and it looks like you didn't even have a chance for dinner, am I right?"

Dave and Felicia followed Nancy's eyes to the dining room, which was perfectly arranged but empty, like a movie set.

Felicia walked casually over and turned off the light. "Yeah, um, dinner didn't quite work out tonight."

Nancy put a hand on Dave's shoulder. Her obvious comfort in touching him took Felicia aback. "Oh, Pastor Morrison," Nancy purred as if she were talking to a small child, "is that *your* little mistake I smell from the kitchen?"

Dave looked back and forth from Nancy to Felicia, unsure what to say.

Felicia broke the ice. "Wasn't that sweet? He went to all that trouble, then forgot to set the oven timer." Immediately she felt bad for lying, but she couldn't take any more image wounds.

"Mom!" Nicholas bounced into the room. "Do you have the enchiladas done yet? I'm starving!"

Felicia heard the halt-screeching jet again in her mind. Nancy cocked her head suspiciously while Dave stared a hole in the floor.

"Let's go see what we can find for you." Felicia scooted Nicholas out of the room, glad for a quick exit strategy.

As she walked away, she heard Nancy say conspiratorially to Dave, "Maybe we need to get you some help . . . you know, with the house and all."

Help! Felicia huffed to herself while she set the oven to bake Nicholas's third frozen pizza that week.

17

Mimi

Monday, June 26
5:47 p.m.

"You've been spending a lot of time in the bathroom, Mom," MJ said as he reached for another dinner roll. Family meals at the Plaisance house—together at the dining-room table with the television off—were a must. Although never gourmet, Mimi's meals were the best she could muster with their budget and the faulty oven. Tonight the menu included chicken cordon bleu, mashed potatoes with homemade gravy, green beans almandine, and homemade yeast rolls.

"Don't reach, MJ," said Mark. "We're trying to teach you some manners. Please ask to have it passed. And let's not talk about the bathroom at the dinner table, please."

"Can I have—"

"May I," Mimi corrected him.

"May I have a roll, and how come you're always puking?" Seven-year-old Mark Jr., also known as MJ, spoke his mind, whenever and wherever he happened to be. This, of course, had always made for interesting comments at church. "I heard you in the bathroom again this morning."

"Enough." Mimi picked up the roll basket and handed it to her son. Then her eyes bored into Mark's: *will you please control your child?*

"MJ, I just said not to talk about those things at the dinner table," Mark said, apparently getting Mimi's visual message.

Everyone was quiet for a moment. Mimi could tell Michaela tried to kick MJ under the table but missed. MJ smirked at his older sister.

"Come to think of it, though, babe," Mark said, "you have been acting kind of strange lately."

"I think I'm coming down with the flu or something," Mimi said casually. "It's going around, and kids can be walking petri dishes. I'm forever picking up something."

"We're not sick," Michaela protested.

"Carriers," Mimi said and passed the mashed potatoes to her.

"Carriers," Megan repeated.

"Thank you, Megan," Mark said in his hush-up tone.

Mimi changed the subject. "I've been thinking, it might be fun to invite the Taylors to dinner this Saturday night." The Taylors were their most loyal supporters in the church, plus they had kids the same ages as MJ and Michaela. "Donna has some new stamps she said she'd lend me for my scrapbooking. It might be nice to show her what I've got and see if she wants to borrow any."

As Mimi started to bite into her chicken cordon bleu, nausea swept over her from the smell. *That's odd. This chicken's never bothered me before.*

Then she realized: it wasn't just the smell. It was the *thought* of eating the chicken.

"You're overworked," Mark suggested, still on the previous topic. "You didn't have to agree to head vacation Bible school this year. And why not take off some time this summer from teaching the young-marrieds class? Let someone else do it. How about Cindy and Gary Golding? I think they'd do a great job."

The queasiness was growing stronger. Mimi tried to suppress the urge to curl into a fetal position on the floor, cry and grit her teeth, or clutch her stomach and moan. Instead she stood, placed her napkin—neatly folded—on the table next to her plate, and said, "Let me get some more rolls." She walked briskly into the kitchen and out the back door. *Breathe deeply*, she told herself. *That will help.* But the more deeply she tried to inhale, the worse the feeling grew.

As she leaned over the porch to heave, she heard MJ entering the kitchen. "Mom, you forgot the basket," he said, his mouth sounding half full. "Mom?"

"Dad," MJ yelled into the dining room, "Mom's puking again."

Lulu's Café

Tuesday, June 27
12:26 p.m.

"I'm just going to have the beef-and-barley soup today, Gracie," Mimi said as she closed her menu and handed it over.

Gracie considered her with narrowed eyes. "Since when do you eat only soup, little girl? For the last several weeks you've been ordering up big sandwiches and fries and—"

Mimi put her hand over her mouth. "Gracie, please stop with the descriptions. I'll be back to my usual soon. I think I have a touch of the flu or something. In fact, Jennifer, why don't you trade places with me? I should probably be on the outside in case I need to make a run for the rest room."

Jennifer slid out so Mimi could take her spot. "I hope I'm not pregnant if you're sharing some flu bug with us," she said half-jokingly. "How long have you had it?"

"Oh, I don't know," Mimi said cautiously. She didn't want the PWs to think she intended for them to get sick too.

Lisa turned to Felicia. "You can forget about me taking the part-time job at your agency that you mentioned last time."

"Oh, really? Why? Did you find something closer to home?" Felicia asked, disappointed.

"No. Joel put his foot down and said I couldn't work," Lisa said sullenly.

"But didn't you used to?" Jennifer asked.

Lisa nodded. "I paid his way through seminary!"

Felicia frowned.

Was she going to broach the subject of Joel's authority? Mimi wondered. She knew some couples viewed the "wives submit to your husbands" passage a little more legalistically than she and Mark chose to interpret it.

"I was hoping we could carpool occasionally," Felicia said.

Jennifer scrunched her face as though she was thinking hard. "What do you mean he 'put his foot down'?"

Lisa looked embarrassed. "He said there's no way he wants me to work outside the home. That it makes him look like he can't support his family."

"Isn't your church giving him a good enough salary?" Mimi asked.

Lisa sighed. "It's adequate, but we've had a lot of families move away since the meat plant closed. The younger families don't seem to understand tithing. So there are money issues, and that's why I thought it would be good for me to get a job, to help out. To be honest, if they cut his pay any more, we'll have to sell my car to make it."

"Whoa," Felicia said. "That is tight."

"Lisa, all churches have their ups and downs. We've had our lean years and our better years," Mimi encouraged. "Of course, I'm never too sure which is which—they all seem pretty lean!"

All four women laughed.

"Oh, hey, Mimi, you'll love this," Felicia said. "Last Thursday I left work early, went to the store, and got home in time to make my enchiladas—"

"You promised to get me that recipe," Lisa interrupted.

Felicia clunked herself on the forehead. "I know, and I keep forgetting to do it. I'll have to sit down and write it out—it's all in my head from years of making it with my mom."

"So what happened last Thursday?" Mimi said weakly. She had to swallow every syllable to keep down her stomach. Just the word *enchilada* was starting to nauseate her.

"Yeah, so I have everything ready: dinner cooking, table set. I even changed clothes and put on a new perfume I'd just bought."

Jennifer shivered. "Oh, I feel something bad coming."

Felicia nodded. "Then Dave comes in and announces that the VBS committee is meeting at our house that evening! And I don't mean a few hours later—I mean a few *minutes*. So of course I get all angry—" Mimi and the others nodded in agreement, "and go into the bedroom, where Dave and I had words. But here's the best part, Mimi—"

"Okay, I'm listening," Mimi said, although she wasn't sure she would be for long. She could feel the bile rising into her esophagus again . . . as it had three times that morning already.

"While we were 'talking,' the enchiladas were cooking. By the time I remembered them, they were black and the house was full of burnt enchilada smell. So that's what the VBS committee got to endure for their two-hour meeting."

Jennifer and Lisa laughed, but when Mimi started to laugh, she felt warm liquid coming up. Lifting the napkin from her lap to cover her mouth, she got up and dashed for the bathroom.

Several minutes later, when Mimi arrived back at the booth, trying to appear casual, as though nothing out of the ordinary had happened, Lisa leaned across to her. "Good grief, should you even be here?"

Mimi nodded adamantly. There was no way she wanted to miss her favorite outing. This was the one thing she really enjoyed being involved in.

"I know I've made some pretty big sacrifices to be here from work, so I imagine Mimi feels the same way," Felicia said, as though she understood Mimi's nod.

Jennifer nodded too. "It isn't easy for any of us to 'sneak off' every other Tuesday, but I think we'd all agree it's worth it."

"Jen," Lisa broke in, "have you been going to church, or what *are* you doing on Sundays now?"

Jennifer took a sip of milk and set down the glass. "Yes, I've been going, but it's been a *struggle*." She hung her head. "Every time I walk through that church door, I feel this fight inside me to run the other way. And then, during the worship services, I find myself overanalyzing everything. I think if there was an award for most cynical person attending a church on Sunday morning, I would win."

Mimi propped her elbow on the table to support her head. "Are you talking with Sam about this?"

Jennifer shook her head. "I've tried. He doesn't get it. He thinks it's the Clomid, but I was having these feelings long before I started on that. I did find someone to talk with, though. Besides you guys, of course."

"A Christian counselor?" Felicia asked.

"He's a Christian and he's a counselor, but maybe not in the way you're thinking," Jennifer answered.

Lisa, Mimi, and Felicia gave Jennifer puzzled looks.

"What do you mean exactly?" Lisa asked.

"He's a priest," Jennifer explained stiffly. "He just happened to be there when . . ."

"There where?" Felicia asked.

"At St. Peter's," Jennifer answered as if it were perfectly logical for her to be in a Catholic church.

"What were you doing *there?*" Lisa asked.

Jennifer explained how she ended up at St. Peter's with her food-donation box, and how she met Father Scott.

"I've never been in a Catholic church," Lisa said, "but I've always wondered what it would be like. Is there incense burning everywhere? Is it dark and musty?"

"Oh, they love their incense and their candles," Felicia said just as Jennifer opened her mouth to respond. "My dad's side of the family is all Catholic except for him. He says he always hated the smells in the church he grew up in. But I used to catch him praying the rosary sometimes when he was worried about something. Made me wonder if he didn't miss Catholicism, or at least some parts of it."

Gracie gingerly placed a steaming bowl of soup in front of Mimi. Once Mimi got a whiff of it, her chest heaved and she covered her mouth just in time. Gracie reached into her apron and handed Mimi a stack of napkins.

"Don't you think you should go home and lie down, Mimi?" Felicia asked as Gracie handed over her usual chicken Caesar salad. "Thanks, Gracie. Mimi, we know how much you want to be here, but you need to rest so you can get better. Go home."

Mimi shook her head, looking away while Gracie deposited a tuna melt in front of Lisa and an omelet at Jennifer's spot. "I know you probably don't believe me," Mimi said defensively, "but I feel fine. It's just this nausea that I can't seem to shake. Maybe it's a stomach virus. Anyway, I want to hear more about your visit to St. Peter's, Jen. What happened? What did you talk about?"

Jennifer took a bite of egg and swallowed it. "He just listened to me share what was on my heart, then we prayed together. If I hadn't known any different, I would have thought he was a pastor from any of our churches."

"He listened, and you prayed? That was all?" Lisa appeared skeptical. "And what do you mean, you 'would have thought he was a pastor from any of our churches'?"

Jennifer shrugged. "All I know is everything he said to me that afternoon jibed with what I've learned in my thirteen years as a Christian. While I was talking with him, he pulled out one of the booklets from the pew—I think he called it a 'missal' or something—and flipped to a passage of Scripture he wanted me to read. It was from Psalms . . . just like we read."

As the women ate quietly for a few minutes, Mimi pondered Jennifer's encounter with the priest. She got the feeling from the sudden hush that Felicia and Lisa weren't too approving of Jennifer's new counselor.

Finally she broke the silence. "Well, I don't know much about Catholic theology, but I do appreciate that they are firmly pro-life. Every time I'm downtown and pass by that so-called women's clinic I see those folks from St. Peter's out there praying with their priest and nuns, and I feel guilty that I'm not joining them."

"I know what you mean," said Felicia, brightening. "I wonder how many lives they've saved just by being there?"

Lisa still looked pensive, but she nodded. "I'm not sure about the Catholic thing, either, but I can agree on that. They've saved a lot of babies and helped a lot of women too."

"You know," Jennifer said slowly, "each of our churches has its own way of doing things. I guess what's most important is that we all believe the same basics."

"You mean that God sent his Son to save us from our sins? And that if we have faith in him we'll go to heaven?" Mimi added.

Jennifer nodded. "Pastor Scott believes that too. And he's certainly been the only light in my dingy faith. Besides you guys, that is," she defended quickly.

"Hey," she added, wiggling her eyebrows as though she wanted to lighten up the conversation. "Guess what Pastor Scott was wearing when I first met him?"

Felicia

Thursday, June 29
8:45 a.m.

"I put a cup of coffee on your desk, but it's probably cold by now."

Felicia slipped by Delores's desk. She didn't need to hear Delores's admonishments. She knew she was late.

"That Jim from the bar is coming at nine, you know," Delores said as she jumped up and followed Felicia into her office.

Felicia sighed as she dropped her briefcase—the new Dooney & Bourke she'd gotten on her last trip to LA—and plopped into her desk chair. Delores continued reciting the day's schedule as Felicia took a swig of room-temperature coffee and flipped on her computer. That's when she noticed the dirt smudges on her hands.

"Delores, could you grab me some paper towels from the bathroom?" She'd interrupted Delores midsentence, but the sudden silence as the woman hurried out of the office gave Felicia a few moments' peace to scan her schedule. Her morning had become a rush after Dave had informed her that the new women's Bible study—the one at noon that he wanted her to go to—had been moved.

To their home.

And, in his ever-increasing "forgetful" manner, he had neglected to tell her until seven that morning. So instead of her usual three-newspapers and a muffin routine, she'd had to berate her husband for his insensitivity, scrub the toilet, dust, and run the vacuum. Now here she was at work with who knows what on her hands, no newspapers read (what if she missed press on one of her clients?), and no time to prepare for Jim from the bar.

"Here you go." Delores handed her some towels. "Eew, what *is* that on your hands? I hope you didn't get it on your suit. I have extra hose, but I can't redress you."

Felicia stopped wiping her hands and looked up at Delores. Was this some sort of mother/daughter routine? "I had to clean the house this morning," she said through gritted teeth. "That is why I am late, and that is why I have a white chalky substance all over my hands. Okay?"

Delores took one step back. Felicia felt a surge of victory.

"What you need is a cleaning lady."

Felicia's twinge of failure was becoming all too common. She tossed the paper towels in the trash and lifted her hands to pump a blob of lotion from the bottle on her desk. "I know, but Dave won't go for it. He says humility is an important part of ministry, and having someone clean our house is not exhibiting humility. He claims people in our church would think we were living too high on the hog."

Delores turned to go back to her desk. "Well, how about the fact that you'd be providing income for someone who might not be able to work somewhere else? I think that's pretty Christian."

That was the same argument Felicia had given Dave. Maybe her thinking and Delores's weren't so far apart after all.

9:05 a.m.

The one day I didn't read the newspapers.

Felicia scanned the article Jim gave her. He had handed out water to the MADD protesters as she'd suggested, and the Cincinnati *Enquirer* had covered it, just as she had hoped. The photo accompanying the article showed Jim handing a bottle to the mother of the boy who was killed.

"Wow, that's some picture. Did she say anything to you?" Felicia asked Jim as she jotted a note to send a box of Godivas over to the *Enquirer's* city editor.

"Yeah. She said a bottle of water wouldn't make up for losing her son. But I noticed the protesters were a little less vocal the rest of the day."

"Good! I think one or two more pushes like that, and your business will be back on track."

"Yeah, but what else can I do? I need to get them off my sidewalk ASAP. People are telling me it's a downer having to cross their lines."

Felicia hesitated, then laid out her new plan to Jim, all the while hoping Dave would be up for it. She had meant to run it by him that morning but had forgotten it in the herculean cleaning effort.

Jim listened patiently, then shook his head. "Pop *only* for three hours? That'll kill me—" He stopped, evidently realizing what he'd said. "Okay, have someone call me to set it up."

11:55 a.m.

Felicia burst through the back door, slipped off her heels, and dashed to the kitchen.

Bless his heart.

Two platters—one with subsections and the other with cookies—sat on the counter.

He knew I wouldn't have time to make anything, so he ran to the grocery store for me.

Ten minutes later, the living room was full of women toting Bibles, journals, and colorful pens. Felicia noticed that some of their Bibles had quilted covers with little handles on them. Others had notebooks that looked to Felicia more like scrapbooks with their colorful covers and personalized pages.

How do people have time for that?

The front door opened one more time as Nancy Borden came in. "Hi, ladies," she said cheerfully. "Sorry I'm late, but Pastor Dave and I had to go over some more VBS plans. And Felicia"—she walked over to pat Felicia's shoulder—"I hope I didn't step on your toes by dropping off those subs and cookies. I had a feeling you wouldn't have time to do anything, you know, with your job and all."

"Hey, Nancy, we're all working women," Libby Gabriel said in mock appall. "Only some of us don't get paid."

Felicia chuckled along with the rest of the ladies but felt her cheeks growing hot. Had Nancy been in their home alone? Did Dave suggest that Nancy get the food because he thought Felicia couldn't handle it? And why were they having so many meetings about this VBS anyway?

Libby started the Bible study by asking Rhonda Barber to read Psalm 72:12: "'For he will deliver the needy who cry out, the afflicted who have no one to help.' Now isn't this the perfect encouragement scripture for us full-time moms?"

Usually Felicia would have been offended at the implication that women with jobs outside the home were not "full-time moms." But she had tuned out well before that and was instead clicking away at her BlackBerry.

One message in particular intrigued her:

Cleaning problem solved.
Will fill you in when you get back.—Delores

7:04 p.m.

Felicia walked into the dining room and dropped the bucket of chicken on the only spot on the table that wasn't covered with piles of papers. Dave and Nicholas were hand-driving a couple of Matchbox cars over the paper piles like mountains.

"Hello, my gorgeous men," she said as she stooped to kiss each of them in midrace, then stood back proudly with her hands on her hips. "You'd better enjoy your driving terrain today, because this house is going to be spotless soon!"

Dave stopped driving to look at Felicia in mock astonishment. "What—did you quit your job?"

His sarcasm reminded Felicia that she needed to address the Nancy Borden food thing with him later. "No, I hired someone."

"C'mon, Felicia, you know how I feel about having someone clean for us. I know it's common in LA, but here it's so . . . statusy. People at church are already raising their eyebrows at your car and your designer this and that."

Felicia glanced down at her new spectator pumps—bought on a quick lunch run the previous day to Macy's—then slyly kicked them off and slid them under the chair.

"Yes, I thought of that. And that's why I scheduled Becky for Sunday morning."

"A Sunday? Let me get this straight. Not only is the pastor's family employing a cleaning lady, but she will be working in our home on a Sunday?"

"I figured that was the only time she wouldn't be seen by anyone at church."

Dave sighed and hung his head. Then he considered Felicia with tired eyes. "We can't be encouraging someone to work for us on Sunday instead of going to church, Felicia. I realize she probably doesn't go to church now, but that doesn't mean—"

Felicia had been eagerly waiting for this moment all day. "Ah, but Dave, she doesn't go to church. She worships . . . on Saturdays. Becky is Jewish."

It felt to her like the perfect solution.

"Jewish."

"Yes, Jewish."

Dave got up from the table and glanced around at the messy living room, his back to Felicia. She could tell he was weighing the relief of a clean house against the potential gossip of a Jewish cleaning lady. Felicia felt time standing still and started hearing the screeching airplane again.

Dave turned to her with the start of a smile. "Let's give it a try. If it doesn't work out, we can always let her go, right?"

Felicia walked to hug him, thinking, *Over my dead body.*

Mimi

Saturday, July 1
11:12 a.m.

"Mom!" Michaela ran into the living room where Mimi was lying on the couch. "Can I wear my purple shirt to the picnic today? Please? I promise I won't spill anything on it."

Mimi rolled over to face Michaela and nodded. "Before you go upstairs to change, though," she said wearily, "would you check to see how many more minutes are left on the oven timer?"

Michaela ran to the kitchen and yelled, "Ten minutes." Mimi rolled back over with her face toward the back of the couch. She just wanted to rest a bit before the community picnic that afternoon. Her spinach lasagna was in the oven. The peach pie was waiting to go in next. She figured that once she put the pie in to bake, she could go upstairs and get ready.

But really, Mimi didn't want to go. She didn't want to face any more people. She was tired of people. She was tired of all that smiling and listening and nodding. She was tired of explaining to everyone how the church and her husband were doing. The only bright light for her was that she'd get to see Jennifer, Felicia, and Lisa. Even though they'd agreed not to act too familiar, just having them in the same vicinity would give her a sense of security.

"We should create a secret code," suggested Felicia at their last lunch get-together. "That way we'll all know it's a special support booster!"

"Definitely," Lisa had agreed. "We can wiggle our noses or sneeze or fidget with our earrings." All the girls had laughed at how silly they knew they were being, but somehow Mimi felt more able to take on the day knowing they were all thinking the same thing. Being a pastor's wife was difficult and, at times, tedious work.

Mimi had drifted off to sleep when she felt a nudge on her shoulder. She lazily opened her eyes to see Mark bending over her.

"Um, Mims," he said cautiously, as though he was considering some confession. He peered into her droopy eyes, then told her it was time to get ready and not to worry, he'd already put the pie in the oven. She slowly got off the couch and headed upstairs to put on her picnic dress—the short-sleeved one with the bright pink flowers and green ivy spread across the bodice. She'd made matching dresses for her and the girls, but she was too tired to force Michaela to wear hers. In fact, she was too tired to care much about anything, even that she overslept and didn't prepare completely for the picnic.

After she splashed her face, retouched her makeup, and curled her hair, Mimi walked back downstairs to the noise of chatter in the kitchen. It seemed everyone was having a family meeting without her. She entered the kitchen and stopped. Mark and the kids immediately fell silent and looked guiltily at her.

"What's up?" she tried to ask brightly, becoming a little paranoid at the looks on their faces. All of a sudden, the kids parted and she could see what they'd been discussing. Her food contributions—the spinach lasagna and her special peach pie with the crust she'd spent hours perfecting—were sitting on top of the counter by the stove, burnt almost beyond recognition. The crispy black crust of each dish looked like tiny Duraflame logs after an evening's fire.

Her family's eyes were wide as saucers with terror. They slowly backed away from the scene of the crime. Mimi, speechless, stared at the charred mess. A lump caught in her throat. Then she turned as if in slow motion to Mark, her eyes pleading for some explanation.

"The oven," was all he could say.

Finally she found her voice. "But you took the lasagna out. Why didn't you tell me then?"

"W-well," he stammered and half raised his shoulders, as if hoping that would calm the brewing storm, "you've been working so hard lately and have been so exhausted, I didn't want to upset you. I wanted you to get a little more rest."

"And the pie?"

"Um." Mark shrugged again.

"Now what are we supposed to do?" she almost pleaded. "I can't take these! And I don't have time to make anything else."

"That's okay, babe," Mark said, trying to sound helpful. "We can stop at the Clucker House and pick up a bucket of chicken. It's on the way."

Mimi opened her mouth to protest, then shut it again. *Great. My culinary skills have been taken over by the Clucker House. Not KFC. Not Popeyes. The* Clucker *House.*

"Well, this is just classy," she couldn't help but snip. "Yes, let's have the pastor of Trinity Methodist Church show up with a fine and tasty bucket

126

of fried chicken from . . . wait—" She held up her hand for dramatic effect. "The *Clucker* House."

She knew that was her only option. That or she could take the burnt mess and serve it, which she knew would never happen. *Never.* Mimi looked again at the dishes, then silently nodded and turned away. She walked back into the living room and stood. Now she really dreaded going. She knew she'd have to listen to people wanting to know where her famous peach pie was. She'd hear them "cluck" their disapproval at her choice of feasting op-tions—Clucker chicken. *How pathetic. I'm ruined.*

Knowing that she had to attend and make the best of their situation, she mustered what little courage and energy she had left, lifted her head high, and decided to put her best face forward. *If it's chicken, it's chicken,* she thought wryly.

She returned to the kitchen and marched past her kids. They were still standing in the same place, as if they feared their mother was going to have a nervous breakdown. She opened a drawer in her china cabinet and grabbed a special blue-gingham linen cloth, then knelt to the cabinet below to slide out a large casserole dish.

"Let's go," she said, resigned to the lower standard she was being forced to accept. "The Clucker House awaits."

11:46 a.m.

Between the strong smell of fried chicken, the bumpy ride to the picnic area at Herman's Park on the outskirts of town, and Mark's insistence on tailgating the Honda Accord in front of them, Mimi thought she was going to be doubly sick as they approached the site. She just wanted to get out of the van.

When they finally arrived and parked on the grass next to the other vehicles, Mimi yanked open her door, smoothed her dress, tucked her blond bobbed hair behind her ears—something she always did when she was nervous—and tentatively stepped out.

"You okay?" Mark asked, coming to her side of the car to remove Megan from her car seat. "You look as pale as a ghost."

MJ started to laugh. "Dad, you said Mom looks like a ghost! Ha, ha, ha, ha, ha!"

"It's an expression, MJ." Mark playfully swatted MJ on the bottom. "It means your mom looks sick."

"I like the ghost thing better," MJ said, still laughing. "Mom, you look like Casper!" He waved his arms around as though he were flying.

Megan joined in, jumping up and down and trying to mimic her brother.

"Remind me again why we had children," Mimi said dryly.

Mark picked up a cooler from the back of the van and walked toward the picnic tables.

"Mimi!" Jennifer headed toward the Plaisance family. "Need some help carrying anything? We just got here, and I put the hubby to work." She smiled brightly. Her curly, strawberry-blond hair was gathered into a high ponytail. She was dressed in khaki Bermuda shorts and a colorful Hawaiian shirt with parrots on it. Jennifer stopped short when she was face to face with Mimi.

"You all right? You don't look so good."

"She looks like a ghost!" MJ called and began his Casper imitation all over again.

Mimi waved everyone away. "I'm fine," she said, a little too abruptly. Then she smiled genuinely to Jennifer. She was glad to see her friend. "I'm just a little tired and maybe a bit under the weather."

"You're not still sick, are you? Maybe you should go to the doctor."

"No," Mimi said, "I'm sure this will pass." She fidgeted with her left earring and winked at Jennifer, amused at their secret code.

Jennifer eyed Mimi skeptically, then fidgeted with her left earring and winked back. "Well, I should get back. It's anybody's guess where Sam placed our food. And anyway," she said with a twinkle, "we're not supposed to know each other too well." As Jennifer began to walk away, she stage-whispered, "I'll fidget at ya later!"

Mark returned and grabbed another cooler filled with sodas, juice, and bottled water. MJ and Michaela had the baseball bats and mitts. Which left the disguised "homemade" chicken, now in a casserole dish, for Mimi. She picked it up and began to carry it—proudly, she hoped—to the potluck table, where all the other food was sitting.

Sure enough, there at the table stood Kitty Katt, royally holding court with her "admirers" from First Presbyterian. Kitty was dressed in a canary yellow pantsuit and matching pumps, her bottle-black beehive shellacked to her head. Her lips were smeared with ruby red lipstick, perfectly lined. Even with her back turned, Mimi could feel Kitty's "holier than thou" energy. Mimi tried to be as inconspicuous as possible, quietly slipping her chicken between two casseroles at the end of the table, farthest from Kitty.

"Hey, Mims," Mark said as he jogged over to her. Kitty's head popped up and she immediately looked at Mimi. "I'm running over to 7-Eleven to grab some more ice. Do you need me to pick up anything?"

Mimi shook her head and darted from the food tables to the picnic table to which Mark had laid claim. She held her breath, hoping Kitty wouldn't follow.

The picnic was getting underway. The town had spared no expense for the day. They'd hired a DJ all the way from Cincinnati. There were balloons and streamers everywhere, and a banner that announced:

RED RIVER'S ANNUAL JULY 4TH PICNIC

The games were already set up so they would be ready to go after lunch. She saw they had horseshoes, volleyball nets, lawn darts, potato sacks for races, and baseball equipment for the adults.

Mimi glanced around for Lisa and Jennifer. Instead she saw Gloria Redkins at the next table, organizing her tablecloth and plates. So Mimi quickly turned her attention to setting out her own tablecloth.

Is this going to be a day of me avoiding everyone?

She didn't hate Gloria. She didn't even hold a grudge against the woman for taking her slot as PTA president. Mimi just wasn't sure what to make of someone who was always so quiet. Gloria wasn't necessarily spectacular or gifted at anything. She brought average meals to the picnic every year and mostly kept to herself and her family. She smiled a lot . . . maybe to cover her insecurities. She wore baggy outfits to cover her slightly plump figure, her brown hair was bushy and streaked with gray, and her face was pocked with scars—the leftover remnants of high school acne.

Maybe I should take her under my wing, Mimi thought. *I could help bring her out of her shell, teach her how to bake something other than tuna casserole or macaroni and cheese . . .*

Mimi stopped herself. *Shame on you. Gloria is fine just the way she is. Maybe you should take lessons from her.* She was shocked. She couldn't believe she was reprimanding herself—over Gloria Redkins.

Just then Kitty sashayed over to Mimi's table. "Well, hello, Mimi," Kitty said with an icy smile as she patted her helmet of hair. Mimi tucked hers behind her ears.

"Hello, Kitty," Mimi replied, hoping she sounded kind, but purposely busying herself with getting the tablecloth on the table so Kitty might get a clue and go away.

"I was looking for your famous peach pie, but I can't seem to find it," Kitty said, obviously not catching on to Mimi's ploy. "Don't tell me your family ate it before you got here." She smiled again.

If someone were watching from a distance, it would have looked as if Kitty were truly the kindest, most sincere person with her expressive eyes, her plastered smile, and the way she flipped around her hands so concerned-like. But Mimi knew better . . . from long experience.

"The mayor has asked me—*again*—to sing one of my special songs for the picnic." Kitty laughed lightly. "I would have asked you to accompany me on the piano, but I wasn't sure if you'd be able to pick up the tune in time. In any case, you'll have to make sure to be nearby when it's time for me to sing so you can hear it. I wrote the song myself, you know."

"Oh, good for you," Mimi mumbled, still trying to sound interested and polite, but starting to feel queasy.

In the background she heard the DJ playing "Who Let the Dogs Out," and a swarm of children repeating, "Woof, woof, woof, woof, woof" to the music. Mimi sucked in her stomach to take the pressure off. All the while Kitty continued talking about her singing ability and how the mayor wanted her to travel to Columbus during the holidays this year to perform for the governor.

Go away, Mimi mentally jabbed at Kitty, hoping against everything that Kitty would extricate herself from Mimi's presence. Instead Kitty slipped around the table to Mimi's side and touched her arm with her perfectly manicured hand.

"You know," Kitty almost whispered, as if she had some juicy bit of gossip to share with Mimi, "I hope you're not still mourning over your loss to Gloria Redkins. I mean, *Gloria Redkins*. She's such a mouse of a woman.

And to lose to her. Well, I'd be devastated if it were me. But everyone's been talking about what a wonderful job she's doing. The next thing you know, *she'll* become everyone's favorite cake baker."

Kitty shot Mimi a saccharine, toothy smile. "I suppose it's a good thing she doesn't attend your church too. Can you imagine having to greet the woman who beat you every Sunday? That's why I do my very best, so I'm never in that position."

Kitty paused and dabbed her ring finger—with the giant three-carat diamond sparkler—at the corner of her mouth.

Just like a feline grooming herself.

"But then," Kitty continued, "*you'd* understand that's a pastor's wife's duty."

"Kitty," Mimi said, trying to keep her temper in check, "It's just the PTA presidency. You're making it sound as though I lost the presidency of the United States. I'm okay with Gloria."

Kitty gave her a surprised look.

"Really," Mimi said defensively.

"Oh, dear, you don't have to pretend with me," Kitty said, ignoring Mimi's words. "We're pastors' wives, after all. We need to stick together. Who else do we have as friends?" Kitty patted Mimi's arm again. "I know how upset you are. It's all over town how shocked you were." She leaned in closer. "Have you ever wondered who *didn't* vote for you?"

Mimi could stand it no longer. She had just opened her mouth to tell Kitty exactly what she thought of her when from the depths of her stomach erupted the projectile "spew," as MJ liked to call it. And its aim was perfect—all over Kitty's canary yellow pantsuit and matching yellow pumps.

Kitty's response was immediate. She began to scream and flail her hands. Her boisterous shouts and jumps got everyone's attention.

"Good aim, Mom!" MJ shouted from across the park.

Mimi felt better than she had in a long time. She grabbed a napkin to wipe her face but also to cover her smile. While she was mortified at what she'd done in public, there was also a part of her that had been vindicated. She'd finally been able to give Kitty what she deserved. *When you care enough to send the very best,* she thought and smiled again weakly.

Gloria ran to Mimi and took her arm. "Here." Her touch was gentle and soothing. "You don't look too good. Why don't you sit down, and I'll go get your husband?"

Mimi grabbed Gloria's arm just as she started to walk away. "Mark's not here. He went into town to pick up some more ice. I'll be okay."

Kitty was still making a loud to-do about her mess and outfit.

"Well, at least you didn't get anything on *you*," Gloria said quietly.

Mimi looked at her, unsure how to take that comment. Then she noticed a slight sparkle in Gloria's eyes.

"I think it makes her outfit look a little better."

Mimi grinned.

"You know," Gloria continued, "when I was pregnant with Daniel, I was sicker than a dog. It seemed as if I was throwing up every time I turned around. But only with Daniel. I never experienced that with any of my other kids."

"Oh no." Mimi tried to laugh it off. "No, I'm not pregnant. I must have some bug I can't shake." She tried to stand and still felt a bit woozy. "Actually, I'm not feeling too well. Would you mind taking me home? I think I'd like to lie down."

Gloria's eyes grew big. "You'd like *me* to take you home?"

"Yes, if you wouldn't mind."

"No, not at all!" She seemed genuinely thrilled by the opportunity. "Let me grab my car keys, and I'll be right back." While Gloria was gone, Mimi motioned to Michaela to come over and told her she was going home. Then she made Michaela promise she'd look after MJ and Megan until Daddy came back.

12:02 p.m.

The drive home seemed to take an eternity. Mimi's head was aching, she didn't have any energy, and she wondered how she was going to get out of the car.

"I really appreciate you doing this for me." Mimi kept her eyes closed and held her stomach. "You didn't have to. You could have stayed."

"Don't worry about it," said Gloria. "I know what it's like not to feel good. The only place you want to be is in a fetal position on the couch, wrapped in at least three blankets, moaning."

The women were quiet for a moment, then Gloria murmured, "I know this isn't the best time, but I did want to talk to you about what happened. You know, with the PTA thing." She seemed uncomfortable broaching the topic.

"The best person got the job, Gloria," Mimi said, and she realized she meant it. "You've wanted that job for several years. It's about time you got it."

They traveled another minute in silence, then Gloria admitted, "I envy you sometimes."

Mimi's eyes opened. Did she imagine hearing those words? "Don't. *I* don't even envy me." She laughed but knew it sounded hollow.

"Not in a bad way!" Gloria hurried to say. "I mean, you have so many talents. You're good at anything you put your mind to. You have the prettiest lawn, you bake the best cakes, you have a wonderful husband and family. Everyone admires you. You're such a selfless, giving person."

Mimi cringed. She wasn't any of those things.

Gloria looked straight ahead as she drove. "I don't do anything particularly well. I'm average. I mean, don't get me wrong, I don't hate myself or anything like that. I have a great family, and I love them dearly and would do anything for them. But sometimes, I dunno. I guess I feel as if God overlooked me in the talents department."

"How can you say that?" Mimi asked. "You have plenty of talents. You're a great mother. You're soft-spoken and gentle and kind. Those are wonderful gifts."

"You're right, and I know that. God has been so good to me. He really has. He's given me everything I've ever wanted. I can't complain. But I know people talk about me—especially now that I won that election."

Mimi didn't know what to say. She'd been one of those people.

"You know, though," Gloria added, "the oddest thing is that through all of that, I still feel my life is filled with joy and peace."

There was that word. *Peace.* Mimi cringed again. She supposedly had the outstanding gifts. Yet Gloria was the one who had peace—something Mimi longed for.

Gloria continued. "I never knew my father. He left when my sister and I were really young. And my mother had to take on two jobs to make ends meet. My grandmother took care of us kids, but she wasn't happy about it—and she never let us forget. When I met Marty, I was a mess. I didn't love myself, and I didn't think anybody else could love me. But he did. And he introduced me to Jesus. I discovered two loves of my life. And I've had such peace since then—even if I don't do everything well."

There was the word again.

"But if you have peace," Mimi said, "why would you envy me? Doesn't that mean you don't have peace?"

"No, I don't think so. Well, no, you're right." Gloria glanced over at Mimi with a smile. "But this is something I've discovered. When I'm grateful for who I am and what I have, I'm at peace. It's when I look at other people and begin to compare my situation with theirs that, you're right, I don't have peace. But the truly amazing thing is that, deep down, even when I feel everything's a mess, God still blesses me with a calm and collected feeling. Does that make sense?" Gloria laughed. "Of course it does! I mean, you're a pastor's wife. You could be telling *me* about God's peace."

"You'd be surprised," Mimi muttered. Then she spontaneously touched Gloria's arm. "You're an outstanding woman—especially considering your past."

Mimi closed her eyes again and breathed deeply. For some reason, she felt safe with Gloria. Before she could stop herself, she confessed, "My father was an alcoholic. I loved him, but he wasn't much of a father to me. When he was drunk, which was pretty much all the time, he made everything out to be a joke. He could never hold down a job, which meant we never knew if and when the bills would be paid. My mother was miserable in the marriage, which caused her to check out completely from our family. She didn't cook or clean or take care of us kids. Every night Dad was in his den with a whiskey, and Mom was on her bed watching TV or reading some silly celebrity magazine. When they were in the same room together, it was either extremely tense or they were having huge yelling matches.

"And since I was the oldest, it fell on me to take care of my brother and sisters. The one thing I wanted more than anything else growing up was peace. I wanted my family to get along. I wanted a mother and father who would hold me and tell me I was a good girl. That everything was all right.

"But instead, every Sunday our family would attend church and act as if everything was great. Then, after we got home, Mom would go to bed, Dad would pull out his bottle, and I'd make everyone's lunch, do laundry, and get everything set for the week. I always thought if I could control things, our family would get along and everything would be the way it was 'supposed' to be. And then I'd find that peace."

It was strange—Mimi didn't cry. In fact, she felt no emotion about telling the story. Finally she risked a glance toward Gloria. "I've never told anyone that before. I mean, besides Mark." The nausea returned. "You better pull over. Now!"

Gloria barely made it to the side of the road when Mimi flung open the car door, leaned out over her seat belt, and heaved. She stayed leaning out of the car for several more minutes after she was finished. Finally she sat up and tried to adjust herself back into the seat. "Thanks," she said weakly.

Gloria reached over and handed her a tissue, then motioned to the corner of her own mouth. "You have just a little bit there."

"Thanks." Mimi pulled down the sun visor and looked at herself in the mirror as she wiped off her mouth.

"I know you said you're not pregnant, but you may want to check, just to make sure," Gloria offered helpfully.

"Thanks, but I'm sure. Mark and I planned to have three kids—and three only. There's no chance we could have an accident."

Felicia

Sunday, July 2

9:00 a.m.

As Felicia walked toward the screen door, she got her first look at Becky. She wasn't sure what to expect. None of the Jews she'd known in LA—and they were plentiful and powerful there—would have stooped to clean their own shoes, let alone someone else's home. So she was curious to find out how Becky came to be cleaning homes in Red River of all places, certainly not the Jewish capital of the world.

"Good morning, Becky," Felicia said with her pastor's-wife smile firmly in place. It was Sunday after all.

"Good morning, Mrs. Morrison. I mean, um, Mrs. Lopez . . . oh, I'm sorry. I forget what Delores told me to say." Becky focused on the ground as she talked.

"Come on in," Felicia said. "We're ready to head out for Sunday school, but let me show you around first."

She led Becky through the house, pointing out supplies and spots that needed extra care. As always, she was thorough and detailed in what she wanted.

Becky continued to avoid eye contact, simply nodding as Felicia ticked off her list of requirements.

"And this is my husband, Dave, and our son, Nicholas," Felicia said as she and Becky made their way into the kitchen where Dave was eating a doughnut over the sink and Nicholas was sitting at the counter tearing apart a Pop-Tart.

"Becky. So nice to meet you," Dave said warmly as he walked toward her with his hand extended. Felicia caught an overzealous note to Dave's greeting, then realized he was in "on" mode for Sunday too. He had learned that people expected the pastor to be happy and glad to see them on Sunday, no matter if he had a cold, they had voted down his latest proposal at council that week, or if he had just stubbed his toe.

Becky glanced up slightly at Dave and mumbled a soft "Hi." An uncomfortable silence covered the room.

Felicia took in a breath. "All right then. We should be going. Nicholas, go get your jacket. Dave, do you have the offering envelope?"

Becky placed her canvas tote bag on the counter.

I wonder what's in there? Felicia watched Becky while waiting for Dave to check his suit-coat pocket.

"Yeah, but what are we taking for the church lunch?" he asked.

Felicia threw back her head and groaned. "Oh, I totally forgot. Uh, maybe I can run to the grocery store for one of those cooked chickens in between Sunday school and church?"

Dave narrowed his eyes. Was he comparing her to Nancy Borden, who surely had a crate full of culinary delights in her car and on its way to church?

"There is no time between Sunday school and church," he said. "Besides, you can't have people seeing the pastor's wife driving away right before the service."

Felicia felt that searing failure again. Would she ever fire on all pistons? She walked into the kitchen and started throwing open cabinets, as if she might find a magical casserole waiting for her on the top shelf. Dave joined her in the hunt.

"They never like anything I make anyway," she said under her breath as she fingered through cans of vegetables and boxes of cake mix. A month ago she had taken tamales she'd made from her mom's recipe to the church's volunteer appreciation dinner, thinking people might appreciate a taste of something different from ham, creamed vegetables, and carb-laden side dishes. But no one touched them. Not even Dave! ("It's impolite to eat what you bring," he'd said to Felicia when she'd confronted him. "People need to see that I accept them." Felicia had huffed, "You show acceptance by eating their Tater-Tot casserole?")

"I can make something for you."

Felicia and Dave stopped rummaging through food and looked at Becky.

"I couldn't ask you to do that." Felicia closed the cabinets, surprised at how easy it was to say one thing and mean another.

"It's no problem, really," Becky nearly whispered.

Dave shrugged at Felicia.

"Okay then. But I don't have many supplies here."

Becky didn't say anything. Felicia wasn't sure if she could get along with someone so silent.

"Uh, well, I'll be back around about 12:15 then to pick it up. Is that enough time for you?"

Becky nodded.

Felicia felt a twinge of anxiety at what Becky might make, but at this point she knew something was better than nothing.

12:21 p.m.

Felicia cradled the warm bowl as she hurried back into the church, heels clicking smartly on the parking-lot pavement.

"Hi, Felicia," called Maggie Bowser as she joined up with Felicia before the doorway. "I'm glad to see that even the pastor's wife forgets things occasionally too."

Felicia looked down at the covered dish in her arms. She hadn't even taken time to peek in it yet, and Becky had been upstairs vacuuming when she picked it up so she wasn't able to ask her.

"You know how it is with a three-year-old. I'm lucky even to make it out of the house some Sundays." Was she blaming her son for her inability to pull everything together in her life?

Reaching the fellowship hall, Felicia stopped briefly to take in the scene. Serving tables were placed end to end, like a runway of food, ranging from green salads and gelatin molds at one end to creamy casseroles and sliced meat at the other. Another table off to the side had pitchers of punch and water. Felicia watched as Nicholas sneaked up to the drink table for what appeared to be—from the red mustache on his face—a second or third hit from the punch pitcher.

Felicia strode over to intercept him but was intercepted herself.

"Felicia, can I take your dish for you and put it on the table?" Nancy Borden seemed to appear out of nowhere, glowing in her cute red-and-white apron that read Made with Love.

"Uh, sure. Thanks." Felicia started to hand over the bowl, keeping her eyes on Nicholas across the room. "Nic—"

"And what do we have here?" Nancy asked as she lifted the lid.

Felicia watched as Nicholas overpoured his cup, creating a sea of red liquid around the other pitchers that dripped onto the new fellowship-hall carpet. She looked away in time to avoid responsibility.

Nancy was holding the bowl in the crook of her left arm and the lid in her right hand as she gazed into the bowl, her forehead scrunched in confusion.

Felicia glanced confidently at the bowl to answer Nancy, but her glance turned into a stare. The bowl seemed to be filled with broth.

"Um," Nancy began.

Great. She heated up a can of chicken broth? I could have done that!

With no response from Felicia, Nancy sighed as she set the lid on the counter next to her and picked up a serving spoon. Little balls of dough rose to the top of the bowl as she released them from the bottom.

Memories of the Jewish deli across the street from her LA office clicked in for Felicia.

Of course. Jewish housekeeper, Jewish food.

"I thought matzo-ball soup might be something different from the same old chicken and potatoes," Felicia announced.

Nancy placed the lid back on the bowl. "How . . . creative. But we're not set up for soup here—people just get one paper plate, no bowls."

A gradual choir of shushing came from the other side of the room. Dave was trying to quiet everyone to offer the blessing.

"Here, you take this." Nancy handed Felicia the bowl and turned to walk away. "I need to get my serving team ready to roll."

Left holding the bowl, Felicia started to run back to the car to leave it when she heard Dave's voice.

"Everyone grab the hand of someone near you as we go to the Lord in prayer." He stopped and scanned the room. Spotting Nicholas, who now had red stains on the front of his white shirt, he motioned for him to join the circle. "Felicia? Oh, there you are. Put down that bowl and get up here, my beautiful bride."

Startled, and with all eyes on her, Felicia reapplied her pastor's-wife smile. She swiveled to drop the bowl on the counter but saw that Nancy and her "team" had filled the space with extra plates and napkins. So she crouched down to set the bowl on the floor, causing her hose to run down the back of her left leg.

"Everyone's been so generous that I can't even find a spot for my bowl," Felicia said cheerfully as she made her way to Dave's side. He grabbed her hand, but it was more like a vise grip than a love clasp.

"Father, we thank you for each person in this room . . ." As Dave began to pray for the meal, Felicia heard shuffling around the kitchen. She glanced up in time to see Nancy Borden dumping the contents of Felicia's bowl in the trash. She caught Felicia's eye and winked. Felicia snapped her head down and squeezed her eyes shut, but she couldn't block out her humiliation.

"And we especially thank you, Lord, for this bounty you have provided for us. Use it to the benefit of our bodies, so we can be strong to witness and share your love. In Jesus's name we pray. Amen."

The room filled with voices and action again as everyone moved to line up at the food tables. Dave turned to hug Felicia. Nicholas saw an escape opportunity and crawled under the table to grab his Sunday-school teacher's ankle. She yelped.

"I saw you putting that bowl on the floor," Dave whispered into her ear. "What did we bring?"

But just as Felicia started to explain, Dave let go of her and turned to face Nancy Borden, who was eagerly waiting behind him. "We're holding the line for you, Pastor Dave," she said sweetly. "I know you want first crack at my chicken-and-potato casserole."

Dave patted his stomach as he followed Nancy to the food tables. "Mmmm, sounds good." He grinned and left Felicia behind, her arms still outstretched as if she were hugging him.

Lisa

Wednesday, July 5
9:42 a.m.

The phone rang in the kitchen, then echoed to the phone in the living room. The annoying sharp sounds seemed to be coming at her in stereo. Lisa was really starting to resent Alexander Graham Bell for inventing such an intrusive, rude machine. *If he's in heaven, and we meet, I think I'm going to deck him.*

One of the most dreadful parts of being a pastor's wife, for her, was that the phone rang constantly. It was no discriminator of time or event. It was the ultimate slave driver, because once she or Joel picked it up, they were held in bondage to what the person on the other line needed or wanted. And that meant her family time, her peace, and her relationships were shot. *All for the ministry*, she would often think with resignation.

Tempted to pick up the phone and drop it back into the receiver, she wandered past it and grabbed a Coke from the refrigerator instead. *I won't answer it.* A heady joy rushed through her at her rebelliousness. She didn't care who it was. It could be Rick Warren or Joel Osteen, for all she cared. It could be Rachael Ray wanting one of Lisa's thirty-minute meals. It could be her mother or the principal at Red River High. No matter. She was doing things on her terms today—and that meant not answering the phone.

She gulped down the cold soda and listened to the answering machine pick up. A soft, crackling voice came over the speaker. It was Bonnie Bentz, an elderly widow who was one of the founding members of the church and known to be a godly saint.

"Oh, dear," Bonnie crackled. "I've never been too good at leaving messages on these things. I always tend to babble . . . well, I guess nobody's home there. You're probably out visiting or doing ministry work. I was calling to see if Lisa wanted to come over and keep an old woman company this afternoon. Maybe have a sandwich and a cup of coffee? But I guess you won't get this message since you're not home. Something's been on my mind a lot lately, and—"

Beeeepp. The machine cut her off.

"And what?" Lisa said out loud. *Why does she want to talk with me?* She was stumped at what Mrs. Bentz could possibly want with her.

"Well, so much for resolve." She grabbed the church directory and looked up Mrs. Bentz's phone number.

11:56 a.m.

"You have a lovely home, Mrs. Bentz," Lisa said as she walked into the older woman's living room. The green chintz walls were cluttered with old photos of family members past and present. A large sepia-toned photograph of Mr. and Mrs. Bentz on their wedding day hung over the fireplace on the outer wall. He was handsome in his military uniform. And she looked so young and happy in her white, lacy gown and veil.

There were older, yellowed portraits of men and women from what appeared to be the turn of the century hanging next to more recent photos of children and grandchildren.

The furniture was old—as if the last time she decorated was in 1963. But the house was neat and clean and appeared to be in good taste—at least for that decade. *Keep something long enough and it comes back into style,* Lisa thought as she took in the mint green and orange couch.

"Thank you, dear." Mrs. Bentz stood next to her as they studied the photos. "It holds a lot of memories. When my Charlie died, everyone wanted me to move to a retirement center. They said it would be easier for me to move on with my life if I left this place. But this house and my husband *were* my life. How would it be easier to lose my husband *and* my memories? I lost him once. I don't think I could lose him again."

Lisa only nodded. She used to feel that way about Joel.

"Come here," Mrs. Bentz continued. "I have something to show you."

She led Lisa into the next room, the dining room. A crystal chandelier hung from the middle of the ceiling over a huge, dark mahogany table. Working her way slowly around the table to the corner, Mrs. Bentz approached a large curio cabinet, filled with scarlet glass tableware, and lovingly ran her hand down its side.

"It's beautiful," Lisa murmured as she studied the intricate wood details. "The craftsmanship is amazing. Look at those roses etched into the doors." She gently touched the wood vines that ran the length of the sides.

Mrs. Bentz smiled. "Charlie made this."

Lisa's head shot up. "He made this? The whole thing?"

"The whole thing. He spent hours in the garage working to get it just right."

"That's amazing. He certainly had a gift."

Mrs. Bentz nodded. "Yes, he did. I tried to get him to go into business doing this, but he said no. He told me that this was a unique one-of-a-kind beauty for a unique one-of-a-kind beauty." Then she winked and chuckled a little. "He meant me, of course. You know, I was quite a looker in my day. At least that's what Charlie always told me."

"How long were you married?"

"Sixty years."

Lisa cocked her head toward this woman who, despite her age, still seemed sharp and spry. "How did you do it?" Lisa said under her breath, not realizing she was talking loud enough to be heard.

Mrs. Bentz laughed. "Oh, don't get me wrong. There were days—sometimes months!—when I wanted to send him packing. We were both pretty stubborn. One time after church we got into an argument, and he got out of the car and walked home. That was a fifteen-mile walk! But we loved each other. And we understood that love isn't a feeling—although when it is, it sure makes life easy and wonderful. But love is a decision. And it becomes most important when you would rather punch his lights out than snuggle up and give him a kiss." She smiled again, then patted Lisa's arm. "How about those sandwiches. Are you hungry?"

Lisa nodded, lost in thought about her own marriage. She wondered if she'd be able to say those kinds of things about Joel after sixty years. She wondered if they'd even make it *another* year. But she knew they would—mostly because she didn't believe in divorce and her husband and her parents would never go for it. It would ruin Joel's ministry too.

So as much as she hated the tug of war she felt, she knew her only option was to stay married. *Only how do I get through that when I'm wilting away?*

Lisa followed Mrs. Bentz through the dining room and into the kitchen, where she helped the elderly woman carry the tray of sandwiches and tomato-lentil soup into the adjoining sun room off the back of the house.

The room had floor-to-ceiling windows that opened to an expansive view of the backyard with Mrs. Bentz's lush flower garden.

"I took the liberty of making iced tea." Mrs. Bentz motioned to the pitcher of tea sitting on the glass table in the middle of the room. The table was already set. And there was an arrangement of roses in a small vase in the center.

"They're beautiful," Lisa commented as she inhaled the scent of one of the roses.

"Thank you. Those are from my rose garden, there in the back." Mrs. Bentz pointed to a small area in the farthest corner of the yard. "Charlie was the rose expert. He won several rose competitions. I don't do nearly as well with them as he did. Those thorns on my poor arthritic hands!" She balled and flexed her hands several times.

"Your husband was gifted at a lot of things." Lisa poured tea into both of their glasses, then sat down.

"He was. You know, after Charlie's death it became easier to talk about him as if he were perfect. But that couldn't have been further from the truth."

Lisa raised her eyebrows in anticipation of a story.

"Well," Mrs. Bentz chuckled, "that's a long tale. And I don't want our soup to get cold. May I say a blessing?"

Lisa sat back in her chair, slightly surprised but pleased. Most of the time, members of the church would ask Joel or Lisa to pray over the meal. This was the first time Lisa could remember that someone else offered to pray. It felt nice.

As Mrs. Bentz offered a soft-spoken prayer, Lisa realized she genuinely liked this woman—not because she had offered to say grace, but because she had a certain charm and easiness that made Lisa relax. Mrs. Bentz had the same talent of hospitality that she'd watched and admired in Joel. But this time the kindness was being offered to *her*.

After the "amen," Mrs. Bentz waited for Lisa to take a sandwich and to fill her soup bowl from the tureen she'd set on the table.

"Ages ago, when our three children were still at home," Mrs. Bentz started, "Charlie got pretty puffed up about his role as breadwinner for our family. So much so that he spent hours away from the house, working overtime and trying to get his automobile-repair shop up and running. I would get really angry with him when he'd miss supper or one of the kids' school functions. And he wouldn't listen to anything I told him. I'd nag, I'd cajole, I'd threaten. Then one day I stopped. I thought, *Okay, God, if you're so big and powerful, do something with my husband to get his attention that he's needed at home with his wife and kids.*

"Well, not two weeks later, Sally, our youngest, brought home a draw-ing she'd done at school. It was of our family. Only Charlie was missing. When I saw what she'd drawn, I asked her why her daddy wasn't in the pic-ture. And she said it was because he was fixing somebody's car and couldn't make it."

Mrs. Bentz shook her head, almost in delight. "The wonder of children. And the wonder of God! I asked if I could show her daddy the wonderful drawing when he got home that night, since she'd be long in bed by the time he came in. So I did."

"What did he say?" Lisa asked, so engaged in the story that she hadn't yet touched her soup or sandwich.

"It wasn't so much what he said as what he did." Mrs. Bentz took a bite of her ham sandwich.

Lisa couldn't stand the suspense. "Then what did he do?"

Mrs. Bentz slowly swallowed, then sipped her tea. "Well," she said, dab-bing at the corners of her mouth with her cloth napkin, "he took one look at that drawing, and when I gave him Sally's explanation as to why he wasn't in the picture, he sat down on the edge of our bed and cried. To be honest, it was difficult for me not to say something, but I knew God was working on my Charlie, and I'd only mess it up if I started jabbering. So I kept quiet so Charlie could hear God."

"God certainly answered your prayer quickly."

"That he did. Bless him."

"So then what happened?" Lisa wanted to know more.

"He apologized—not only to me, but to our children. Then he swore he'd never again put his business or anything else above his marriage and family."

Jealousy washed over Lisa. She wanted that from Joel.

"Now, dear one, tell me. How is your marriage going?"

Lisa blinked, unsure of what she was being asked, or how to answer it. They'd now entered uncomfortable territory for Lisa. What was she supposed to say? "It's going absolutely terrible. Thanks for asking"? Or maybe, "Right now, I'm thinking about chucking my marriage and this church, and taking the kids and running away to a commune in San Jose"?

She knew she couldn't be truthful. If there was one thing she had learned from being a pastor's wife, you never, *ever* tell the truth to one of the church members when life isn't going well. Church members don't want the truth. They want to know that everything's great with the pastor and his family. Otherwise they can't sit under his preaching and teaching and leadership. After all, if he can't keep his own personal problems in order, how is he supposed to help them?

"It's fine. Quite well, actually," Lisa lied. She purposefully avoided looking across the table at her hostess's eyes.

Mrs. Bentz remained quiet. She took a sip of her soup, then set down her spoon. Finally she tapped her index finger on the glass table. "I'm wondering if life at the Barton household is really as good as you say."

Immediately Lisa lifted her eyes to meet Mrs. Bentz's. She wasn't sure if she felt relieved that someone had finally noticed and cared about the state of her marriage, or defensive that this person would find out the truth and blab it to the entire congregation.

That's all I need. "Why do you ask?" Lisa tried to sound reassuring.

"Well, last week when I was sitting in front of you at church, I thought I heard you mutter a few things that caught my attention."

"Mutter?" Lisa was confused. "What do you think I said?"

"When Pastor Joel announced his upcoming sermon series on marriage God's way, you snorted and whispered, 'Yeah, right, like you'd know.' Or something to that effect."

Oh no. She did not hear me say that . . . did she? Lisa's heart began to pound and her breathing quickened. *I'm in so much trouble.*

Mrs. Bentz smiled gently. "Don't worry, dear. Your secret is safe with me. I was the only one who heard the words. Although several people did hear the snort, I think." She shrugged, almost comfortingly.

"You know, Lisa, I've never been a pastor's wife. So I know you have challenges I can never completely understand. But I've been a Christian for most of my almost ninety years on this earth, and I've sat under a number of different pastors. And the one thing I've noticed more often than not is that all those pastors had marital problems at one point or other.

"Now, let me be clear," Mrs. Bentz rushed to admit. "I'm not saying pastors are synonymous with marriage problems. What I'm saying is that pastors are like everyone else in this world—human. And we all have trouble in marriage sometimes. That's nothing to be ashamed of. In fact, I often wonder if God made men and women different so that through their differences they would fight and wrestle and, if they jump in with both feet, end up stronger. But pastors often try to hide their struggle. That's not right. But I understand. A lot of church members couldn't take the messiness of real life. We Christians want everything to be neat and tidy. We don't like mess." She chuckled again. "Another sandwich?"

Lisa shook her head.

"If you're struggling in your marriage, which from that snort I'd say you may be, it's okay to admit it. And it's okay to seek help. I'd never think less of you—in fact, I'd think more of you! And those who gossip and act surprised, well, they're not worth your time anyway."

Amazed again at this woman's insight and gracious manner, Lisa placed her napkin on the table and sighed. "You're right. I didn't mean to snort in church. I just . . . I'm tired of living a lie." She waited to see how her companion would react, but Mrs. Bentz only nodded slightly, giving no hint of surprise or shock at Lisa's words.

"When Joel and I got married, we had such big dreams for the ministry. And it was *ours*. We believed God had called us both into the pastorate. But when Joel got the senior pastorate here, it grew into this monster. I was no longer part of the ministry team." Lisa had been holding in her confession for so long that now she started to talk faster and faster, spilling all her hurts and disappointments.

"I love Joel. And all I want is for him to love me. But I can't get through to him. Everything is about the church and the ministry and his reputation in the community."

For the next hour, Lisa ranted and complained until she was spent.

Throughout the entire time, Mrs. Bentz spoke only to clarify something Lisa said. Otherwise she listened patiently, nodding at the appropriate moments.

"I'm sorry to dump all this on you, Mrs. Bentz. I probably shouldn't have. Joel would be so angry if he found out."

"Nonsense," Mrs. Bentz said. "You needed to release. I've seen it building for several months, and I've been praying for you. There is nothing for you to be ashamed of. You have every right to want to be loved and cherished. To feel honored. And that's something he's not providing, which he should be. I know your husband is a good man and a good pastor. He's just lost his way a bit right now. Would you like some advice from an old woman?" She smiled.

Lisa could only nod. Her throat had started to hurt from all that talking.

"My niece is a Christian counselor who practices down in Cincinnati. Why don't you go and talk to her? Joel probably won't go with you. That's okay. You go for yourself. You've lost within yourself that understanding that you deserve to be loved. That you don't have to apologize for it. Honey, God doesn't expect you to take second place to the church. I don't find that to be biblical at all.

"If he loses you, he loses his ministry. I always used to say, 'What good is doing everything for God's kingdom if you can't serve your mate?' Why not do what I did with Charlie? Pray for God to show your husband how important you are, and how he's ruining the one relationship he needs more than any other."

Lisa soaked up Mrs. Bentz's words like a sponge. Unlike the "advice" Lisa had received from her mother, Mrs. Benz's instruction was heartfelt . . . not some hollow cliché.

For the first time in months, Lisa felt hope stir within her at the wonderful possibility of getting her marriage back on track . . . and herself and the kids firmly entrenched once more in Joel's heart.

23

Jennifer

Sunday, July 9
9:45 a.m.

Jennifer sat in her car, watching two others get out of theirs and gather on the sidewalk at the Southwest Ohio Regional Park sign, as instructed by the sheet she'd picked up at the Red River Public Library.

At least I wore the right thing, Jennifer thought as she looked over the group and then down at her sweatshirt, jeans, and tennis shoes. She hadn't been sure what the dress code was for birding on a Sunday morning.

Jennifer squinted at the clock on her dashboard. *9:45.* Sunday school would just be letting out so people could make their way to the sanctuary for the 10:00 a.m. worship.

Wonder if anyone will notice I'm not there?

A few more potential birders flocked to the sidewalk.

There was a lump in Jennifer's throat as she recalled her conversation with Sam that morning. She hadn't told him she was skipping church until he came out of the shower and saw her pulling on jeans.

"Did you forget what day it is?" he had asked jokingly. "Does that medicine you're taking have you all kooked up or something?"

Sam could be so insensitive sometimes!

"No, I know very well what day it is," Jennifer had answered matter-of-factly. "Sundays are to be set aside for getting in touch with your spiritual side, and that's what I plan to do from now on."

This wasn't an original thought—Jennifer had read it on an infertility bulletin board for people who need to de-stress their lives to get pregnant. It sounded good to her. At this point, anything away from that church sounded good to her.

But Sam had seen right through her. "Is this some attempt to shun God because you haven't gotten pregnant yet?"

Nailed!

"No, I just thought it might be nice to experience God in a different way," Jennifer had stated. "There is nothing in the Bible that says I have to go to church every Sunday like clockwork."

Jennifer's stomach lurched as she thought about the hurt look on Sam's face when he realized she wasn't going to church with him. She hated disappointing him, and she knew she was possibly forcing him to lie about why she wasn't at church. After all, no one would understand the pastor's wife eschewing church for birding on a Sunday morning.

Jennifer wasn't even sure she understood, but she got out of the car anyway and joined the group.

"Ah, a newbie! Welcome! I'm Brad," a tall, thin man in khakis and a green T-shirt said enthusiastically as Jennifer approached.

She hated the word *newbie*. It sounded like a cartoon robot or something.

"Hi," she said cautiously when everyone turned to look at her. "I'm Jennifer."

Brad looked at her like he was taking inventory. "Okay, newbie Jennifer."

Ugh.

"I see you are without binocs and a field guide," Brad continued. "Wendy, will you share with newbie Jennifer today?"

Is he going to say that every time?

"Sure," said a petite brunette who appeared to be in her late forties. She moved closer to Jennifer.

"Okay, troops, let's move it out," Brad directed, swooping his hand through the air.

The group of thirteen made its way into the woods, following a trail marked Oak Run.

"So, Jennifer, what do you do?" Wendy asked pleasantly as they hiked toward the back of the group.

"I'm a homemaker." Jennifer gave herself a mental pat on the back for not saying she was the church secretary. It was freeing not to be a church "anything."

"Oh, so what does your husband do then?"

"He's a pa . . . a pathologist." She couldn't believe how much she was lying nowadays!

"A pathologist? So he's a doctor, then?"

Is a pathologist a doctor?

Wendy didn't give her time to answer. "Which hospital is he at?"

A few people turned and gave them dirty looks. No one else was talking. Several had binoculars pointed into the trees as they walked. Jennifer knew she would trip and break a leg if she tried it.

"My brother's an X-ray technician over at St. Luke's," Wendy added.

"Let's stop here for a minute," Jennifer heard from the front.

Whew! Saved by the Brad, she thought, amused and glad she didn't have to answer any more of Wendy's questions.

"Now," he instructed, "we try to be as quiet as we can. Then the birds will feel welcome to come into our presence and will let our spirits commune with them."

"Let our spirits commune with them?" What exactly does that mean?

She sneaked a peek around. No one else seemed confused. What harm would it do to play along for a bit? She was there, after all, wasn't she? But she couldn't shake the concept that Brad was sounding a bit too New Agey for her comfort level.

The group stood silently, continuing to peer through their binoculars.

"There's a bird right there," Jennifer said a little too loudly as she pointed to a northern set of trees that no one was observing.

"Good, Jennifer," whispered Brad as the group swiveled in the bird's direction. "What do you think it is?"

Jennifer's bird knowledge was limited: cardinal (only because it was red), crow, hummingbird, Big Bird . . .

"Don't know. A sparrow maybe?" That was the only other bird she knew.

The others chuckled. Jennifer looked around for answers. Why did she feel like she was back in ninth-grade French class?

"The sparrow has a distinctive song, and that's not his tune," Brad said. "Why don't we close our eyes for a few minutes? Sometimes, though we might not be able to see birds, we know they're there because we can hear them when we're quiet enough to listen. Their songs tell us who they are."

Everyone but Jennifer closed both eyes. She kept one eye open, a practice she'd started years ago to keep track of who was going forward during the altar call. It never made sense to her when the preacher called for "all heads bowed and all eyes closed." Who was going to go pray for people at the altar if they couldn't see they were there?

An all-too-familiar feeling interrupted Jennifer's thoughts. She knew what it was—this visitor always arrived at the most inopportune times. While everyone's eyes were closed (and some heads were bowed), Jennifer sneaked away back down the trail and headed for the park restroom.

Nine days late. I was really hoping . . . but Dr. O'Boyle did say the medicine could take a few months to get into my system and be effective, she tried to convince herself as she walked, attempting a positive attitude.

With each step, her feet dug deeper and deeper into the mulch-covered path, stomping down her hope and filling the space with despair.

Tuesday, July 11
10:45 a.m.

"I haven't seen you at any Masses. Did I miss you and your husband?"

Jennifer cleared her throat as she set her purse on the coffee table in Father Scott's office. While she had shared her inability to get pregnant and its effect on her faith during their first meeting, she had conveniently forgotten to tell him that she wasn't Catholic.

Or that her husband was a Protestant pastor.

At the church across the street.

And here they were at their agreed-upon second session. She'd been wrestling for a few weeks with whether or not she should tell him who she really was at this meeting.

"Yes. I mean, no. I mean . . . oh, Pastor Scott." Jennifer rubbed her forehead as she dropped onto the blue sofa across from where he was sitting. She wondered if her brain might explode from the stress of her life recently.

"Were you staying away these past weeks because you thought you weren't worthy to join us? Jill, did you forget what I said about God honoring your journey?"

The last thing the priest had said to Jennifer as they parted back in June had indeed stuck with her. "None of us has 'arrived' when it comes to faith," he'd said. "God honors the journey. You just keep seeking and asking him to show himself to you, and he will. You'll see."

His simple, kind words had been a balm for her wounded soul.

Jennifer dropped her hand from her head and met Father Scott's eyes. His warm gaze made her smile, something she hadn't been doing much lately.

"I need to tell you something," she said. "Something important."

"Should I wear my stole then?" he asked as he started to rise from the chair.

Why was he always asking her about that stole? The only "stole" she'd ever seen was her elderly neighbor's rabbit fur collar. But she was pretty sure priests didn't wear fancy furs.

"I don't think so . . . Pastor Scott, I'm not Catholic."

Father Scott appeared puzzled. "But—"

She figured now was the time to tell all. "And my name isn't Jill. It's Jennifer. My husband is the pastor of Red River Community Church, right across the street."

Now Father Scott looked concerned. "Ahhh . . . I've met your husband, then."

"You have?"

He nodded. "At the city pastors' prayer breakfast."

The city's pastors' prayer breakfast was an ecumenical monthly event open to all ministers in Red River. Sam always came home with good reports from their meetings. Jennifer tried to think when the last one had been.

Father Scott shuffled his feet. "I don't go much anymore." There was a pause, then, "They ask me a lot of questions about Catholicism . . . but I'm not so certain some of them really want to hear the answers." He looked up. "It makes it difficult for me to relax with my fellow pastors."

"Oh, I know just how you feel," Jennifer said. She told him about Kitty Katt's monthly pastors' wives' teas—and why she didn't go. She talked about the anxiety she sometimes felt as a pastor's wife with no one to turn to.

Father Scott gave her a knowing look. "Is that why you came over here to pray? Because you can't be seen praying in your own church?"

Jennifer rolled her eyes. "It's not that bad. They still let the pastor's wife pray. But I do feel alone when it comes to talking about my deepest feelings."

She thought of the PWs and what a positive difference they had made in her life. After all, up until the time she'd met Father Scott, the PWs were the only people she could be honest with—without any guilt or worry.

"My husband is not only the pastor, he's also the church counselor. But I can't go to him for counseling, so who else can I go to? Not anyone else in the church. I wouldn't dare let them know their pastor's wife is going nuts."

"You're not going nuts."

With just those few words, his calm voice worked its way into the emptiness inside her.

They were silent for several minutes as Jennifer reflected on the previous Sunday.

She began to tear up. "Can you believe I let my poor husband go off to church while I went birding—of all things?" She combed through her purse for a tissue.

Father Scott reached behind his chair to grab a box of Kleenex, then tilted it toward her so she could pull one. "It's possible to find God in places other than church, and sometimes that can mean getting back to nature, his creation."

Had he been reading the infertility bulletin board?

"So what did you learn?" he prompted.

"Pretty much nothing. We were just starting to find birds when I—" She frowned. She had a tendency to start a sentence before she knew what the end would be. And there was only one ending to this sentence . . . something she didn't want to say in front of a guy. Even if he was there to help her.

"When you what?" Father Scott asked.

"When I . . . had to go to the bathroom."

"So didn't you rejoin the group after that?"

"No. No, I wasn't feeling well."

Father Scott considered her with her sad eyes. "Oh, you mean you started your period? So that medicine didn't work, then?"

Jennifer looked down, embarrassed.

"Hey, I grew up with five sisters," the priest said sympathetically. "Life happens! But I'm sorry to hear that. I know you said last time you were hoping this would be the month."

Jennifer sighed. "Yes, so I decided just to go home. Besides, the whole 'you have to be quiet' thing was starting to get on my nerves."

"Why was the quiet bothering you, do you think?"

"Maybe because it was forced," Jennifer explained in a disinterested tone. She should have known birding would leave her uninspired—her fun-loving nature didn't jell well with silent activities. "The leader, Brad, said something about being quiet and shutting our eyes because it's easier to find the birds by listening than by looking."

Father Scott sat back in his burgundy leather chair, nodding as if he was relieved, but he didn't say a word.

"What?" Jennifer asked, annoyed. Obviously he had captured some revelation that he wasn't sharing with her.

"Don't you see it? That was God's message for you this week."

"Wha—" Jennifer stopped herself and thought about what she'd just said. Metaphorical messages had never been her strong suit. Back in high school lit class, she was always at a loss when the teacher asked for the "real meaning" behind the stories they read. To this day, she stuck to biographies for her bedside reading—no symbolism there.

Father Scott seemed to sense her quandary. "How much time have you spent in prayer lately? And I mean real, down-on-your-knees kind of prayer, not just the good-night prayers at bedtime?"

Jennifer stared at the priest, then looked away. "I'm tired of praying. A baby is the only thing I've ever really asked for, and God isn't giving it to me. After all I've done for him—turned my life around, worked at the church, married a pastor." She took a breath that came out almost as a sob. "Sometimes I think God is punishing me for my past."

Father Scott leaned forward. "I see we have more ground to cover than I thought. What is this about turning your life around?"

Jennifer bit her lip. She'd revealed more than she'd intended. "Well, before I was a Christian, I was very promiscuous. As soon as I was eighteen, I moved in with this guy I was dating so I could get out of the house as fast as I could." She went on to explain the emotional abuse she'd endured from her mentally ill mother and the physical attacks from her indifferent stepfather.

"Things were okay for a few years. But then one day this guy I was living with hit me. And it got worse and worse until it finally dawned on me that there I was, right back where I'd started, with some guy slapping me around. So eventually I went to the women's shelter. The night I showed up, the shelter volunteers were from Red River Community Church. They were so nice to me that I started going to the church."

"And that's when you began your faith journey?"

"Yes. They led me to Christ, then gave me a job in the church office. A few years later I sensed God calling me to ministry, so I enrolled part-time at Cincinnati Bible College while I was still working at the church."

"What kind of ministry?"

"That's just it. I never got to find out because about that same time Sam came to the church as pastor. When we started dating, I dropped out of college."

"Why?"

"When we got serious, we made a decision to spend more time on our relationship. I loved him and wanted to support his ministry, so I figured it was worth giving up college. Plus, I wasn't even sure what I wanted to do at Bible college."

Father Scott appeared lost in thought for a moment. As she watched him think, it occurred to Jennifer how different they were—not just as a Catholic priest and a Protestant pastor's wife, but because he was a deep ponderer and she a "say it like it is" realist.

Finally he spoke. "So God delivered you from an abusive relationship and provided a good Christian husband, but because he hasn't provided you with a child, you've decided to give up on him?"

Jennifer felt like someone had shot her in the heart.

Father Scott leaned forward again. "What was your prayer life like back when you decided to go to Bible college?"

"Oh, I was a new Christian then, so I was really into my daily devotionals." She stopped. *Daily devotionals? How long has it been since I've done those?* "And I was meeting once a week with other abuse survivors to talk and pray." She hadn't talked to them in two years, she realized as she was saying it.

"And your prayer life now?"

"Basically nonexistent." Jennifer had never been so honest with anyone, not even Sam. Father Scott was so easy to talk to. "I'm just so busy—*was* busy—running the church office and going from church function to church function, that I can't seem to find time for devotions. And it's hard to go to church prayer meetings. I can't be open and honest there. Besides, I think God has given up on me."

Her brain told her that last statement wasn't true—how many abused women had she counseled over the years on that very topic?—but her heart beat with abandonment.

Father Scott tapped his fingers on the arm of his chair. "Sounds to me like you need to spend a little less time looking for what God is doing—or, according to you, *isn't* doing—in your life, and a little more time listening to what he might be saying to you. Like the—"

"The birding! That's what you meant!" Jennifer was reenergized at figuring out Father Scott's spiritual lesson.

When he stood up, she reached for her purse to leave. "No, please stay seated. I would like for us to pray together. I will start, and you finish."

He came around and stood next to her, his hand lightly on her shoulder. Jennifer glanced at the clock—11:20, only thirty minutes until she was supposed to be at Lulu's.

I'll have to make this quick, she thought.

But once Father Scott started praying—beginning with, "In the name of the Father, the Son, and the Holy Spirit" as he crossed himself—Jennifer forgot her interest in time. When she started praying, she felt like a new Christian again. Awkward, unsure what to say. After a minute or two, though, she began to experience the intensity she hadn't felt since her Bible college days.

After their "amens," Jennifer stood to face him. It felt like someone had removed a twenty-pound weight from her back!

When Father Scott lovingly opened his arms, she gladly wrapped hers around him in a friendly embrace. As she stood there, feeling safe and warm, she wondered if this was what it would have felt like, as a child, to be encircled by the arms of a loving father.

"I know you Protestants don't really do confession," Father Scott teased as they ended their hug. "But I hope you remember what you're feeling right now. Our time here and that hug was God working through me, an ordinary human being, to bring you closer to him and to show you how much he loves you."

Jennifer wasn't sure how she felt about "confession"—especially the kind Father Scott was talking about—but she knew one thing for sure: prayer *did* make her feel better.

Yet she was still cautious. It was one thing to talk to God, but she wasn't ready to go gung-ho for him yet. The idea of joining in worship and praise to a God who wouldn't give her the one thing she desired was more than she could bear.

24

Lulu's Café

Tuesday, July 11
12:21 p.m.

The women were already seated in their usual spot, sipping their iced teas and Diet Cokes, when Jennifer rushed in, tinkling the bell over the front door.

Gracie looked up from pouring a patron's coffee and called in a mock rough tone, "Oh, it's just you, Jennifer. You're late, girly! They're all already here and chatting up a storm. It's probably all about you."

Gracie was wearing her usual pink waitress uniform with the white apron tied around her paunchy waist. Her standard pen was stuck halfway behind her ear and poked into her hair. She broke into a wide smile and winked at Jennifer.

"I know, I know!" Jennifer retorted, also smiling. "Are you getting me that glass of milk, or do I need to bring in my own cow?"

It felt good to be here among friends, who accepted her and loved her for who she was. And even though she felt guilty about being late—she hated being late for anything, but especially for her biweekly lunches—she knew they'd understand.

They always did.

Mimi grinned in welcome and waved as Jennifer hurried toward their booth.

"I'm sorry I'm late," Jennifer said before she reached the women.

"No problem. I'm sure it's a good story!" Mimi was dressed in a silky, emerald button-down shirt that looked a little too snug.

Is Mimi gaining weight? Jennifer wondered, but she was distracted when Mimi motioned toward Felicia. "Guess who's got a cleaning lady?"

"No kidding?" Jennifer sat next to Felicia. "And Dave's okay with that?"

Felicia started to respond, but Mimi butted in. "She was just telling us that she's Jewish and comes on Sundays. Isn't that a hoot? That way nobody from the church will know. Tell her the story, Felicia."

Felicia's white teeth shone beautifully against her olive skin. "Well," she started and recapped her story so Jennifer could catch up.

When Gracie placed a glass of milk in front of Jennifer, she interrupted Felicia to say, "Thanks, Gracie."

Gracie lifted her eyebrows, as if to say, *You gals ready to order, or are ya still too busy gabbing?*

Lisa lifted her finger and mouthed, "Just a few more minutes."

Gracie shook her head and muttered, "You women talk more than anybody I know. Long-windedness must run in pastors' families."

"Oh! And I didn't tell you guys this part yet," Felicia continued, seemingly oblivious to what Gracie had said. "So I get to the church with this tureen filled with something, and Nancy Borden grabs it from me and looks inside. Guess what Becky had made?" Before anybody could respond, she gushed, "Matzo-ball soup." She grimaced. "Well, they already think I'm a bit off anyway."

"And you helped seal the deal." Jennifer touched Felicia's arm in a mock act of concern.

"Oh! You looked just like Kitty Katt when you did that," Mimi said brightly.

Lisa eyed Jennifer. "What made you so late today?"

"I visited Pastor Scott again. He's been so helpful and comforting. When we prayed today, I felt something for God I haven't felt in a long time."

"That's good," Mimi said.

"But I'm still not ready to—" Jennifer shook her head.

"To trust God again?" Lisa interjected.

Jennifer nodded and took a sip of her milk.

Everyone turned quiet for a moment, which seemed to be the cue for Gracie to reapproach the table. "Okay, PWs, we're not here to camp. What'll it be?" She removed the pen from behind her ear and took her order pad from a pocket in her apron.

"Okay," Felicia started. "I'm game. I'll try that grilled salmon special you've got listed on the chalkboard up front." As Gracie started to jot down the order, Felicia stopped her. "Wait. Tell me the truth. Is it any good?"

Gracie said loudly, "Oh sure, it's the best. Very fresh." She looked quickly over her shoulder, then whispered, "It's left over from three days ago. Really fishy. I wouldn't eat it."

Felicia nodded. "Thanks. I guess I'll stick with salad."

"Chicken Caesar, it is."

"No, I think this week I'll try the chef salad—unless that's not good either?"

Gracie cracked a smile. "It's good. Did you want me to top that with the salmon, then?"

"Smart aleck." Felicia laughed.

The others ordered and returned to their conversation.

"Honestly?" Mimi half whispered, almost as if fearing someone would overhear her confession, "there are times when I daydream about not having to go to church. I mean, I love our church and Mark's preaching. But I wonder how peaceful and relaxing it would be to have those extra hours to myself."

Felicia nodded, "*Oh* yes. No little ruffian to have to look after."

Lisa laughed. "To be able to sleep in just one Sunday—and not because you're sick! Or I could lie on the sofa and actually watch what I want on TV. Full and unlimited use of the remote control. And the best part? No ringing phone interrupting my schedule!"

"And I could enjoy a clean house without anybody messing it up!" Mimi laughed gleefully.

"I would pour myself a hot cup of coffee and read not only the local papers but the *LA Times* and *The New York Times* too," Felicia joined in.

Jennifer smiled politely. "I hate to burst your bubble, friends, but there's not much to do on a Sunday morning. Believe me—I've checked it out. And all I could come up with was birding . . . what I did last Sunday. I even bought a pottery wheel this week, figuring I'd 'worship' God through creating a clay pot. I hoped it could turn into something I could do on Sunday mornings."

"How'd it go?" Lisa asked.

"Not so great. I couldn't get the stupid wheel to work right, and the pot kept collapsing. But I did make a mighty fine mess."

I could never be this brutally honest with Sam or with any of my other friends—and especially not with the people from church, Jennifer realized. *They'd all be aghast at my admission.* But the PWs seemed to understand. And while she knew they didn't necessarily approve of her choice to skip church for now, she also knew they weren't judging her for it.

"We're praying for you," Lisa had told her several weeks ago. And Mimi had sent her a beautiful card with a photo of a sunrise on the front. She'd written these words on it:

Hang in there. We know you'll get through this.
And you'll come out much stronger on the other side.

How grateful she was that God had placed these women in her life. Was that how he was looking out for her?

She quickly brushed that thought from her mind. *Even if you are looking after me*, she told God, *I'm still not happy with you.*

Her disappointment with God flared again when Felicia changed the subject. "So what's going on with the Clomid?"

Jennifer exhaled sharply. "Let's just say Stayfree made another appearance at my house."

Felicia nodded sadly.

But Jennifer tried to blow it off. "Yeah, well, why get angry about it? It's not like that's making God change his mind."

When the women grew quiet again, Jennifer felt uneasy and slightly guilty. She watched Mimi tuck her blond hair behind her left ear and bite the inside of her cheek. Lisa took a sip of her iced tea, then smoothed her napkin.

"Sorry," Jennifer offered. "I didn't mean that. It's just . . . I don't know. Never mind. Let's talk about something else."

Lisa eyed Jennifer closely, as though trying to decide on something. "It's okay to be angry at God," she finally said. "That's better than being absent from him. You know, the Old Testament prophets said some pretty harsh things to God. At least you're keeping the lines of communication open with him. That way he can still work in your life."

"Honestly, I'm not sure I trust him enough to work in my life right now."

"Have you told him that?"

"Hardly!" Jennifer half laughed more to cover her discomfort than for any other reason.

"Why don't you?" Lisa pressed gently.

"Now you're starting to sound like Pastor Scott."

"Well then," Felicia said, "I'd say he's a pretty smart guy."

Jennifer sighed. "I'm just not there yet. But don't worry, I'm working on it. Let's talk about something more enjoyable than my views on faith."

"Well, if you want to talk about something incredibly ridiculous," Mimi threw in, "Gloria Redkins thinks *I'm* pregnant! Isn't that a kick?"

Felicia's eyes opened wide in surprise. "Why would she think that?"

"Oh, it's silly." Mimi grabbed her tea. "Just because I threw up all over Kitty Katt at the July Fourth picnic down at the park—"

"Whoa!" Felicia stopped her. "You vomited on Kitty?" She threw back her head and laughed. "That's priceless! I wish I could have seen her face."

Mimi nodded conspiratorially. "I would have enjoyed it more, had I been feeling well."

Jennifer furrowed her brows. "That's right. You *were* pretty pale that day when I saw you. MJ kept saying you were Casper."

Mimi waved away Jennifer's comment. "I must have picked up some bug. I'm feeling fine today." The PWs eyed her suspiciously. "Really." She looked from one to the other. "Okay, well, maybe I'm a *little* nauseated today. But it's *nothing.*"

Jennifer watched Lisa catch Felicia's eye and nod.

"I can't have another baby anyway," continued Mimi. "I can barely handle the monkeys I have."

Jennifer smiled in that friendly, pastor's wife sort of way, while she inwardly cringed. *Great, God, you're doing well here. Give her another child and keep me from having just one. Yeah, that's super.*

Mimi

Tuesday, July 11
1:36 p.m.

On her way home from Lulu's, Mimi drove past a billboard advertising St. Luke's Hospital's maternity ward. Come Birth with Us, it read in large black letters. A happy mother was holding a baby. Gloria's words echoed through her mind. *"You may want to check, just to make sure."*

No, she reassured herself. *I just had my period last . . . it was just . . . when was the last time?* Her mind was blank.

Suddenly her heart slammed into her chest. *Okay, calm down,* she reprimanded herself. *You're not thinking clearly. Just because you can't remember the last time doesn't mean you're pregnant. You don't get morning sickness.*

But another part of her brain screamed, *Aaahhh! What if it's true? What if you are pregnant? After all, Gloria said she was really sick with only one of her children.*

Panic rose within Mimi. She drove past a Walgreens, and after losing—

or winning?—the mental tug of war, she did a U-turn and sped back to the parking lot.

She glanced around to make sure she didn't know anybody and hustled toward the pregnancy kits at the back of the store. There were dozens. *Which one's the most accurate?* she wondered as she felt the panic again.

Finally she grabbed one of each kind and, with arms full, headed toward the checkout. The clerk, a greasy-haired, pimply teenager who looked like he hadn't bothered to shower that morning, snorted when she dumped her items on the counter.

"A little paranoid, lady?" He snickered.

Just hush and ring me up, she wanted to say. Instead she said, "One can never be too sure" and mentally added, *especially if they grow up to be smart-aleck clerks.*

"You sure there weren't any others back there you missed?"

She gritted her teeth but said nothing.

"Hope you have enough urine for all those," he said as he loaded the boxes into a bag. "Do you think if your husband helps, they'll still read positive?" Mimi gave him what she hoped was her meanest look, grabbed the bag, and walked briskly from the store.

She threw the bag into the passenger seat, mentally committing to writing a letter of complaint to the manager, buckled up, and drove off. As she headed home, she glanced at the bag. Then she pulled into the McDonald's drive-up and ordered a large iced tea to get that sample supply jump-started. She tried to reassure herself, *This is just a precaution. I'm probably thrown off my cycle because I've been sick.* That thought made her feel a little better.

Mimi drove past Gladys's house and decided to let Megan stay with the babysitter a little longer. Mimi needed to be alone and uninterrupted. And since Michaela and MJ were at their friends' houses, and Mark was at the church preparing for next Sunday's sermon, she figured she had a good hour and a half before anybody arrived home. The iced tea should do the trick by that point.

Mimi pulled into the driveway, grabbed her purse, the drugstore bag, and her large drink, and headed into the house and straight for the bathroom.

3:45 p.m.

"This is all your fault!" Mimi yelled at Mark as he walked into the bedroom.

As soon as she was sure she was pregnant, Mimi had called Mark and told him he needed to come home immediately. When he got to the top of the stairs, she blurted out that she was pregnant.

Mark asked if she was sure. She pointed to the dipsticks arrayed on the nightstand, blue lines showing on all. "Six tests can't be wrong, Mark."

He broke into a wide grin and threw his hands in the air like a football official's touchdown call. "Score!"

"This is all your fault!" Mimi said again.

"What?"

"You *knew* I was ovulating."

"I don't keep track of those things."

"You took advantage of me. I was too exhausted to say no."

"Come on, Mims. This is great news."

"Great! Great? For whom exactly? We decided three was it. Not four. Three. Three is all I can handle, Mark. This one will put me over the edge. I want peace and calm—something I haven't had being a wife and mother. I want a *life*. I barely have one out of diapers. I barely get a full night's sleep.

174

I can barely keep track of the ones we've already got!" She stared at him hard. "I don't *want* another child."

Mark stood silent.

Mimi gulped hard at the realization of what she'd said.

"You don't really mean that." When Mimi didn't answer, Mark asked, "Do you?"

"Yes. No." Mimi closed her eyes and sighed. "I don't know." She slumped onto the bed and put her head in her hands. Finally, when she lifted her head to look at Mark, her eyes were brimming with tears. "I'm so tired."

"I know."

"No," Mimi said, resigned and frustrated. "You don't know. You don't know what it's like to slave away every day trying to . . . to be the best mother . . . a great neighbor and committed citizen . . . a good Christian and pastor's wife. Having everyone watch every single thing you do and judge it. As if I don't judge myself harshly enough!"

"Yes, I do understand that."

"No!" She stood. "See, the difference between you and me is that you get paid. Your job is to be the pastor. I'm the bonus—with no benefits, no pay, no life of my own."

"Wait a minute. What exactly are we talking about here? Another baby? Or your issues with being a pastor's wife?"

"Yes. All of it." She walked over to him and tapped his chest. "Let me ask you something, Pastor. When was the last time you had a member of your congregation tell you how to raise your children? Or question how you could let your kids color during the service? When was the last time you had a member of your congregation make some comment about the new car you purchased—with a 'joke' about how they're paying you too much?"

Mark simply shook his head.

"See, Mark? If you don't keep a clean house when the council comes over, you don't receive the dirty looks or snide comments. If your kids aren't well behaved at McDonald's, you don't receive the parenting advice the next Sunday morning. I do. *I* do."

"Well, what do you want to do? It's not like you can become unpregnant. And it's not as if I'm leaving the ministry."

"Did you know a lot of pastors leave the ministry because their wives can't take it anymore?"

"Is that what you're suggesting?"

She sighed again. She had to get ahold of herself. Everything seemed so out of control. Deep in her heart, she believed children were a gift from God. Deep in her heart she loved being part of her husband's ministry—*her* ministry. And deep down she told herself to buck up—this was another challenge, and she would rise to the occasion. She would succeed at this just as she had at everything else. She breathed deeply and told herself to calm down. *Get it together, Mimi.*

"Mark," she finally said, calmer now, "I would never ask you to give up being a pastor. I think it's the stress talking. Finding out I'm having another baby—my *fourth*—is overwhelming for me." She stroked Mark's cheek. "Of course I want this child. Of course I'm grateful for the blessing."

That seemed to work the magic. Mark's shoulders relaxed. He took Mimi by the shoulders and drew her to him. "That's my girl." He kissed her forehead. Then he let go of the embrace and headed out of the room. "Where are the kids? I have to tell them. They'll be so excited!"

Mimi told Mark where they were, then watched him bound down the stairs, two at a time. She looked around her crisp green and cream bedroom, with its pleated draperies and neatly decorated walls. "That which does not kill us makes us stronger," she said, leaning over to smooth the bedspread. "I just hope this doesn't kill me."

Felicia

Thursday, July 20
7:12 p.m.

Felicia smiled and tapped her fingers on the steering wheel as she bounced along to the new Casting Crowns CD while zooming home on I-71. It had been a good day. A very good day.

That morning Felicia had met with Brandon Brooks, First Baptist's singles-ministry director, to explain the same plan she'd shared with bar owner Jim. Felicia had heard Brandon talking with Dave about a comedy outreach ministry he wanted to start. His idea was to rent a space in Cincinnati one night a week for local Christian comedy stand-ups in an effort to build more of a singles ministry that would result in a Saturday-night contemporary service in Cincinnati. He and Dave both agreed that a singles ministry in sleepy Red River would not be nearly as effective as one in the larger city.

So when Felicia shared that Brew-Ha-Ha would supply the space for "Ha-Ha at Brew-Ha-Ha" plus serve only soda on Monday nights from six to nine, Brandon was thrilled. Felicia was equally excited because it was the first time she had significantly helped one of the church's ministries. And she knew the bar's hosting of an alcohol-free event would improve its image and play well in the media.

And she couldn't wait to share her success with Dave. Finally he would see that she was able to be a good professional *and* a good pastor's wife . . . it was all coming together!

But after she parked in the driveway and started walking toward the house, she peered in the living-room window and saw Lauren, the church secretary's teen daughter, helping Nicholas stack Lincoln Logs on the floor.

"Mom!" Nicholas called as he knocked over the blocks in an effort to get to her quickly when she walked in the door.

"Hi, Lauren. Hi, Nicholas," she said as she hugged him. "Where's Daddy, big guy?"

Lauren got up off the floor and smoothed her pants. "Hi, Mrs. Morrison. Pastor Dave called me to come over. He and Mrs. Borden had to go for coffee to talk about the VBS some more. I hear this year's going to be bigger and better than ever!"

"Yeah, well, as much as they've been meeting, you'd think they were planning the Olympics or something." Felicia regretted her derogatory tone, but it was too late.

Lauren giggled. "That's funny, Mrs. Morrison."

"What's funny?"

"About planning the Olympics."

Felicia felt that strange chasm between wanting to know more and being afraid to ask. She decided to take her chances. "What's funny about that?"

Lauren got a curious look. "You know," she started slowly, "the VBS theme? It's *Going for the Gold*."

Felicia realized she didn't even know the theme for the VBS, let alone the plans.

"Oh, right." She nodded knowingly, then kicked off her shoes and grabbed her purse off the floor. "Now how much do I owe you? And do you need a ride home?"

"It's ten dollars, and Mrs. Borden said she'd swing back by and pick me up when she drops off Pastor Dave."

Felicia's mind whirred like a top as she flipped through her purse for a ten-dollar bill. *She picked him up to be alone with him? And she brought the babysitter? Am I even needed here anymore, or am I just taking up space?*

Finding two fives, Felicia took a deep breath before handing them to Lauren. "What time did they—uh, I mean, he—say he'd be back?"

"Any time now." Lauren picked up her book bag and headed toward the door. "He said he was hoping to beat you home so you wouldn't even miss him. But it's still light out, so I'll just walk home."

So I wouldn't "miss him," or so I wouldn't catch him on his date? Felicia wondered as she watched Lauren walk away, down the street.

CHAPTER
27

Mimi

Monday, July 24
10:21 a.m.

"Dad, Mom's cryin' again," MJ not so subtly yelled across his mother's body on the couch. Mimi had just settled down for a minute's rest when MJ came bouncing a ball through the living room. She had asked him to stop and told him that he knew better, then Buster showed up and thought it was playtime. Buster had grabbed the ball and jumped onto the couch—and Mimi.

"Get her that box of tissues," Mark called from his home office in the back of the house. It was his day off, but he often spent hours on Mondays studying for the following Sunday's sermon.

"I can't find it."

All the yelling back and forth only served to make Mimi cry harder. She put her hands over her head, then began to scream, and jumped off the couch. "If you don't take the dog and that ball and anything else you have hanging around down here causing a mess, I'm going to ship you to Singapore. Now!"

MJ's mouth dropped open.

"I mean it," she continued. "I know someone at the post office who ships off little boys—*and their fathers.*" She raised her voice loud enough to make sure Mark could hear.

"Where's Singapore?" MJ said in a tiny voice.

"Far away."

MJ gulped.

"I try hard to keep this house from being condemned by the EPA, only for you and your dad to mess it up again."

"What's an EPA?"

"Ask your father. Now scoot."

Mimi wiped her eyes and picked up her husband's Bible and sermon notes. She marched them into his office. "Is this your study?" she asked, gesturing toward the book-lined walls.

"Huh?" Mark looked confused.

"Your office. Is this it?"

"What are you talking about?"

"This." She held up the Bible and notebook. "This belongs in here, not floating around the rest of the house."

Just then the phone rang. "I'll get it!" came MJ's voice from the kitchen.

"Mom! It's for you. It's Mrs. Beesom," MJ yelled seconds later.

Why's Alice calling me? Mimi wondered as she picked up the receiver. Then it hit her. *The food pantry. Today.*

Mimi looked at the rooster clock above the sink. *10:30.* She was supposed to have been there forty-five minutes ago to help set up.

She dove right in. "Oh, Alice, I'm so sorry. I completely forgot to call you. I—" All of a sudden, she got choked up.

"You all right?" Alice asked, concern in her voice.

Mimi nodded, knowing Alice couldn't see her but feeling unable to do anything more.

"Mimi?"

Mimi nodded again. "I'm just . . . so . . . happy you called. I've been running behind and didn't get the coffeecake baked."

"That's okay. We'll take a rain check. Can you still make it over?"

Mimi looked down at her "cleaning" outfit—paint-stained jeans and an oversized Kings Island T-shirt the kids had given her last Christmas. She hadn't even taken a shower yet that morning.

"Uh, sure. Yes. Absolutely. I'll be there." She hung up and realized she wasn't even sure where the food pantry was.

11:21 a.m.

Less than an hour later, Mimi stepped into the food pantry looking much better than she actually felt. She'd grabbed a shower, quickly blown her hair dry, donned a pair of khaki pants and a pink blouse, and applied some light blush and mascara. Mark had given her directions to the pantry, so she was able to make it there in twenty minutes, find a parking spot in the back of the rundown building, and enter through the back entrance. Fortunately she had baked several coffeecakes a few months back for just such an emergency—thanks mostly to the overly hot, dysfunctional oven. She'd been able to defrost one in the microwave before she'd hopped in the shower.

Alice was the first to greet her and shush away her apologies for being late. "It happens. Don't worry about it," was all Alice said.

When Mimi held out the cake as a peace offering, Alice squealed in delight. "Oh, Mimi, I don't know how you do it, but you always come through." She winked and led Mimi through the warehouse, pointing out perishables in the large, glass-plated refrigerators on the far end that covered most of the wall. They navigated around crates of coffee, cereal, rice, macaroni, tuna, and canned stew.

"I had no idea this was such a large establishment," Mimi uttered, impressed.

"Yep. Even Red River has the poor. But we're really a district point, so we get families from all over the area, not just from Red River."

"Our church donates food here once a month."

"I know. And trust me, we all appreciate that. We also get food from corporations and other organizations and churches. The funniest thing happened not too long ago. A woman stopped by and donated a thousand dollars. But the catch was it had to be for one specific person. We told her we really couldn't do that, and maybe she should consider just giving the person the money. She was adamant, though. She said that if we didn't accept her money for this man, she would have her husband pull all funding to the pantry. Her husband is some bigwig pastor. The Presbyterian church, I think."

Mimi cocked her head and slowed her walk. "Alice, do you remember the woman's name?"

"No. But it was a funny one, I remember that."

"Katt?"

Alice lit up. "Yeah, I think that was it. Oh, of course, you'd know, huh? What with you being a pastor's wife too. I probably shouldn't have said anything."

"No no. That's fine." Mimi didn't want to appear too eager to wrestle information about Kitty. But this juicy tidbit was too good to be true. "Do you know the person's name?"

"No. It wasn't as interesting as hers. All I remember is that it was a man. He's come in before—midthirties, I'd say. Nice looking, though." Alice got a glint in her eye. "You don't think they're . . ." She stopped herself. "Sorry. I shouldn't have said that. But what I don't understand is why somebody like that woman would be attached to somebody who gets his food from this place."

"Yes, it is interesting, isn't it?" Mimi couldn't wait to tell the PWs.

Wonder what Kitty Katt is up to?

28

Lulu's Café

Tuesday, July 25
12:07 p.m.

Just get through this lunch without crying, Mimi kept telling herself as she sat with the PWs in the back booth at Lulu's. She had purposefully not worn mascara, just in case. She didn't want to look like the '70s rocker Alice Cooper, with black runs smudged under her eyes.

As soon as everyone arrived, Felicia launched into a tirade about Nancy Borden, the woman Felicia thought was trying to steal her husband—"from right under my nose! I mean, that's gall. And what's worse is Dave is so gullible! He just goes about his business with her as if he's completely unaware of what she's trying to do. And lately he's been making these snarky comments about how Nancy's so involved in ministry and how he wishes I would be. Like he's comparing me to her! I'm so tired of hearing him say, 'You're the pastor's wife. You should do this,' or 'You should be involved in that.' You know what? I am a person—not a job description. And if he really had his eyes open, he'd realize that I *am*

185

involved in ministry—but because it isn't what he envisions, it apparently isn't acceptable."

She went on to tell the women about her idea of using Brew-Ha-Ha as the new outreach ministry for singles.

"That's a wonderful idea," said Jennifer, who was sitting next to her with one leg tucked under her body. "Why wouldn't he like that?"

Felicia paused. "Because I haven't told him about it yet."

Lisa scrunched her face as though trying to understand. "How come?"

"Because he's too busy spending time with Nancy Borden. *Alone,*" Felicia shot back fiercely.

Jennifer and Lisa both clucked their disapproval. "That's trouble with a capital T," Lisa said.

"What is it with these women who throw themselves all over our husbands? Maybe those wives at the seminary were right about the rock-star syndrome you mentioned that time, Felicia," Jennifer joined in.

"My mother said it's because they see something in pastors that they don't have at home. A strength, a godly leadership," explained Lisa. "They think strong, spiritual men are sexy."

"Well, Dave *is!*" Felicia said, a bit defensively. "But he's mine. That means hands off."

Mimi sat barely listening to what they were saying. She'd felt disconnected from most things since she'd seen the blue lines on those pregnancy tests she'd taken two weeks ago. She'd held on with a stubborn hope that those test results were wrong—even though Mark kept reminding her that six tests wouldn't lie.

So Mark had made her an appointment to see Dr. O'Boyle for confirmation. When the gynecologist had examined her and given her the "happy" news, Mimi had burst out in heartbroken sobs. It was as though the news had turned on a fire hose, instead of a spigot, in her emotions. Dr.

O'Boyle had mistakenly assumed that Mimi was delighted by the prospect of bringing another baby into the world. But Mimi could only nod and choke out, "My husband will be so thrilled to hear my announcement." Then she tucked a mental note into the back of her brain: *Never let that man touch me again.*

"Mimi," Jennifer said, tearing Mimi out of her detached mental state, "you haven't heard a word we've been saying."

"Hmmm?" Mimi muttered.

"We were talking about how you and Mark had agreed to generously donate five thousand dollars to each of us for our Alaskan cruise," Felicia said.

"Uh-huh," Mimi said absently. "That's nice."

"Mimi." Lisa turned in her seat to face Mimi directly. "Earth calling Mimi. Honey, what's going on with you?"

Mimi blinked a few times, desperately trying to focus, yet fearing the fire hose would erupt again.

Lisa's smooth hands reached over and gently held Mimi's face. "Mimi?"

"She's not on drugs, is she?" Jennifer offered. "She mentioned last time she was feeling sick. Maybe the doctor gave her some medicine that makes her loopy."

"I don't think that's it," Lisa said, pulling her hands away.

Mimi shook her head slightly. Tears brimmed, threatening to spill onto her cheeks. She blinked again. "I'm okay." She was finally able to force the words from her lips.

"No, I don't think you are," Lisa whispered to her.

Mimi opened her mouth to speak, but no sound would come out. Finally she mouthed the words to Lisa.

Felicia leaned in slightly. "What did she say?"

Lisa shook her head. "'I'm' something. *What* are you, honey?"

Mimi whimpered, "I'm preg—"

"She's pregnant," Jennifer said with an edge to her voice.

Mimi dropped her head into the napkin in her hands to hide the sobs.

"Well, that's just great," Jennifer said nastily. "Good for you, Mimi. How about that? You got an oopsy. You and Mark did it without even trying."

Mimi looked up in time to watch Felicia shoot a harsh look at Jennifer.

"No," Mimi said between gasps. She'd started to cry so hard that she felt as if she were hiccupping. "She's . . . right. Jennifer . . . should . . . be . . . the . . . one . . . having . . . this . . . baby. Not me."

Jennifer's face immediately went white. "I'm so sorry, Mimi. That was horrible of me. I didn't mean it."

Mimi tried to get her emotions in check. "I know . . . you didn't." She hiccupped again.

"Please forgive me. I was wrong."

"Of course I do. We're friends."

Jennifer grew teary-eyed. She lifted her face slightly and blinked several times.

"That doesn't work," Mimi said through her own tears. "I've already tried it."

They both laughed. Jennifer grabbed her napkin and blotted at her eyes.

Just then Gracie sidled toward the table carrying a tray stand and a large round tray with four plates of food. When she got to their table, she expertly opened the stand with one hand and put the tray on top of it. She picked up the first plate and started to lean across the table, then stopped short.

"The food's not that bad," she said, cocking her head.

When they all laughed again, Mimi felt as if she was starting to get back under control.

Felicia made up some excuse about their having a crying contest to see who was more believable.

"They both look pretty bad, if you ask me." Gracie finished placing the plates. "I'm almost afraid to ask if you need anything else."

"No, thank you, Gracie," said Lisa.

Gracie's face turned serious. "If it's something bad, I'll sure say a prayer for you. I'm not really on speaking terms with God, but if it's about you PWs, I bet he'd listen. You're all good girls," she said as she knocked on the table. Then, looking extremely uncomfortable—she was never completely easy talking about God, she'd told them over and over when they'd try to talk to her about their faith—she cleared her throat, grabbed the tray, and hustled away.

"One of these days God's going to get hold of that lady," Felicia said as her eyes followed Gracie.

"She has a good heart," Mimi agreed.

"Shall we?" Lisa said, and they all nodded.

Mimi knew Lisa meant it was time to pray a blessing over their food.

"I'll do it," Jennifer piped in.

Mimi's eyes widened. She saw the surprise on Lisa's and Felicia's faces too.

"Well, it's the least I can do, considering what I said to you," Jennifer protested.

Mimi bowed her head along with the others and listened to Jennifer say a quiet, simple prayer of thanksgiving for food and friendship.

Mimi wiped her eyes again. She picked up her egg-salad sandwich and held it as she said, "I just don't do well with things that are unplanned. You know, things I can't control."

"That's definitely pregnancy," said Lisa before she popped a ketchup-covered french fry into her mouth.

"Mark and I had a pretty heated argument over it," Mimi continued. "He asked me what I wanted to do—as if I had a choice."

"You do, technically," Felicia said jokingly as she tore open a package of saltines. "Many women give up their children for adoption."

"I'm desperate, but not that desperate. Although I *have* considered giving up my husband and other children at various times."

"I admire those women," Jennifer said. "They realize they can't give their child what he or she needs, so they choose a better life for their child, hoping and praying for a wonderful family."

"Have you considered adoption yet?" Lisa asked Jennifer.

"Sam and I have discussed it, but we're trying to exhaust all our natural-birth options first."

Mimi took a last bite of her sandwich. "I know everything will be okay. It will work out. I mean, that's biblical, right? *All things* work together for good?"

"I certainly hope so," said Jennifer.

"Me too," sighed Mimi. "Me too."

When the women were finished eating, Felicia dove her arm under the table, coming back up with her purse. "Okay, girls, time to go," she said as she dug out her car keys. "The Ciao Bella Spa and Lisa's afternoon of beauty await!" The others reached for their purses, and Felicia took a final swig of water.

While they were making their way to the cash register, Mimi noticed that Lisa looked nervous. Letting Felicia and Jennifer go ahead, she grabbed Lisa's elbow. "Hey, you *are* looking forward to your makeover, aren't you?" she whispered. "I know Felicia is really excited about treating you. And we've all been looking forward to this since we started talking about it a few weeks ago."

Lisa toyed with the receipt in her hand. "I'm really grateful to Felicia," she said in a low voice, "but I've never been to a spa before. I'm not sure I'll like it. And I'm not sure it will work to get Joel's attention. He doesn't notice anything I do anymore. I hope it's not a big waste of everyone's time."

Mimi put her arm around her and pulled her along to the register. "Hey, even if it doesn't do anything for Joel, at least you will feel better about *you*. Plus we get to spend an extra few hours together. I see no waste of time in that, do you?"

Lisa nodded but still seemed uneasy . . . and a bit scared, like a deer caught in a car's headlights.

Lord, give this woman confidence so she can become a beautiful butterfly for her husband today, Mimi prayed as she handed her money to the cashier at the restaurant. *And let her know that no matter what happens, she is loved— by me, by you, and by Joel.*

Ciao Bella Day Spa

Tuesday, July 25
1:27 p.m.

Felicia was like a pied piper leading Lisa, Mimi, and Jennifer down the strip-mall sidewalk toward the Ciao Bella Day Spa. "Now I haven't been to a day spa here in Ohio yet," she said, "but I expect it will be similar to the ones in LA where you get your own locker for your things, and they give you a comfy robe and slippers to change into."

Red flags popped immediately into Lisa's head. "You mean they want you to take off your clothes and walk around naked?" she asked innocently. "I don't think—"

"No, silly, you have your *robe* on!" Felicia said, sounding slightly exasperated. "But you're naked under that. How else do you think they can massage you?"

Lisa wished her cell phone would ring with one of the kids calling to say he or she needed her immediately. She did not like the idea of walking around someplace half-nude. And she was not excited about some stranger "massaging" her either, especially since Joel hadn't touched her in a long time. It seemed like a sad reminder of the intimacy she missed so desperately.

Felicia held open the spa's glass door so the three others could file in. As Lisa surveyed the interior, she regained some self-assurance. *This place is just a glorified beauty salon,* she thought, admonishing herself for being uptight about it.

The spa was basically one room. In one corner were two basins with chairs on either side. Next to the left chair was a plastic basket full of nail polish bottles. The other chair, in front of a wall mirror, joined a metal cart that held hair spray, combs, curlers, and other hair tools.

In another corner, she saw two counter-high chairs. Shelving behind one chair held cosmetic cases and brushes. Behind the second chair was a door with a sign: Massages Here.

The front right corner was home to a couple of folding chairs and two simple-looking upholstered love seats. Magazines were stacked on the floor. To Lisa's left a gum-chomping receptionist sat at a small glass table, talking loudly on the phone while she doodled on the open page of the appointment book. A potpourri burner near the edge of her desk provided a rose scent.

Lisa smiled and turned to tell Felicia how much she liked the spa already, only to find Felicia standing inside the door with a sour look. Her eyes were darting around in obvious dismay.

Lisa dropped her smile. "What?" she asked Felicia. "Did I do something wrong already?"

Felicia erased her disagreeable expression. "No no." She smiled at Lisa. "It's not you, it's—" She exhaled and moved toward the receptionist, clutching Lisa's hand as she did so. Lisa glanced at Mimi and Jennifer, who were already ensconced on a sofa, happily flipping through glossy celebrity magazines.

When the receptionist saw them standing in front of her, she said into the phone in an annoyed tone, "I've gotta go. I have people here."

Felicia seemed to ignore her attitude. "My friend has a one-thirty appointment for the half-day beauty package," she said, handing over her MasterCard. "Her name is Lisa Barton, and I hope you will take extra special care of her."

Was it Felicia's lack of confidence in the spa that brought on her diplomatic request? Lisa wondered.

The receptionist gazed out the window, then down at her appointment book. "Massage with Mandy, Brittany for mani and pedi, and Adam for hair and makeup," she said blandly.

"Adam?" Lisa asked. "Is that . . . a woman?"

The receptionist rolled her eyes. "Have you ever met a chick named Adam?" She handed Felicia back her credit card. Lisa heard Felicia take in a sharp breath.

"So I suppose there's no chance you'll be giving her a robe and slippers *here*," Felicia said, putting the card back in her wallet.

"This isn't a hotel," the receptionist responded in what appeared to be her typical surly voice.

Felicia crossed her arms. "May I speak to the manager, please?"

The receptionist crossed her arms, mimicking Felicia. "I *am* the manager. Is there a problem?"

Felicia sighed. "Well," she said to Lisa, with a forced brightness to her voice, "this should be an experience."

"Go knock on the massage door over there," the receptionist said as she dialed her cell phone. "Mandy's probably in there waiting for you."

Lisa walked over to the Massage sign, waving to Jennifer and Mimi as she passed.

"You go, girl!" Mimi cheered.

Lisa knocked, and the door opened to a closet of a room that was sauna warm. A sheeted table took up most of the space. Relaxing guitar music wafted through the air from a CD player in the corner.

"Hi, I'm Mandy." The woman inside extended her hand. Lisa was surprised at how soft her hand was and made a mental note to ask what brand of lotion she used.

"I'll step out so you can undress," Mandy said cheerfully. "Just get under the sheet facedown, and put your head in that doughnut at the end."

As Mandy pushed the door open wide to leave, Lisa thought she heard Felicia say, "Ugh, this place is a dump." Which surprised her, because she thought it was quite nice so far. She hadn't been in a beauty salon in years, let alone a place like this where they did everything.

Lisa took off her tennies, khakis, green polo shirt, and bra, and finally her gold stud earrings and L necklace. When she got down to her underwear, she wasn't so sure. *Am I supposed to go completely naked?* she wondered. *Why would I take off my panties? She's not going to massage my tush, is she? Or anyplace else down there for that matter?*

Leaving her underwear on, Lisa climbed onto the table and scooted around until her face was hanging in the "doughnut," as Mandy had called it. Seconds later, a knock sounded on the door, and Mandy cracked it open. "All clear?"

"All set," Lisa said, although the padded doughnut was pressing against her cheeks, making it difficult for her to talk.

I thought massages were supposed to be relaxing, she thought as she listened to Mandy pump something on her hands and rub them together. *This feels like a torture contraption.*

But when Mandy's hands, spread with warm oil, pressed down on Lisa's back and swirled around to her neck, she couldn't help but let out an "ahhh" that was so heartfelt it made Mandy giggle.

"Under a lot of stress lately?" Mandy asked, rubbing deep into the crevices between Lisa's neck and shoulders.

"Married to it," Lisa said.

An hour later, her clothes back on and with "a new sense of well-being," as the spa brochure said ("They have a *brochure?*" Felicia asked with disbelief when she saw Lisa reading one), Lisa was sitting next to one of the sinks, her feet in a tub of warm water and her left hand stretched out to Brittany, who was trimming her cuticles. Lisa's right hand rested in a bowl filled with a soapy solution.

"What color you want?" asked Brittany, an Asian immigrant who clearly did not have "Brittany" on her birth certificate. She pushed the plastic basket full of polish bottles to where Lisa could see them.

"Uh, I don't—"

"She wants red, the hottest red you've got," Mimi said, seeming to appear from nowhere. Mimi, Jennifer, and Felicia had left the spa for an ice cream cone after hearing Lisa's effusive account of her massage, so Lisa hadn't expected to hear Mimi's voice that soon.

"Red?" Lisa was unsure. Red seemed kind of trashy. She didn't want to go over the top for Joel. After all, she'd have to live with those nails for a while.

Mimi moved around to where Lisa could see her. "If you're going to do this thing, do it right. Mark loves it when I put on red polish. He likes me to run my nails down his back—"

"Okay, I get it," Lisa interrupted, not wanting a full account of what Mimi and Mark did in their private time. "Red it is."

Mimi plucked two OPI bottles out of the plastic basket, then held them for Lisa to inspect. "Do you want"—she brought the bottles close to her eyes so she could see their small titles—"Better Off Red" or "Sleeping Single in a Double Red?"

Lisa threw back her head in laughter. "I think they both sound pretty appropriate, don't you?"

Mimi held both bottles to Lisa's arm. "I like the Sleeping Single one. It matches your skin tone best."

"Good afternoon, ladies!" a voice rang out.

Lisa leaned out and Mimi turned to see a gorgeous man, who appeared to be in his forties, walk into the spa. He was wearing a shiny black shirt with purple flowered buttons down the center and snug black jeans. His blond hair was tipped in black, and perfectly combed.

He marched right over to Lisa, who drew back slightly at the power with which he approached her. "So you must be my makeover girl."

Lisa could smell his citrusy cologne.

"I'm Adam. I came in especially for you today. So once Brittany's done"—he peeked over her hands to see the progress—"we'll get you in the chair and figure out how we're going to transform you."

Adam swung back to talk quietly with the receptionist, whom Lisa figured out was "Dana" from others talking to her. Lisa motioned with her head for Mimi to lean down to Lisa's ear and whispered, "Is he . . . a . . . homosexual?" Lisa had never met a homosexual. That she knew of anyway.

Mimi shrugged and whispered back, "The ones on those TV makeover shows sure seem to know what they're doing. I wouldn't worry about it."

"Oh! Okay," Lisa said, trying to keep her voice low. This whole day had been about throwing caution to the wind, so a gay man doing her hair and makeup seemed par for the course.

After Brittany put the top coat on Lisa's toes, which were separated by pieces of foam, she helped Lisa walk over to the salon chair. "You hold my arm. I help you," she told her.

Lisa spotted Jennifer and Felicia, working together on a crossword puzzle. Mimi took Lisa's chair at Brittany's station to ready herself for a pedicure. "I don't really care about getting my toes painted," she told Lisa. "I just want the foot-massage part."

Adam was busying himself at the metal supply cart. Hearing Lisa sit, he spun around with an expression of excitement. He studied Lisa for a minute, causing her to ask uncomfortably, "What?"

"I'm just looking at you, darling," Adam purred, then spun around again to his cart. He pulled out a drawer with hair-color samples, flipped through a few, then turned and held a few next to Lisa's head.

"What cologne is that you're wearing?" Lisa asked, trying to make conversation. "I might want to get some for my husband this Christmas."

"Oh, darling, you don't want this for your husband, unless he's looking for a husband himself," he said good-naturedly, bending back down to sort through his cart. Wide-eyed, Lisa caught Jennifer's eye and they grinned at each other across the room.

Adam escorted Lisa over to the sink, seated her in the chair, and leaned the chair back. When he told her he wanted to surprise her with the color, she started to jump up, afraid of what color he might select. But he gently pushed her back down.

"Trust me," he said. "I have a sister in Phoenix with your coloring. I put this rinse on her, and she looked *fab*ulous." He stretched out the *fab* part of the word when he said it.

While the color set, Adam took Lisa back to his chair so he could apply her makeup. Before he started, he asked, "Do you want a daytime or an evening look?"

Lisa started to say "daytime" because she didn't want anything too heavy. She didn't wear much makeup—just a little powder and some tinted lip gloss. But before she could answer, Felicia called from the waiting area,

"Give her your nighttime 'come hither' look." Jennifer and Mimi let out a few catcalls in agreement.

"Wow, you must have something really special planned for that hubby of yours tonight." Adam winked.

Even he'd probably be surprised at the outfit I have planned, Lisa thought. But looking at the hand-painted flower buttons on his shirt, and the pointy boots on his feet, Lisa reconsidered.

By the time Adam was about half done with Lisa's makeup, the three other PWs were standing in front of her. He wouldn't let her look in a mirror until "the big reveal," as he called it, so she had to gauge his success by the looks on the girls' faces. And if their expressions were any measure, Lisa thought she must be looking fantastic.

Thirty minutes later, Adam was gliding around Lisa's chair, tiny styling scissors in his hand. He had already cut and blow-dried her hair, but he said he needed to do just a few more "nip and tuck" pieces before he spun her around. The PWs had returned to the sofas, but they were watching from a distance. Lisa caught Mimi's eye, and Mimi gave her a thumbs-up.

Adam put down his tools and stood in front of Lisa. He placed a hand on either side of her chair, then leaned in toward her. "Darling, I think you look ravishing, and not because I did the work. If that husband of yours isn't blown away, I'll give you my number—and that's saying something." He chuckled at that unlikeliness, then stepped back and spun Lisa around to face the mirror.

"Ta-da!" he called from behind as the PWs rushed over.

Lisa took a second to focus on herself. Was that her? The reddish rinse he'd put on her hair gave it a healthy shine, and the cut—oh, the cut—took her hair from long and bushy to shoulder length and bouncy. Her hazel eyes sparkled with their tan and gold shadow, and her lips looked luscious in a deep, wine-based red.

Felicia, Jennifer, and Mimi were so caught up in their *oohing* and *aahing* and congratulating of Adam that Lisa thought she might get away with the tears in her eyes. But when the green eyeliner started to dribble off, Adam took notice.

"Oh no, you don't like it," he said with earnest alarm. "What can I do to change it, darling? How can I make it better for you?"

"Lisa, if you don't like something," Felicia said as she walked around the chair to face Lisa rather than looking at her in the mirror, "let's let him change—"

Lisa grabbed Felicia's hand and shook her head vigorously so Felicia would get the message. She was afraid if she tried to speak, her tears of joy would turn into a full-fledged cry, ruining all of this wonderful day.

As she looked again at Lisa, Felicia's face changed from concern to delight. "I think we're done here," she said, smiling over at Jennifer and Mimi. "Let's get Cinderella home so she can wait for her handsome prince."

Lisa

Tuesday, July 25
6:00 p.m.

Lisa pulled into the driveway. She still couldn't believe she'd let Felicia and the others talk her into a makeover. Every time she looked into the rearview mirror, she hardly recognized herself. Her now reddish-brown hair was silky and styled so it framed her face perfectly with wispy fringes. Her eyebrows were neatly plucked and shaped. She was wearing a shimmering face shiner that added the perfect touch of pink to her cheeks.

Lisa smiled at her reflection. Then she looked down at the package sitting next to her. She lifted her neatly manicured hand and touched the brown paper bag with Lover's Lane splashed in pink curly writing across it. *If this doesn't get his attention, nothing will.*

She checked her watch. *Six o'clock.* Callie and Ricky were spending the night with Lisa's mom and dad, so she didn't need to worry about that interruption. And she'd called Joel. He was set to come home within the next half hour. Plenty of time for her to prepare herself and the house for her romantic adventure.

Once inside she grabbed the roses she'd just bought and depetaled them, taking care not to accidentally catch her fingers on the thorns. Next she took out the new scented candles she'd purchased. Jennifer had told her lavender and jasmine were great for romance, so she'd splurged on four of each kind.

After she carefully placed the petals along the hallway and leading to the bedroom, she finally unwrapped the Lover's Lane purchase and held it up. For a moment she had second thoughts, afraid the garb would be too sleazy. Then she realized, *I'm married, for goodness' sake. I'm doing this for my marriage.* She went into the bathroom and slipped into her sexy nurse's costume, then eyed herself in the mirror.

Even though the tag said size 12, what she usually wore, the outfit was skintight. She purposefully hadn't worn anything that revealing since before Callie was born fourteen years ago. Although she was a perfect size 6 before she started having kids, with each one she gained more weight and lost less, and then her metabolism slowed. Plus when she was depressed, she ate. She'd been doing a lot of that lately.

She started to unzip the back zipper. *I can't do this. I look terrible*, she thought, looking at the little bulges around her midriff and thighs. Then she remembered something Felicia had said at the spa. "He'll be so surprised and excited, he won't notice that your body isn't Jessica Simpson's. And believe me, he'll forget about the church right away."

She stopped mid-zip. *He used to not be able to keep his hands off me. Maybe this will remind him of when we were first married.*

She fixed the zipper and looked again in the mirror, then chuckled. *If my mother knew what I was planning, she'd have a heart attack. So what does a sexy nurse say? She needs him in the operating room STAT? Do I call him "Doctor"?* she thought whimsically.

Hearing the front door open and shut, she looked around frantically, wondering if she'd forgotten anything. Then she hopped on the bed and tried to set her pose. She decided to lie straight out, with one leg bent and an arm raised above her head. Then she thought that looked silly. So she turned on her side facing the door, bent her knees, and placed her head on her hand. That didn't work either. So she sat up, knees curled under her.

In her rush and anxiety to find the perfect posture, she didn't notice at first that Joel wasn't following the petals upstairs. So she settled into her first option and waited. And waited. She still didn't hear his footsteps on the creaky stairs, even though she was sure she'd made the clues obvious for him.

Should I go down and find him? she wondered, then talked herself out of it. If she did that, it would ruin the effect. No, she'd wait. He'd have to come upstairs eventually. She fixed her hair so it flowed neatly on the pillowcase. The flutter of the candles on the dimly lit walls was hypnotizing. Her eyes fell closed and reopened a few times. She stifled a yawn.

This is ridiculous, she thought and sat up. If she lay there any longer, she was going to fall asleep. So she cut her losses and walked downstairs. The candles were lit along the hallway, and she could detect the faint scent of jasmine and lavender. She was careful not to step on any of the petals.

Spying Joel sitting in the living room, reading the newspaper, she stepped into the archway. "Hey."

"Hi," he replied without looking up from the paper. "Where are the kids?"

"I sent them to Mom's for the night."

"Why'd you do—" Joel lifted his head from the paper and stopped.

Lisa thought his jaw might fall to his chest. A nervous flutter took over her stomach, so she knew she needed to dive in or she'd back out on this marriage-saving endeavor.

"I thought we could spend the evening together. Just the two of us."

Joel stared at her, looking almost unsure of what to do or say. It seemed to her like an eternity until he put down the paper and stood.

Lisa wanted to say, "It's about time, mister," but thought that might be a mood killer. Instead she just smiled in what she hoped was a seductive way.

Joel stopped. "Why are you making that face?"

"What face?" She tried to smile again.

"You look like you have something in your eye."

"It's nothing," she said and pulled him close to her. She placed her freshly manicured hand on his chest and rubbed lightly. "I've missed you, Mr. Barton." Then she gently and slowly kissed him.

He responded hesitantly to her kiss and awkwardly started to put his arms around her.

She was just beginning to enjoy the moment . . . when the phone rang.

Joel's shoulders stiffened, and he began to back out of her embrace.

"Just let it go," she said. "This is our time."

"It could be important."

"Then let them call back later."

"Lisa," he said, extricating himself from her tightening arms, "I have to answer the phone."

She dropped her arms and watched him retreat toward what she now viewed as her enemy. She refused to stay and listen to the conversation—she didn't even care if it was a wrong number or a sales call. She was finished. The night was ruined. He'd made it abundantly clear, yet again, that she was not the priority. He was married to the church, and she was just his mistress.

Lisa trudged back up the stairs, ignoring the petals and candles. She walked into the bedroom, shut the door, and unzipped her costume. Then she stood in the middle of the bedroom and stared blankly at the bed. There were no tears. No sighs.

When she heard the front door open and close, she knew that, once again, she had lost.

31

Felicia

Friday, July 28
5:42 p.m.

The red dress. No, that's too much for a pastor's wife. The blue dress is better.
Wait, what's wrong with wearing a little red dress—the one that's cut a little too
low here and a bit high there—for a night out with my husband?

Felicia stood in front of the bedroom closet in her pantyhose and bra,
running her hands through her silky, black hair like an actress trying to sell
hair color on TV. "You'd think we were going out on our first date, not our
seventh anniversary," she said aloud to herself.

"Hey, I like *that* outfit," Dave said as he approached her from behind
and wrapped his arms around her bare waist, kissing her neck.

Felicia played like she wanted to escape. "Yeah, well, I'm not sure a restaurant like Jean-Robert would be too thrilled with my getup in a room full
of men in expensive suits and ladies dressed to the nines."

Dave let go and gently turned Felicia toward him. "Jean-Robert?" he
asked with a disappointed tone. "All the way in Cincinnati? Aw, come on,

Felicia. That's an expensive French place—not where a pastor eats."

"Hey, you said I could make reservations anywhere I wanted for our anniversary, and that's what I wanted," Felicia said as she turned back toward the closet. "We haven't eaten at a really nice restaurant since we moved from LA. And Red River sure doesn't have much to choose from." Felicia thought about Lulu's Café and wondered what Dave would think of that place. "Besides, where is it written that a pastor can't have a nice meal out occasionally?"

"I know, but isn't there something a little less high-end? Like maybe a home-cooked meal type of a place that's not so froufrou?"

Slipping the red dress over her head and down around her body, Felicia turned and motioned for Dave to zip her up as she wondered about his sudden fascination with home-cooked meals. In LA, they had tried a new restaurant every weekend—he'd never mentioned wanting a "home-cooked" meal.

Then again, in LA there was no Nancy Borden.

As Felicia turned to face Dave, she switched into secret desperation mode and decided to try a little reverse psychology. "If you don't want to go, we can cancel," she murmured. "But I thought it might do us some good to get away, even if it's just for a few hours."

Dave put his hands on her shoulders and looked her up and down. Then he smiled. "How could I not take *mi amor* where she wants when she looks like this?" He kissed her lightly. "Now what am I wearing? I know you've probably picked out something already to avoid CBD."

CBD was Felicia's nickname for Dave. She'd discovered early on in their relationship that he was color-blind to nearly every dark color, so she'd started to call him Color-Blind Dave, which got shortened to CBD at some point.

"Oh, actually I haven't. Go see what Nicholas is up to, and I'll pull something together for you."

As Dave trotted out of their bedroom, Felicia walked back toward the closet, catching her image in the dresser mirror. She stopped for a moment.

That new Pilates workout is finally knocking away the pregnancy pooch, she thought as she faced her reflection, then turned sideways and patted her tummy. *Of course, the control tops don't hurt either.*

Felicia hummed as she started sorting through Dave's end of the closet for a suit and clean shirt. A night out was just what she and Dave needed, she assured herself. They needed to get out among "other" people for a while—away from the chance they would run into people from church. Not that Felicia feared what the church people might say to her. It was what they *didn't* say that bothered her the most.

She pulled Dave's black suit and purple tie from the closet, then reached farther back to get his new white shirt, causing her to lose her balance and drop the suit on the floor. Sighing, she crouched down to pick it up. But as she replaced the jacket on the hanger, she noticed a piece of paper in the breast pocket. Slipping it out, she opened the note (folded four times!) and read:

> *Dear Pastor Dave,*
> *Thanks for the shoulder rub. It worked wonders!*
> *☺ Nancy*

Felicia sat backward on the wood floor, too stunned even to notice the small run that had started down the front of her left leg.

Mimi

Friday, August 4
3:09 p.m.

Mimi stared at Mark uncomprehendingly. He'd just surprised her with the news that he'd spontaneously asked the church council to come to their house to hold their meeting—and dinner was included.

"You volunteered our house and my cooking. Tonight." She still couldn't believe what she'd heard him admit.

Mark shifted uneasily. "I thought it would be a nice change. We've done this before, and it was never a big deal."

"Yes, but that was with advance warning."

"Well, this is advance warning."

"Mark, three hours is not advance warning."

"But you can pull something together, babe. Everyone got excited when I suggested it."

"You mean, when June called them about it." June was Mark's secretary at the church. A retired schoolteacher, she enjoyed volunteering at the church and helping print the Sunday bulletins, type Mark's sermon notes, and do little administrative odds and ends.

"Well, yeah," he admitted.

"You are so unbelievable."

"What's the big deal? Just throw something together. You've got all those casseroles in the freezer, ready to be defrosted and thrown in the oven."

"What's the big deal? Here"—she pointed toward the La-Z-Boy rocker in the living room—"have a seat, so I can tell you about the big deal." She set her hands on her hips and walked over to him. "First of all, I'm pregnant, which means I'm tired, nauseated, and just overall cranky. Second, just this morning alone, I've dealt with MJ breaking Mrs. Crowder's upstairs window because he wanted to see if he could throw that far. Megan was chasing Buster and fell and tore up her knees and bloodied her favorite Tweety Bird shirt. I still don't know which was the major tragedy for her—her knees or the shirt. Michaela smarted off because I wouldn't let her go to Angie's house until she finished her chores. I've had three people call, asking me to volunteer for different committees at the church—doesn't anybody else volunteer for things? Must it always be me? Do I have *sucker* written across my forehead? And let me remind you the oven's running hot and I've been burning everything lately. Also, the shower is backing up, the basement flooded from the water hose when I tried to water my flowers out front, and . . . do you want me to continue?"

Mark sighed and massaged his neck. "It's one night. I'll help. I can't uninvite them."

Mimi turned on her heel and stormed into the kitchen, muttering.

5:13 p.m.

The next two hours before her guests arrived got only worse. Buster chewed Mimi's favorite shoes. Megan dripped her Popsicle across the kitchen floor.

Michaela dared MJ to shake a can of orange soda and open it, which he did. In the living room. While Mimi was standing there. The soda exploded all over Mimi, the beige couch and carpet, and the mauve lampshades. When MJ realized what had happened, he took off running outside, with Mimi yelling behind him. Mimi had to decide what to do: run after her son and hang him on the clothesline, or try to clean up the orange mess. Figuring MJ would have to come back in the house at some point, she rushed to grab towels and spray stain remover before orange soda became part of her decor.

With forty-five minutes to go, Mimi grabbed a casserole and a cake from the freezer, swiped from the basement some jars of peaches she'd canned last summer, calculated the oven's heating discrepancies, set the timer, and headed upstairs. That was when the phone rang. She was tempted to let the answering machine pick up but decided it might be Mark telling her all the council members had come down with the flu and wouldn't be able to make it.

Instead it was Rita, a "needy" woman in their congregation, who was sweet but terribly unstable. She'd often call Mimi and Mark at the most inconvenient times to cry on their shoulders about her spiritual doubts (the same ones over and over), her inability to make her husband get a job, or any other number of things. Mimi knew Rita needed help. But that didn't make her lack of boundaries any more tolerable. And once Rita got you on the phone, there was no getting off. Not even rudely.

"Oh, Mimi," Rita whined into the phone. "Oh, Mimi, I'm at my wit's end."

Join the club, Mimi thought.

"Oh, oh, I don't know what I'm going to do."

"Rita, now isn't a good time for me. Can you call back a little later?" Mimi felt a twinge of guilt about pushing Rita off, but she knew Rita's emergencies were rarely that.

"But you're the pastor's wife. You can help me. I have nowhere else to turn."

"It's just that I'm expecting some of the council members over soon, and I really need to prepare for that."

"I won't take but a moment. Actually, can I come over?"

"No! I mean, that's not a good idea right now. I'm sure whatever it is that's bothering you will still be there later this evening. Or tomorrow morning. Why not call the pastor back then?"

"Oh, dear. No, that wouldn't work at all," Rita melodramatically howled over the phone. "Mimi, do fish go to heaven? One of our fish went belly up, and John took it and flushed it down the toilet. But I'm just not sure that's right."

Mimi sighed and ran her fingers through her messy mop of hair. She checked her watch. *I love being a pastor's wife. I love being a pastor's wife,* she mentally chanted over and over.

"Do you think Pastor Mark would do a sermon on animals? Maybe John would come to church then. What if the fish wasn't really dead, but only sleeping? Would that be murder then?"

Mimi began to tune her out. This had become her life. Rushing around, trying to get things done. Why even bother? What difference did it make? There would always be a Rita to mess it up.

EEEEEeeeee. The high-pitched scream of the smoke detector went off.

Not again. "Rita, my house is burning down. I have to go." She dropped the phone in the cradle and ran to the kitchen, with MJ, Michaela, and Megan all chasing behind to see what was going on. Sure enough, smoke was pouring from the oven. She raced toward the back door to fling it open and grabbed a broom from the closet to fan the detector enough to silence it.

Ding dong, the front doorbell sang out.

"Someone's at the door," Michaela said.

Mimi threw open the oven door, pulled out the burnt chicken and broccoli casserole, and stood frozen. There were the black and crusty remains of supper—supper for the church council. Supper that would impress them that their pastor's family had it all together.

Ding dong.

"Mom," Michaela said above the din of the detector.

Mimi dropped the casserole onto the stovetop and sank to the floor, still holding the broom handle with the bristles pointed toward the ceiling. Hot tears streamed down her cheeks and over her nose, racing down her neck, and onto her collar.

Finally the smoke detector ran out of steam and blurted a few more times before becoming still.

Footsteps fell on the back porch. Mark entered.

"Hey, guys!" he said brightly. "What's going—"

"Something's wrong with Mom," Michaela whispered.

Megan tugged at Mimi's sleeve and then threw her arms around her. Even MJ kept silent.

Mark stepped to Mimi, gently removed the broom from her hands, and set it on the floor. Then he knelt beside her. "Hi, babe. Are you still having a bad day?"

For an instant Mimi considered decking him. Instead a tiny wail escaped from her lips as a flood of new tears came rushing out. In the background she could hear the doorbell ring again. Her eyes locked on Mark's.

"I'll tell the council that we need to reschedule the meeting and dinner, okay?"

Mimi stared hard at Mark, then glanced around at her children and the kitchen, stopping at the oven. She wiped her eyes and cheeks. "No. Invite them in."

"But—"

"Michaela, please go answer the door and escort our guests into the living room. Your father and I will be there in a moment." She offered her hand to Mark to help her stand.

"What are you doing?" Mark said.

"You invited the council over, and we're going to entertain them." She forced a smile. "Go ahead and start the meeting in the living room, then I'll call everyone to the dining room when supper's ready." She shooed Mark and the kids out of the kitchen.

"MJ, go upstairs and clean up," Mark said. "Put on a different shirt and wash your face and hands."

Mimi looked down at her stained blouse, then grabbed her ponytail and quickly fixed it to include the stray hairs that had fallen out. She looked out toward the living room, where most of the council had now gathered and were talking. There was no way she could get upstairs to change her clothes and fix her hair properly without being seen. She decided to grab her red full-body apron and put that on. Only it still didn't cover all the spills and stains on her shirt.

These folks are in for a real treat. She opened the freezer door and started to grab another casserole. Then she stopped . . . and eyed the burned casserole sitting on the stove. She looked back out toward the group. A slow grin crossed her face.

6:02 p.m.

Mimi smiled brightly as she entered the living room to announce supper was ready. She made no apology or acknowledgment of her disheveled hair, smudged mascara, or messy clothes. But the oddest thing for Mimi was that nobody seemed to notice, or at least, if they did, they made no mention of it. They all greeted her pleasantly and stood, ready to eat.

The dining-room table was exquisite—set with Mimi's best china and silverware. White candles lined the middle of the table, shimmering with their firelight. There were steaming rolls, fresh garden salad, peaches, and directly in the middle of the table sat the burnt casserole with a large serving spoon sunk into it.

The council members all glanced at the casserole, eying it as if unsure what it was, then glanced at one another. No one said a word about it. Mimi stood at the edge of the table, closest to her husband. "Our oven's been running hot, as you might remember Mark mentioned several months ago. But I'm sure you won't mind the casserole. If you just scrape off the black parts from the top, it will be fine." Mimi smiled again. "Coffee, anyone?"

"Aren't you and the kids joining us?" one of the council members asked, motioning to the seats around the table.

"Oh no," Mimi said pleasantly. "We're running out to Applebee's. We have a gift certificate. I'm sure you won't mind?"

After Mimi poured everyone's coffee, she gathered the kids and escorted them to the car. She couldn't believe what she'd just done! Not only had she ruined the meal, looked a mess, and left the house in a shambles, but she'd rubbed it in by admitting that they were going out to eat! She expected to feel horrible and guilty and ashamed. But the strangest sensation spread over her as she put the key into the ignition. She'd erased any pretense of perfection—that was certainly ruined now. But deep down, even through the tug of war she felt for approval, there was something else. It was a quiet feeling, but there all the same. She hadn't felt it before. And as new as it was, it felt good.

Freedom. And just a hint of peace.

Mimi laughed out loud. "Kids, I'm hungry. How 'bout after dinner, we get dessert?"

The children's cheers filled the car as they drove away.

Saturday, August 5

6:11 a.m.

The next morning Mimi wasn't feeling all that great anymore about what she'd done. The guilt was eating at her, flooding her mind with doubts and accusations that she'd failed. She was sure word would travel fast at church about the little spectacle she'd created for the church council.

Mimi sat at the dining-room table early in the morning before anybody was awake and sipped her decaf, glad that Mark had cleared off the table and put the dirty dishes in the dishwasher the night before. She looked at the ceiling and shook her head.

This is it? This is everything I've worked so hard for? A ceiling that's peeling and an oven that burns everything I put in it! I got a college degree. I'm an adult who has become a teenager asking her "parents" for money and watching a church council decide whether they'll give it to me or not.

Suddenly Mimi's urge to escape became so strong that all she wanted was to get in her minivan and drive. She scribbled a note that she'd gone to run errands, picked up her keys and purse, and walked quietly out the back door, making sure not to wake anyone. She wasn't sure where she would go. She only knew it had to be out of Red River. So she headed north, out of town, and toward the lonely roads of farmland Ohio.

After about a half hour, she pulled off the road next to some dairy cows grazing. She got out and walked over to the fence next to the animals.

A cow has its purpose, she found herself oddly thinking. *To provide milk.*

Every day they're out here eating grass and hay, then every day they give milk. That's their job.

As though they knew she was thinking about them and were annoyed by her presence, a few of the closest cows mooed and turned away.

She gazed up at the puffy, white clouds lazily drifting by. "I don't know what to do, God," she finally admitted. "I can't keep going on this way. My life is totally out of control. Mark's been right all along. I feel as though I just start to get my life in order, and something rushes in to mess it up again."

She realized that wasn't quite the truth. "Okay, the truth is," she whispered, "my life is never under control. The more I try to manage it, the less I can. And now I have another baby on the way. I barely have enough time to handle my other three." She thought of the scrapbooks she kept for each child and the letters she wrote to each of them in their own special journals. Now a fourth one.

And there, standing next to the lonely field, surrounded by cows, the absurdity of everything hit her. Her scrapbooks and baking and piano playing. Her heading all those different church and community boards and functions. All of it so her life would ultimately matter.

She walked up to the rough-hewn wooden fence and grasped the top rail. "I want my life to count, God," she yelled into the pasture. "And I know that my life already matters to you. That I don't have to do anything to make you love me. But why doesn't that seem enough to me?"

The silence seemed deafening.

"Are you even listening? Do you see me?"

Again, more silence.

She dropped her head and dug her shoe into the dirt. *Help me,* she pleaded silently. *Please help me stop this madness.*

She thought of her friends Felicia, Jennifer, and Lisa. *Friends.* She hadn't had real friends in so long that she'd almost given up on believing that would ever be possible. Now, more than anything else, she wanted to talk to them.

Mimi ran back to the minivan and searched her purse for her cell phone. Tapping into the directory, she scrolled down to the first PW's name: *Felicia.* She consulted her watch. *Seven o'clock. I hope she's awake.*

The phone rang three times before Felicia picked up.

"Felicia. I'm so glad you answered."

"Mimi?" Felicia sounded tired.

"Yes."

Felicia breathed a sigh of relief. "Thank goodness, it's you. I thought it would be someone from the church calling Dave. You know, someone in the hospital. Someone upset about something."

Mimi chuckled. It was so good to hear a friendly, understanding voice.

"What's up? You okay?"

"No. I need to talk to someone. I think I'm having a nervous breakdown."

"Well, it's about time, girl! You've been pushing and pushing yourself."

"I know it's early, and I know everybody probably can't get together. But do you think the PWs can meet me this morning at Lulu's?"

"You bet. You want me to call the others?"

"If you would, I'd *really* appreciate it."

"No problem. We'll see you in about an hour?"

"Okay." Mimi paused. "Felicia? Thanks. You're a friend."

"I know. We have to stick together. We're all we've got. I'll see you soon."

Panic struck as soon as Mimi hung up. *What if I've done the wrong thing?* She'd never been completely vulnerable with anybody before—not the PWs, not even Mark.

But it was too late now. So she got back in the minivan and set off slowly toward Lulu's. She decided not to think about what she'd just done or was getting ready to do. Then a voice inside her head reminded her that the other women had been vulnerable with her. Now it was her time. *Maybe this will be your chance at finding some peace*, the voice whispered to her soul.

"Okay, God," Mimi whispered back. "I'm going to trust you on this one. Please don't let me down."

33

Lulu's Café

Saturday, August 5
8:04 a.m.

Mimi was already seated at their booth in the back of Lulu's, nursing her cup of coffee, when Jennifer and Felicia arrived and headed straight toward her. Jennifer looked as though she'd just rolled out of bed. Her strawberry-blond curls were matted together, and she was wearing an oversized Pink Floyd T-shirt and flowy workout pants. Felicia was dressed in red velour pants and jacket, her hair in a ponytail topped with a Dodgers baseball cap. Both women touched Mimi's hands and smiled sympathetically as they scooted into the seat across from her.

"Hi," Mimi said weakly.

Lisa arrived and sat next to Mimi. She leaned toward her and planted a kiss on her cheek. "Hi, honey. Felicia called and said you needed some help. I got here as soon as I could."

Mimi nodded, ashamed.

"We're here for you," Jennifer said.

Mimi looked at each of them. She knew it was now or never. Time to get real with her friends. Her best friends.

"I hate baking."

The women were silent. Jennifer's eyes narrowed slightly.

"What?" Felicia asked finally.

Mimi nodded adamantly. "I do. I hate baking. I hate the mess. I hate the time it takes. I hate that our stupid oven doesn't work right and that the church is so chintzy that they won't give us the money to buy a new one. A nice one. They told Mark—they actually *told* him—that since I obviously have been able to use it so well, with my *fabulous* baking, that they don't think we really need one."

Mimi continued almost in a whisper, as if she were ashamed or afraid someone would hear. "Last night Mark took the liberty of inviting the church council for supper without asking me about it first."

Felicia half snorted, trying unsuccessfully to hide a smile. "Is that a prerequisite for pastors—that they spring things like that on their wives?"

Mimi pushed on. She didn't want to be interrupted or she might chicken out on telling the whole story. "Yesterday was a terrible day. The kids were monsters. I had horrible morning sickness. And the oven overheated again, so the casserole I'd put in for dinner was scorched. I mean, scorched like me spending the day at the beach without sunscreen scorched." Mimi held out her pale arm to make her point. "And that's exactly how I served it."

Lisa gasped, then all the women laughed.

"I just set it down in the middle of my perfectly set table, along with my china and silver and beautiful candles. You should have seen the looks on their faces."

"You didn't!" Jennifer said.

Mimi nodded. "Then I took the kids and we went out to eat."

Felicia clapped her hands together. "That's spectacular!"

"It felt good at first. Until I realized what I'd done."

"What did you do wrong?" Jennifer said. "You just made a point."

"But what if I hurt Mark in the process? He's the one who really has to deal with the church council members all day long. What if they hold it against him?"

Nobody answered, but they all sobered a bit. Mimi knew they'd all been in that position at one time or another.

"The truth is," Mimi continued, "I guess this lifestyle is wearing on me. I didn't realize when I got married that I would be living in this fishbowl, and that everyone in the church was going to spend their lives watching how I run mine. And critiquing it. I spend my entire time second-guessing myself!"

The women nodded understandingly.

"I'm constantly thinking, *Should I have said that? Should I have done that?*" Mimi said.

"It's a terrible, lonely feeling, isn't it?" Lisa smiled sympathetically.

"Hey, since we're telling secrets," Jennifer piped in, "Sam and I hate potluck meals!"

They all laughed again.

"I don't know where that food was prepared," Jennifer said, wincing. "They could have made the tuna casserole while their cat, Fluffy, was sitting on the counter breathing all over it. Yet my husband and I are expected to eat it and smile. It gets tiring having to be 'on' all the time."

"You know what bothers me?" Felicia asked. "It's that I feel judged every Sunday. I feel the women checking out my clothes and hair. Or looking at how my husband's dressed. If I don't smile at someone, *or* if I smile *too much* at somebody, the uproar that takes place is unbelievable. A couple from our church invited us out for lunch two Sundays in a row. Anybody could have tagged along. But several couples accused us of having favorites at the church. You can't win!"

Mimi nodded. They understood exactly what she was feeling! "Maybe this baby has my emotions so mixed up I can't think straight."

"Or maybe God is using your pregnancy to get your attention about your overcrowded, people-pleasing life," said Lisa. "I'm not saying that to offend you, please understand."

The women sat quietly for a moment. Mimi wondered what they were thinking.

"Mimi." Lisa waved her fingers in front of Mimi's eyes, as though she were trying to get her attention. "I want you to hear something, and this is really important. We love you. Not because you're the best cook and domestic genius in Red River. Not because your scrapbooking projects and home canning outdoes ours and could win every county fair in Ohio. Not because you succeed at everything you do or because you'll handle this baby the same way you've handled your others—lavishing love and comfort on it. We love you for *you*. And *we* think you're a success no matter what."

Mimi glanced at Felicia and Jennifer, who both grinned sweetly and nodded.

"I'll be the first to tell ya that life doesn't turn out like we might plan," Jennifer said assuredly. "But I'm starting to see that's okay. You can't keep trying to make things happen the way you want—that's a trip to nowhere."

Mimi sighed with relief. They'd accepted her and the truth she'd shared. "I've never had real friends before . . . until now. And I want you to know that," she said, feeling as though an elephant had suddenly fallen from her shoulders. And just as suddenly she became ravenous. "Let's order.

All this confession and tears and talk about burning things have made me starved!"

The women laughed and Jennifer motioned for Opal, the waitress. It was Gracie's day off.

"Since we're doing this early morning sort of confession," Lisa said somewhat hesitantly after they'd placed their orders, "I have an update on my Lover's Lane evening."

"That's right, I forgot!" said Felicia. "What happened?"

"What *didn't* happen, you mean?" Lisa said without a trace of emotion. "The phone rang."

Jennifer and Felicia nodded.

"And he answered it, right?" Jennifer supplied, even though they all looked like they knew exactly what had happened.

Mimi knew immediately, instinctively, that in a pastor's house, a ringing phone was all at once something to be feared, dreaded, and avoided. It rarely brought peace and rest to the family who received it. But she also knew phones were part of a pastor's ministry. A counselor could tell you to make an appointment to discuss your crisis. A pastor couldn't. He was a church family's main support. Shepherd and leader, spiritual advisor and comforter. And so was his family.

But even so, Mimi thought, *there* are *boundaries!*

"How can I compete against God?" Lisa placed her hands squarely on the table. "I mean, it's a losing battle."

They all nodded. Mimi knew the problem wasn't God; it was Joel's misplaced priorities.

"Want us to go rough him up?" Jennifer said, putting her fists into the air and whipping them around.

Lisa smiled with the rest of them. "I appreciate you trying to cheer me up. But this time, I'm past that. I'm leaving him," she stated flatly as she stared out the window between Jennifer and Felicia. "I love him—or at least I love the person he used to be. But I can't take it anymore. It's destroying me to see him continue to act this way."

Mimi started to open her mouth, but Lisa continued before she could say anything.

"I feel like such a hypocrite. How can I serve and honor God when I'm such a mess? I can't even keep my marriage together! And I don't respect my own pastor—who can't keep *his* personal life in order! He's even doing a series on family life. Last week he told our congregation how to have a God-honoring marriage. Can you believe that? How would *he* know?" She laughed bitterly.

Finally Mimi spoke up. "Wait a minute, Lisa. Not five minutes ago you spoke words of comfort to me. You made me feel as if I had hope to have a different life. A God-honoring life. How can you say that and then tell us in the next breath that you're leaving your husband?"

"I don't know what else to do!" Lisa looked genuinely distressed. "I've tried everything. The makeover, the nurse's outfit, prayer. Nothing's worked. I've even been to see a counselor."

"Well, don't give up! Go back. A counselor won't solve your problems in one visit," urged Mimi.

"So you feel like God has deserted you? Is silent? Not listening to your breaking heart?" Jennifer asked, but they felt to Mimi more like statements.

"Yes," Lisa said. "And you know the saddest part? I don't even cry over it anymore. It's gone on for so long that I feel as if he's killed a part of me."

"But our God specializes in resurrections!" Mimi said, remembering a recent sermon Mark had given on the topic of hopelessness.

"You know, I've wanted to believe that for so long," Lisa said. "I've said that to so many other women. And I've grown up hearing my mother say it to desperate women. But it's different when you're actually *in* that position. It seems as if there is no hope. It's a dark, lonely place to be."

"Please don't give up," Mimi pleaded. "Talk to him one more time. Please."

"Send the kids off to your mom's and kidnap him for the evening," added Jennifer. Go to a restaurant in another town or to some other place where no one from church will bug you. Then spill your guts. Tell him the truth. At least give him that."

Lisa nodded slowly. "Okay."

Just then Opal arrived with their food.

"Well," Felicia said hesitantly after she finished spreading grape jam on her toast, "since we're on the topic of ruined marriages, let's talk about mine, shall we?"

Mimi's head popped up.

"I think Dave's having an affair."

"No!" said Jennifer.

"With that Nancy?" asked Lisa.

"With that Nancy," said Felicia with a resigned tone. Her eyes glistened with tears. "I hate what I've been reduced to. A blubbering idiot." She told them about the notes she'd read from Nancy and the meetings Dave and Nancy were having that were *supposedly* about VBS.

Jennifer picked up her fork and started stabbing her napkin with it. "Why don't you confront him, Felicia? You've been talking about this Nancy for months, and you never *do* anything about it. Well, *now's* the time to take the bull by the horns and find out what's going on."

Mimi chimed in. "I don't understand, Felicia. You're such a take-charge sort of woman. Independent. Full of confidence. You're so competent in the business world, yet you can't confront your husband about something that breaks up ministry marriages all the time?"

Felicia vehemently shook her head. "It's all circumstantial evidence. I can't prove it!"

"Are you kidding me?" Jennifer choked out angrily. "*Circumstantial evidence?* You have to trust your gut. And if your gut is telling you something's wrong, then something's wrong. Don't give me 'circumstantial evidence.'"

"No," Lisa said calmly, looking straight at Felicia. "Maybe the truth is that you don't want to believe it. It's better to be in denial. To make excuses or try to hold on to the mist, pretending that it's something solid. I understand that. I've pretended for three years that my husband was just busy, not wanting to believe that maybe he doesn't love me anymore."

"Whoa, whoa, now wait a minute!" said Mimi. "This is getting too muddled! I can't control this many issues with all of us. We've already got you taken care of, Lisa. You're going to talk to Joel and ask him straight out if he loves you. You're going to tell him how you're feeling. We got mine done, we got yours done." She gestured toward Lisa. "Now we focus on Felicia. Jennifer, we'll deal with you next, all right?" She placed her hands on the table to gain her composure.

"Now," she said, going into "fix it" mode. She tucked her hair behind her ears and lifted her chin. "Felicia, you're going to go home and squeeze the blood out of him until he fesses up, do you hear me? You're going to lay it all out and take him through visually what will happen to his life and his ministry if he's doing *anything* immoral. You've done that kind of image analysis with the Brew-Ha-Ha owner. Just pretend Dave is in the same situation—he's your client. This is business. And *whatever* happens, we will stand beside you one hundred percent." Mimi gave a short breath, pleased with herself. "There."

Felicia dabbed at her eyes. "You're right, you're right. I know you're right. God doesn't expect me to sweep my husband's infidelities under the rug." She squared her shoulders, then let them fall. "Help me."

"Of course we will!" the women said together.

Felicia smiled weakly.

Mimi turned next to Jennifer. "Anything you need to tell us?"

"Well, you know. Just the same old, same old. I can't have a baby, and I'm struggling in my faith. But other than that, hey, I'm great!"

"Would it be okay if I said a little prayer for us?" Lisa asked. "We hear so much about how the evil one wants to destroy our families—especially those of us in the ministry. And we need each other. We need God's strength."

"That would be really nice," Felicia said, fresh tears welling up.

Lisa closed her eyes and quietly began. "Thank you, God, that you've helped us find each other." Her voice trailed off. When she spoke again, her voice broke with emotion. "You know that I've prayed for true friends for so long. And you've blessed me with these wonderful women. You knew how much we'd need one another to rely on. How important friendships are. Help Mimi truly know she doesn't have to prove anything to anybody. Help Felicia have the strength to confront Dave and find out what's really going on in his life and in their marriage. And you know my prayer. That you would bless me with another ounce of hope for my relationship with Joel. Melt his heart. And precious Jennifer. She has such an honest, pure desire for a good thing. Fulfill that desire of her heart. Don't be silent in our lives, Lord. Father, help each one of us not to live lives of quiet desperation, but to be filled with the joy only you can give completely. In Jesus's name, amen."

"Amen," Mimi and the others echoed.

"Thank you, Lisa," Felicia whispered.

Lisa's prayer warmed Mimi inside. Even in this little café in the middle of nowhere, God had shown up. "You know," she told them, as they prepared to move out of the booth, "you've helped me see that no one has life completely under control. Just when we think we do, everything changes."

Jennifer smiled, took one more sip of coffee, and stood. "That's the honest truth."

Mimi was leading the way toward the cash register when Jennifer grabbed her arm and pointed.

Across the street, a woman in familiar-looking yellow pumps and matching outfit exited a run-down apartment building. She took a few steps away from the building, straightened her outfit and hair, then glanced up at one of the windows on the second floor. A younger man at the window waved.

Kitty Katt blew the man a kiss and got into her car, which was parked on the street in front.

Mouths agape, Mimi and the others eyed each other in wonder.

"Well, well," Felicia said. "I think we should have a little chat with Mrs. Katt in the near future."

"Absolutely," Jennifer agreed.

"Let's not jump to conclusions," Lisa said. "It may be very innocent. We don't know. It's 'circumstantial,' right, Felicia?"

"At eight thirty on a Saturday morning? Alone? In some stranger's apartment? Blowing kisses? Come on, Lisa," Felicia said. "You have to admit it's pretty suspicious."

"Kitty Katt has a little secret," Jennifer said.

"And it's time to"—Mimi giggled at what she was about to say—"let the Katt out of the bag."

"Ohhhh!" they groaned.

CHAPTER

34

Mimi

Saturday, August 5
9:52 a.m.

Mimi got out of the car and walked through the house toward Mark's home office. His desk was overflowing with papers, books, and three Bible translations, as well as his computer, and about a dozen photos of Mimi and the kids. She always got on him about how messy his office was, but he always said it was the one place he could be himself without her feather duster and vacuum following him around.

She stood in the doorway unnoticed and watched Mark reading his Bible. *He is a good man. A good pastor and husband.* Finally she sniffed just enough to get his attention.

"Hi!" he said, looking up from his reading. "I was wondering where you'd gone. You came home and went straight to bed last night, and then you were already up and out by the time I got up. Are you all right?"

Mimi nodded and handed him a bag of muffins she'd picked up on her way home from Lulu's. "They're not homemade, but you can pretend. Where are the kids?"

"I dropped them off at Gladys's."

Mimi's jaw dropped. "All of them?"

"Yep." Mark walked around the desk and put his arms around Mimi. His warm embrace felt so strong and wonderful. So safe.

"We need to talk," he said at last, partially releasing her from his grasp. "And I don't want our little rugrats interrupting us. I realized something last night while I was eating our overly crispy supper. I haven't been all that supportive of you lately. Instead of listening to you, I've 'processed' you. I've tried to make you change without looking at what's been driving you."

"Wait, Mark." Mimi interrupted him. "This isn't you. I've done some thinking and praying about this . . . trying to figure out what's wrong with me. Why I can't ever seem to be satisfied and slow down my life. Why I feel as though I'm constantly reaching for something, but that something is never enough and I always need more. I spent the morning driving around. I think, for the first time, I got vulnerable with God. And that's what I need to be with you too."

They sat on the matching forest green chairs on the other side of the office and faced each other.

"I can't do everything," she said simply. "I thought I could. And I've been acting like I could, but I can't. I'm so tired, and I don't want to try anymore. I know that for things to be different in my life, I need to make some radical changes."

She paused, waiting to see how Mark would react to her words. He was intently gazing at her and saying nothing, which made her feel a little unsure. But she'd already gone this far . . .

"I have a few confessions to make."

At this announcement, Mark sat back, a flicker of fear crossing his face.

"No no, it's nothing like that," she reassured him. "It's just that . . ." Could she really admit this? She blurted, "I hate to play the piano. I only took it up because I thought that's what a pastor's wife was supposed to do."

Mark started to laugh. "You hate to play the piano? That's your confession? Next you're going to tell me you hate to bake too."

Mimi nodded. "I do! Oh, Mark, I really do."

Mark stared at her blankly for a moment—as though he were trying to process her admission but was unable to.

"Mark?" Mimi started tentatively.

Mark seemed to snap out of it. "Mims, that's okay. We can do TV dinners for all I care."

"No, wait. There's more." She gulped, feeling silly. "I've always wanted to learn to play the bagpipes."

He laughed again. "You're kidding! You've never told me that."

"Well, come on, Mark. What pastor's wife plays bagpipes? Although I suppose it would work well for funerals. But really, it's not appropriate."

"Who says?"

"Well, everybody knows that."

"Mimi, listen to me." Mark was still smiling. "If you want to take bagpipe lessons, do it. If you don't want to bake another cake in your life, that's okay. If you want to quit every single committee and just show up on Sunday mornings and take your place in a pew, I don't think God will hold that against you. And if anybody in the church does, well, that's their problem."

"Really?"

"Really. Mims, I married you because I love you. Not because I thought you were good pastor's-wife material. You get the raw end of the deal a lot in this, and I know that. A lot of times it eats me up inside. People want us to fit their expectations, but that's not what God calls us to do. He calls us to follow him. But when we get caught up in the 'church scene,' doing what we think pleases other people, it fills us with a whole lot of empty."

"But I'm so afraid of messing up. Like last night. I feel *awful* about that. And I probably got you into trouble."

Mark laughed again. "No, you didn't. As a matter of fact, I wish you'd have stuck around. You know what they said? 'It's about time we found a flaw in your wife. She's not perfect.' And they loved that! They loved the fact that you have bad days, too, and that you finally let it all hang out. Those council members left our house last night with more respect and admiration for you because you didn't try to cover up what you were feeling. And," he said with a twinkle, "you earned us a new oven. And *you* get to pick it out."

"Are you serious?" Mimi couldn't believe what Mark had just said.

"It's true. They did say, though, that if you ever need a new dishwasher, to make sure not to serve them dinner on dirty plates to make your point."

Mimi laughed. "If only I'd known that was the way to accomplish things, I'd have handled it sooner."

"Mims, church life is supposed to be about growing and being real and doing community together. And doing community means there will be messiness. You can give up control and enjoy life—messiness and all. Or you can miss out on the joys of life by trying to control it."

"Which still only ends up getting me pregnant!" she said, then winked and grinned.

"You don't always have to make up for what you didn't have when you were a kid, Mims. Your drive to be everything to everybody doesn't get you anywhere. We can only find peace when we completely lean on God and let everything else go."

"Always turning pastoral on me."

"Well, hey, I have to practice on somebody before I turn my pastoring techniques on an unsuspecting church."

Mimi kissed Mark's hand, then held it to her cheek. "You're a good pastor."

"No, *we're* good pastors. We're a team."

They sat enjoying each other for a minute, then Mimi said rather reluctantly, "Well, I guess we should go rescue Gladys."

"Why? She's taking them for the day so you and I can get some alone and lazy time together."

"Can that include buying a new oven?"

"Well, I was thinking more that we could . . ."

Mimi gave him a pretend evil eye.

"It's not like you can get pregnant," he said in a halfway defensive tone.

"I'll tell you what," Mimi said, offering a compromise. "How about you give me a long foot massage and we'll discuss it."

"That works too," Mark said, standing and offering his hand to Mimi, who took it and pulled him down to her.

She kissed him on the lips, then whispered, "Can we order a pizza too? With onions and green peppers and everything else the kids hate?"

"You bet we can. And I'll even clean up."

"Tease." Mimi laughed and stood. A weight that had been pressing her down was slowly lifting. She breathed in deeply, truly contented for the first time in a long time.

CHAPTER 35

Jennifer

Sunday, August 6
8:56 a.m.

"We're going to be fine," said Sam, grabbing Jennifer's hand as they made their way from the car to the church entrance. It was thirty minutes before Sunday school, so the lot was nearly empty. His voice was slightly patronizing.

"I'm just not sure what to say to people." Jennifer's stomach flip-flopped. "I don't want to lie, but I wouldn't expect anyone to understand where I've been the last month. But it's good to get my reappearance over now, so it isn't a big thing at Derek and Lucy's wedding next week."

As they reached the door, Sam stopped and faced her. "Hey, this hasn't been easy for me, either. It's been pretty tough having a wife who's been distant from me when I've needed her." He glanced behind her toward the parking lot, where people were arriving, and his facial expression changed.

He forced a smile. "Everyone can use a little vacation now and then. But let's do it together next time, okay?"

Jennifer nodded dutifully, but she knew Sam still didn't understand what was going on with her. The weeks away from church hadn't been a little getaway. It was much deeper than that.

Sam held open the door and Jennifer started to walk in, but they were met by an anxious Marian Bell. Marian was always at church early on Sundays to practice that day's songs on the organ. She was a bit of a fixture at the church—first to arrive, last to leave.

"Oh, Pastor, I'm so glad you're here," she said breathlessly, brushing by Jennifer. "The air conditioning won't come on. They're calling for eighty-five degrees today. We have to get it working!"

Marian had a tendency toward overreacting. Sam and Jennifer's home phone had once rung at 1:00 a.m. on a Saturday. When Sam answered, it was Marian, calling to say that she and Gene, her husband, had driven by the church on their way home from the airport and it looked like someone had broken in. The door was open, lights were on, and she even saw people in dark clothes running around outside. Sam assured her that it was just the youth group doing their annual overnight initiation party for seventh graders.

Sam dropped Jennifer's hand and trailed off with Marian to see about the A/C. Jennifer wandered into the church office and glanced around. Sam had hired a temp to fill in during Jennifer's "leave of absence," as he had termed it. Jennifer had a strange desire to sit down at the desk and start working—it was all she had known for thirteen years—but she also felt empowered to know she didn't have to.

She decided to skip her usual Sunday-school class—they had changed books, and she wasn't sure what they were using now—and go to the group that used a set curriculum instead. Although this class tended to appeal more to older people, Jennifer was attracted to its lack of discussion. She'd rather sit back and listen today.

"What an honor to have the pastor's wife join us," said Jerry Smatters as she walked into the classroom.

"That's 'Jennifer,'" she said with a smile, but the words came out slightly more snarky than she had intended. She slipped into a row.

"Glad to see you back again," Edith Myers said from across the room. "Hope you're feeling okay."

Jennifer thought she saw Edith's eyes look down at Jennifer's stomach while she was talking, but then she told herself to quit being so paranoid.

After Sunday school—as nonparticipatory as Jennifer had hoped—she made her way into the crowded narthex for the preworship fellowship. Her plan was to quickly but smoothly wend through the chatty groups, smile firmly in place, then take her seat and read her Bible. Or at least pretend to read it.

But as she sauntered through, she couldn't help but notice that as people gave her a little wave or pat on the shoulder, they all seemed to be glancing down at her stomach. Being home and not working had allowed her more time in front of the TV with the occasional bowl of ice cream or bag of chips, but surely she hadn't put on that much weight in the last month! Had she?

Sucking in her gut, Jennifer slipped by the final few people and strolled down the center aisle of the church to a chair in the fourth row. She was always careful to sit toward the front, but not the very front. In her opinion, there was a fine line between being a supportive pastor's wife and being an obnoxious one. Sitting in the front row fell in the last category.

"Hi, Jennifer. Glad you're back! Sure is warm in here, huh?" Pastor Derek said as he hurried by, loosening his tie, but not so fast that Jennifer couldn't see his eyes zip down to her abdomen and back up to meet hers.

She reached down and bloused out her shirt a bit more around the waist of her skirt.

If they only knew. I started my period yesterday! Maybe I'm bloated. Or am I just hypersensitive? Is it that stupid Clomid?

She didn't have to worry about losing herself in fake Bible reading. Evidently Marian decided the lack of air conditioning was good reason to get the service started early, so she began the prelude worship music. People began filtering in.

"Good morning!" said Pastor Derek from the pulpit once everyone was seated and the choir had taken their places behind the altar. "Let's all stand and sing 'Great Is Thy Faithfulness.'"

Oh, great, we have to start with that of all songs, Jennifer thought.

After a few more songs, an offertory, and a prayer, Sam strode up to the pulpit for his sermon. He caught Jennifer's eye and smiled. She smiled back.

I love that man, even if he doesn't "get" me all the time.

"Before I thrill you with my wisdom and insights," he said, causing several to chuckle, "I want to recognize today as Family Commitment Sunday. We're going to have each part of our families stand in groups so we can reflect on what each one means. First, let's have the dads, the spiritual leaders in our homes, stand. And let's give them a hand."

Ugh. Family Commitment Sunday. Next to Mother's Day, my most dreaded Sunday at church.

The applause had just died down when Carl Tompkins, one of Sam's racquetball partners, called playfully from the other side of the church, "Hey, Pastor Sam. We noticed you were still standing. Are you trying to tell us something?"

Jennifer's heart leapt into her throat. What was going on? Did everyone think she was pregnant?

"I'm sure we will have an announcement soon," Sam said, looking at Jennifer again.

But this time she responded with wide eyes.

A woman behind her patted her back, then said conspiratorially in her ear, "It's smart to wait until after the first trimester to say anything."

Stunned, Jennifer sat in her seat without moving for the rest of the service. She had no idea what Sam said in his message. Her mind was whirling. She was sick to her stomach. And worse, her soul ached more than she ever imagined it could. She'd trusted Sam, and he—of all people—had betrayed her. What had he told them about her absence?

After the service, she shook hands, smiled, and talked with people, but it was as if she were a spirit looking down on herself. Did they really think she would hide a pregnancy? Didn't they know if she ever saw that little blue line on the dipstick, she would be shouting it from the rooftops?

She was never so glad for inoperable air conditioning. Instead of lingering, everyone poured out of the church and into their cars. Windows went up immediately to get the cool air blowing.

"Whew, that feels good," said Sam, climbing into the driver's seat. Jennifer had started the car and kicked on the A/C while she waited for him to gather a few things from his office.

He put the car into gear. "So what did you think of my sermon today?"

Jennifer stared at him. Surely she wasn't the only one feeling the churning tension in the half-cool air.

He's not looking at me, she noticed. *He knows he's in trouble.*

Jennifer looked away and out the window.

"Is something wrong, Jen?" Sam asked, eyes on the road.

Jennifer continued studying every house they drove by. *Plum. Yes, I do like that color on a house. Maybe a beige trim would be . . .*

"Jennifer!"

His high-pitched tone startled her. "What?"

"I asked you what you thought of my sermon today. Where are you?"

Why not throw it out there? Maybe this is just one big misunderstanding.

"Why does everyone think I'm pregnant?" she asked against her better judgment. "What did you say?"

"I didn't say anything . . . *really.*" He gave her a nervous sideways glance. "I think . . . people came up with their own theories—"

"Oh, and everyone came up with the exact same theory, right? No one thought of anything but me being pregnant?" She couldn't help her sarcasm.

Sam's words were soft. "I didn't know what to say to people, so I sort of okey-doked them when they asked where you were. I didn't want people to think it was any more serious than it was, so—"

"So you let them think I'm pregnant? Of all things!"

"Jen—"

"Shut up, Sam. Just shut up." She had exhausted her words.

When Sam pulled into their driveway, Jennifer leaped from the car when it was barely stopped. She slammed the car door, the front door, and the bedroom door. As she threw herself on the bed, she could hear the door slams still ringing in her ears, a tune she'd experienced almost daily growing up with her battling mother and stepfather. As a child, she'd promised herself that she would never, *ever* slam doors or yell when she was older, especially when she had kids.

Jennifer heard Sam flip on the TV in the living room. He hadn't even bothered following her into the bedroom.

No wonder God doesn't want me to have a child. Look how I'm behaving! God knows I would be a terrible mother, just like mine was.

CHAPTER 36

Felicia

Sunday, August 6

12:02 p.m.

As Felicia rose to leave the Sunday service—from her usual spot in the second pew on the right side—she felt a sense of dread. For her, the after-church Meet and Greet was the most difficult part of being a pastor's wife. And there were many difficult parts.

"But you're a PR lady. That should be easy for you," her mother had said when Felicia called her to complain after their first month in Red River.

"Mom, public relations is a *profession*," Felicia had retorted, trying not to sound condescending. Being the first college graduate in her immigrant family, she was perhaps overly conscious about not throwing her education in her parents' faces. After all, they were the ones who had worked hard to pay Felicia's tuition at pricey UCLA. "I write press releases and plan events, but that doesn't mean I like making small talk and being on display for all the church ladies to whisper about my clothes or hair or whatever."

"Ah, Fifi." Felicia hated that nickname but knew it was said with love.

"Just remember where you came from and hold your head high. You are a beautiful Latina with a good-looking husband and a sweet little boy. So what if someone wants to look?"

Felicia smiled as she remembered her mother's simple advice. She arrived at the church door just in time to grab Dave's hand and give him a peck on the cheek.

Nicholas went running by. "Mom, I'm going outside to play on the swings with Josh."

Felicia stepped away from Dave as she called to Nicholas's back, "Nicholas! Give me your suit jac—"

"Honey, have you met the Jamisons?" Felicia whirled around to see Dave beaming as he stood next to a handsome older couple. "They decided to move down here from Cleveland to be closer to their grandchildren. Larry is retired from National City Bank."

Felicia warmly and dutifully shook their hands. As the couple moved on, Dave leaned in to Felicia's ear, "He retired as the CEO—big bucks. Maybe he can fund that new education wing all by himself!"

Elbowing Dave in the side, Felicia turned to see a wave of people leaving the church sanctuary, small children in tow. Some stopped to say hello. Others looked more interested in lunch than lingering.

"Felicia, I don't think we've met," said a confident, well-dressed woman who appeared to be in her midthirties. She approached Felicia with her hand out.

Felicia shook it and smiled, but she heard something eerily familiar in the woman's tone.

"I'm Tonya Lancaster," said the woman as she stepped back to reveal an equally polished blond, "and this is Kathi Snow. We know you haven't had much of a chance to get involved yet here at church since you and Pastor have only been here a year, so we—"

Felicia suddenly was able to place the tone. It was the tone she most feared, the one she usually saw coming a mile away. She'd missed it this time because it was delivered in such a pretty package.

It was the "we want to invite you to something" tone. But this time she knew she wouldn't be able to use one of her pocketed excuses with Dave right next to her and able to overhear.

Glancing to her right to see that Dave was telling one of his pastor's jokes to a rapt audience of five, Felicia quietly drew Tonya and Kathi away from his earshot.

"I'm sorry, I couldn't hear you very well with Dave in one of his stories," she said as she noticed Nancy Borden exiting the church doors and heading straight toward Dave.

"No problem," Tonya said cheerfully. "Anyway, we wanted to invite you to our Bible study."

A bell rang in Felicia's head. Not another ladies' Bible study! Hadn't she visited all of them yet?

She glanced over to see that Nancy was two people away from Dave. She had to make this quick. "Well, you know, I work during the days, so—"

"Oh yes, we know. This Bible study is on the third Tuesday evening of every month at seven thirty. Here are the directions." Tonya pushed a piece of paper into Felicia's hand. "Hope you can make it!"

While Tonya and Kathi turned to rejoin their husbands, Felicia took two giant leaps back to Dave's side, just in time to shake Nancy Borden's hand.

"Oh, I hope you found your red bowl by the back door," Nancy said in mock friendliness . . . or at least it seemed that way to Felicia. "I washed it the best I could, but that stoneware gets so stained when it's not properly maintained."

Felicia started to answer Nancy, but two girls from the youth group bounded up to ask if they could borrow Nicholas to use for some sort of "prop" for their afternoon babysitting seminar. *You have no idea what you're getting yourselves into with that little rascal,* Felicia thought as she listened to their request.

That's when Nancy made her move to get Dave's sole attention. Felicia tried to focus on the girls and what they were saying, but she noticed Nancy had dropped her voice as she talked.

"I got that surprise gift," she said as if she were talking to her high-school boyfriend. "Roses are such a treat!" Then she patted Dave's arm and walked away.

Roses! Felicia fumed as she wrote down her phone number for the youth girls. *I can't even remember the last time he got me roses!*

Jennifer

Jennifer climbed the five steps to St. Peter's church offices and opened the door. The quaint entryway had two sets of doors—she had just come through one set—with a small waiting area in between them. On one wall was a window that slid horizontally, with a bell next to it. If the secretary wasn't at her spot behind the window, a visitor could ring the bell to get someone's attention behind the locked second door.

"You wouldn't believe how many times I've been awakened by that bell," Father Scott had told her a few weeks prior when she rang it, only to have him answer the door.

"Oh, I bet I can," said Jennifer. "We don't live in the church office like you do, thank God, but we've had our share of middle-of-the-night wake-up calls from people in the church who needed Sam."

This time Jennifer hadn't needed to ring the bell because the secretary nodded as she saw Jennifer enter. This was Jennifer's sixth visit to Father Scott, so Barb, the secretary, recognized her.

"Father will be right with you," she said after she slid open the small window.

Jennifer was curious about how Father Scott's parishioners called him "father." She had never called anyone "father" in her life. In fact, even thinking about the word made her stomach knot into a ball. According to her mom, her birth father had left when he found out she was pregnant with Jennifer. Neither Jennifer nor her mother had heard from him since. And her stepdad? He certainly was no "father."

But ever since she'd met Father Scott, she'd started to think about the word again. About the true meaning of it. About safety, warmth, and a truly listening ear. About blessing, peace, and love. About admonition about what was right, yet acceptance and belonging . . . these were the things she saw in Father Scott. The things he said came about because he knew and walked with the Father of all.

The door opened. "Come on in, Jennifer," said Father Scott with his usual warm smile.

As she walked toward his office, Jennifer handed him a medium, nonfat cappuccino from the coffeehouse down the street. After their second meeting, when Jennifer had revealed she wasn't Jill and she wasn't Catholic, she had tried to pay him for his services. He'd refused. When she'd persisted, he'd said she could buy him off with a cappuccino. It had become a tradition. She figured that was a pretty cheap fee for a counseling session.

Jennifer had really enjoyed their talks, and she was impressed with Father Scott's knowledge about marriage and family life. "You sure know a lot about husbands and wives for someone who's never been married," Jennifer had blurted out one day after he'd said something particularly insightful about her interaction with Sam.

"It's kind of like a doctor who delivers babies—you don't need to have a baby to know how to bring one into the world," Father Scott had responded.

"You had to use *that* example with me?" Jennifer had asked, playfully rolling her eyes. Father Scott was the only person she could joke with about her infertility issues. It felt good.

"Yeah, I figured you could relate since it's *all* you think about these days," he'd said with a grin.

Other sessions weren't so jovial, such as the time two weeks previous. He'd handed her a sheaf of paper and a pen, then said, "I have to help Barb with something, but while I'm gone, I want you to write down all the bad things that have happened in your life. One on each piece of paper."

Jennifer had been taken aback. She fingered the sheets in her hand. "That could take awhile. I'm thirty-five—lots of years for bad things."

"Yes, well, just write the ones that have really stuck with you. The terrible things your mother said to you when you were a child, for example."

Jennifer had felt a dull *thud* in her stomach when she thought of her mother. She had buried most of those memories long ago. Or had she?

An hour later, when Father Scott returned with a metal bowl and some matches, Jennifer had a pile of papers on the coffee table in front of her—each sheet with a scrawled sentence or two on it—and a mountain of crumpled up tissues next to her on the sofa.

He didn't say a word to her as he quietly sat down on the other side of the table and placed the bowl next to the pile of papers. Picking up the first one, he read,

My mother told me that my father left her because of me,
and that's why I was worthless and always would be.

Father Scott looked up at Jennifer, then tossed the paper in the metal bowl and stretched out his hands. "Almighty God and Father," he prayed, "give Jennifer the knowledge that she is your best creation. Regardless of the circumstances, she was created as your child. Remind her that you knew her and formed her in her mother's womb. And with her openness to your leading, you will continue to mold her into the woman you intend her to be."

After reading aloud what was on each slip of paper, praying for every one and then throwing it into the bowl, Father Scott lit a match. As he dropped it into the bowl, he looked at Jennifer. "God is greater than all of your pain, Jennifer. He doesn't just heal it—he takes it away. God *is* faithful."

That day had been a significant turning point for Jennifer. Even though she had known for years that Jesus, God's Son, suffered and died so she would not have to, seeing the burning paper had made that sacrifice a reality for her. Only God himself could have taken her messed-up ways of thinking, based on years of pain, and so dramatically changed her. There was no doubt in her mind about that. But she couldn't get over the last little hump of cynicism. If God truly did care, why wouldn't he grant her this *one* desire of her heart? Women were having babies all around her. Their bellies were popping out with seeming ease. Why was it so difficult for Jennifer to get pregnant? Why wouldn't God grant her a child? Especially if he was the almighty Father who cared so much about her?

As she and Father Scott sat down this day for their session, Jennifer wondered what new and interesting technique Father Scott might have up his sleeve. Symbolism was definitely part of the Catholic approach, and she was starting to get the hang of it.

"Jennifer," he said, "I want this to be our last session."

Jennifer peered at him, looking for a joke in his statement. She saw only seriousness. "W-why?" she asked in a small voice. "Have I become a burden on you?"

"No, of course not," answered Father Scott, his normally pleasant face clouding. "But I think you have become a burden on yourself."

Jennifer sat motionless as she considered his words.

"We've undertaken a good faith journey these last weeks. I've watched you confess your heart, and I've seen you recognize Jesus's cleansing power all over again. We've talked and we've prayed. Last week you told me you felt like you were falling in love again with God, right?"

Jennifer nodded, but inside she felt drained of all energy. Why was this trusted counselor—the only "father" she had ever opened her heart to—sending her away?

"All of that aside, I sense that you still aren't trusting God about this baby thing. And that's why I want this to be our last time together."

"Well, excuse me for not meeting your timeline," Jennifer fired back. "I didn't realize this journey had a destination. Didn't someone say that we never 'arrive'?" She recognized the tone—the one she was using a lot with Sam these days—as having a mixture of sadness and self-justification in it.

Father Scott sighed. "I'm not abandoning you, Jennifer. I know you are sensitive to that—"

"Well," she interrupted, "just what are you doing then by telling me I can't come to see you anymore?"

He captured her eyes with his gentle ones. "I know you Protestants don't practice confession, but I think you've seen the benefits from it when we've had our discussions here. In a sense, we've shared several weeks of your confession. Well, there is a second part to confession that we haven't shared, and that's penance."

Oh, great, Jennifer thought bitterly. *Is he going to teach me how to say that "Hail, Mary" thing now?*

"No, I won't make you do a 'Hail, Mary,'" Father Scott continued with an uneasy chuckle, as if he'd read her mind. He was good at that. "We're a little more action-oriented in our penance these days."

His verbosity was wearing thin on Jennifer. *If he doesn't want to talk to me anymore, why doesn't he just shut up and let me leave?*

"I want you to do two things," he said carefully. "One, you should get reinvolved with that women's shelter. You are in an ideal position to relate to those women.

"And two, I want you to stop praying for a baby. In fact, don't even pray for yourself at all. Focus on praying for others. Pray for the families in your church. Pray for expectant mothers you know. Pray for anything or anyone except yourself."

Jennifer relaxed. She could see where he was going now. Their sessions had taken a lot of her mental and emotional energy. "Okay, but what does that have to do with my seeing you again?"

"Jennifer," he murmured, "you have let your whole life become a testament to selfishness."

She flinched, not understanding his statement.

"You want a baby," he continued, "but because you haven't been given one, you are ignoring your husband, your church, your friends—and most importantly, God. It's time to set that aside. Let God handle it, just like he's handled everything else in your life.

"If you continue to visit me, we will continue to talk about this baby you want. So that's why I think we should stop these meetings. Instead, use this time to help at the shelter. Or get to know your husband again without seeing him through fertility glasses."

Jennifer knew Father Scott was right. Even she was tired of reading endless Web-site advice on achieving pregnancy. And she was pretty sure that the Clomid was turning her into a three-eyed goon. But she was sorry to see her time with Father Scott ending. She would miss their conversations . . . and the way his gentle, straightforward nature touched her heart and strengthened her faith.

"Okay, I will head out into the world alone," she said in a mocking, but friendly, tone. "But before I leave, can we discuss just one more thing?"

Father Scott appeared dismayed, as if he thought Jennifer hadn't heard a word he'd said.

"No, I don't mean about the God and baby thing," she said. "I want to know about that stole. What exactly is a priest's stole, and why do you keep asking if I want you to put it on? And I promise to let you explain before I jump all over you like the guys at the pastors' breakfast."

Father Scott ambled across the room. He picked up what looked like a long piece of fabric, or some sort of sash, then turned to face her. "I'm glad you asked. As you can see, this is not a fur garment, like ladies wore in the fifties. That's probably the kind of stole you're thinking of." He chuckled. "This is actually something we priests wear to hear confessions because . . ."

CHAPTER 38

Lisa

Friday, August 11
5:13 p.m.

Lisa waved good-bye to Callie and Ricky and watched the car pull away. They were spending the night with Lisa's mom and dad, so Lisa and Joel could get some alone time. This evening would hold no romance, Lisa was sure of that. Instead, Lisa wanted to talk to Joel. One more time.

She was nervous. Joel didn't know about this surprise evening. It was better that way. At least he couldn't duck out, saying he was busy.

Once she'd watched her mother's black Ford 500 disappear around the corner, she rushed upstairs and into her closet. At the very back, on the top shelf, she grabbed the new journal she'd purchased, per her counselor's suggestion, and flipped through the pages until she came to the letter she'd written Joel.

Since she wasn't as good as Joel at communicating verbally what she was feeling, the journal allowed her to take her time and communicate exactly what she was thinking and feeling, without being interrupted or cut down.

Next she changed into a simple white silk blouse and beige Capris, with her favorite sandals. After a peek in the mirror, she carried her journal downstairs, placed it next to her purse, and sat on the couch, waiting and watching out the front window for Joel to pull into the driveway.

She had to wait only five minutes. Before he was able to get halfway up the walk, she was out of the door, on her way to greet him. "Hi," she said brightly. "I have a surprise for you. We're going out for dinner—to that new Olive Garden across town. Come on." She grabbed his arm playfully and ushered him back to the car. "No cell phones. The kids are at Mom and Dad's. And I won't take no for an answer."

6:41 p.m.

"I love that you love being a pastor," Lisa told Joel after they'd finished eating their ravioli. They'd each just ordered a cup of coffee and the tiramisu. Since she knew she couldn't put off her speech anymore, she decided it was now or never. "I really do. I support you in that. And I know that God has called you to be in the ministry. I'm proud of you when I watch the way you interact with others. You have such a gift."

Joel smiled. The compliments seemed to be working. Even though she did mean them, tonight she was using them to soften the blow.

She took a deep breath and noticed her hands were shaking ever so slightly. "But the truth is, Joel, you're always connecting with other people and not me. When you're connected with somebody else, you're intrigued, involved, and invested with that person—and I feel excluded. If you share a common interest with someone, like Frank and his fishing boat, and you're functioning on a deep level with him, that's a part I can't get to. And, over time, I've learned that's the way it is. At church, all these people are standing in line to talk to you after the service. And sometimes I think, *Why don't I get to be in line?*"

Joel started to respond, but Lisa shook her head. "Wait. I have something to say, and if I don't get this out, I never will." She looked at him almost pleadingly. "Please," she half whispered.

She pulled her journal out of her bag and pushed it across the table to Joel. "I started writing in this journal about a month or so ago. I want you to read it. But I also need to say a few things." She told him how much she loved him and how she loved and missed the times when they were first married. She told him how much she missed him now, and how difficult it had been to sit under his teaching when she didn't see him practicing what he was preaching.

"I know that my behavior at church of late hasn't been respectful of you. And I know my behavior directly reflects on your ministry. Right or wrong. And for those things, I'm sorry. But I've been learning a lot about myself lately, mostly through counseling and prayer. And I've discovered that I'm okay. My desires for you and for us are okay. But what's going on in our marriage isn't. And something has to change. The truth is, being a pastor's kid and being a pastor's wife are way different. I thought I could handle being married to a pastor since I'd watched my mom do it. But I'm not so sure I can. Right now I'm feeling disillusioned with the whole pastorate . . . but mostly with you.

"I understand that we can't sit together during church. That's part of the job. And I'm okay with that. But sometimes I secretly watch husbands and wives who sit together during the service, and I feel a terrible green-eyed monster grow in me. I see the husband put his arm around his wife—so protective, so loving, so gentle. It speaks so many words. You never do that.

You never put your arm around me. And you certainly never show any public signs of affection toward me. And honestly, I'm okay with that too."

Joel half snorted. "I'm a senior pastor, Lisa, in case you forgot. I can't go around feeling you up in public."

"First of all," Lisa huffed, "it's not 'feeling me up.' It's holding my hand or putting your arm around me. And we're *married*. I'm not just a woman in your congregation. I'm your *wife*, in case you forgot. But I'm not even talking about public displays. When was the last time you kissed me? Or nibbled my neck like you used to? The truth is, Joel, you haven't for a long time. I can't even remember when. I'm starved for affection. And I know one thing for sure. I don't want to be in this marriage anymore."

CHAPTER

39

Felicia

Tuesday, August 15
7:19 p.m.

"Ah, thank God they're gone already," Felicia said to herself as she walked in the kitchen door and tossed the mail on the counter and her briefcase on the floor. Dave had taken Nicholas to a Reds game, and they wouldn't be back for hours.

Felicia's mind burst with ideas for the precious few hours. She was plotting a bubble bath, followed by a bag of microwave popcorn and the chick flick she'd taped off TV two weeks ago, when she noticed the blinking light on the answering machine.

She tapped the button. "Hi, Felicia. This is Tonya from church. I wanted to remind you about our Bible study tonight at seven thirty. Sure hope you can make it."

Felicia's head snapped up to the kitchen wall clock. *Seven twenty. Just enough time to get over to Tonya's house.*

Excuses. Felicia could think of zillions of them. But would it be right for the pastor's wife to use one to miss a Bible study?

Felicia sighed and walked over to a basket of energy bars she kept on the counter, just for times like these. She grabbed one, along with her keys, and headed for the car. As she drove, she wished she'd had time to change out of her business suit and into something more "small-town ladies' Bible study." Or at least to grab that new quilted Bible cover—

"My Bible!" Felicia groaned as she realized she'd forgotten it. She checked the clock to see if there was time to return home. *I guess it's better to be on time and Bible-less than late,* she reasoned. *But what will people think about the pastor's wife not having a Bible at a Bible study? They'll probably think I have a Bible attached to my hip. Or that I have the whole thing memorized.*

"Lord, help me have a good attitude about this," Felicia prayed out loud. "I want to do your will, but I can't get everything to work out these days."

She pulled up to Tonya's at 7:29. *Good thing I didn't go back for my Bible,* she thought as she climbed out of her car. In LA, 7:30 meant 7:45 or 8:00. But Felicia had learned the hard way that 7:30 meant 7:30 in Red River, Ohio.

"Felicia! I'm so glad you could make it!" Tonya called from the doorway as she leaned against the screen door to hold it open.

Felicia was surprised to see Tonya in a tailored navy blue suit and crisp white shirt. Tonya also was wearing hose, but she had furry slippers on her feet.

"Hi, Tonya. I almost didn't make it. That Cincinnati commute can be awful sometimes."

Tonya patted Felicia's back as she walked by her. "I know. It took me nearly thirty minutes just to get on 71 from downtown tonight."

Felicia stopped and turned to Tonya. "You work in the city?"

"Yeah! I'm marketing director at Fifth Third Bank."

"Hey, maybe we should start a downtown branch of First Baptist," Kathi said as she walked up to them. "I work over at *Cincinnati* magazine on Vine."

Felicia turned from Tonya and Kathi to scan the room. Eight more women were gathered on sofas and chairs, in various states of postwork dress. And there was not a quilted Bible cover in sight! She noticed one woman reaching into her purse to turn off a cell phone as the one next to her finished up a message on her PDA.

Tonya pulled Felicia lightly by the arm. "Now I know you probably didn't have time to eat. Come in here and make yourself a plate."

As Felicia eyed the table full of food in the next room, she felt guilty. They hadn't mentioned that this was a carry-in dinner. But as she drew closer, she chuckled. The table was full all right—of every fast-food container in Red River!

"Now this is *my kind* of potluck!" she exclaimed to Tonya.

"Well, it's not gourmet because we're all working stiffs too," Tonya said. "But I'm glad it looks good to you, because we want it to be our gift to you every month."

The living room quieted as all ears and eyes focused on Tonya and Felicia. "Felicia, we know how hard it is to be a working wife and mother—we all do it every day. But on top of that, you also have the church. We just want you to know how much we love you and appreciate what you do. So assuming you like us"—Tonya extended her arm out to the group as some women giggled—"we want you to come to this Bible study and not lift a finger. As our love gift to you."

Felicia was stunned. A year into Dave's pastorate in Red River, and no one had ever acknowledged her. She tried to paste on her pastor's-wife smile, but tears filled her eyes instead.

"Wow, um," she finally managed. "I don't know what to say. I'm . . . really touched."

She felt awkward standing there alone, with tears trickling down her face. She had never liked appearing vulnerable in public.

An instant later Tonya draped an arm around her shoulders. Two other women came over to hug her.

"Why don't we all gather around Felicia for a minute and pray for her?" Tonya said. Then she grinned and gestured toward the steaming buckets of chicken and containers of fries and coleslaw. "And we can use it as a good excuse to bless this party of salt and fat on the table too."

Felicia watched as each woman got up and stood next to her, like a mini-brigade. For the first time, she understood what Jesus meant when he said, "For where two or three come together in my name, there am I with them."

He was there. In Red River.

Saturday, August 26
3:35 p.m.

"Whatever happened to that ladies' Bible study at our house? Nancy happened to mention that it was moved to Libby Gabriel's. Does that mean you stopped going?" Dave asked as Felicia handed him another clean, wet saucepan.

They were standing at the kitchen sink scrubbing and drying pans from dinner two nights previous.

"It's not like I purposefully kept it from you, Dave," Felicia said, her back to him as she rinsed a pot. "It just never came up."

Dave muttered something inaudible under his breath, flung his dish-towel in the drainer, and stalked away.

Felicia spun around and followed him, flinging dish soap across the counter and onto a sack of apples. "What was that you said?" she asked, more accusation in her tone than she'd ever used on anyone . . . Nicholas included.

Dave turned slowly. Anger was washed across his face like spilled paint. "I said"—he raised his voice—"like 'it just never came up' that you didn't want to be a pastor's wife?" He slammed his fist on the counter.

Felicia remembered gratefully that Nicholas was visiting Jake, Melinda from the day-care center's son, whom he'd met there.

"What do you mean, 'didn't want to be a pastor's wife'?" she said, piercing every word as if darts were spewing from her mouth. She threw the dripping sponge toward the sink to punctuate her question, but it landed with a *splat* on the toaster instead.

Dave raised his hand to rub his forehead. "I mean, you have never signed on to our ministry, Felicia. It's as if you have your job and I have mine. But that's not how it works in ministry. This needs to be a partnership."

"No way, Dave. You can't put this off on me. This is not some two-for-one thing. When we met, you were in sales. When we got married, you were still in sales. You never asked me to help with your job then. But two years into our marriage, *you* decided to go to seminary. I worked *and* had a baby while you went to school. Then it was *your* choice to be a pastor. And now you think I should drop everything to help you do a job you chose? When was the last time you stopped by *my* office and helped stuff envelopes?"

"Help stuff envelopes?" Invisible bullets were shooting in both directions now. "I can't even get you to go to a ladies' Bible study. Do you think I would expect you to lower yourself to stuffing envelopes?"

"Oh, I get it. So you want me to 'lower' myself, is that it? I don't see you having trouble spending the money I bring in from my job—which is twice what you're making, need I remind you? Or do you think your pastor's salary is what paid for that new TV you love so much?"

They both glanced over at the fifty-inch flat screen in the family-room corner. Dave had insisted it was too ostentatious for a pastor's house, but Felicia had surprised him with it anyway for Father's Day. "We can invite the youth group over for movie parties," she'd assured him when he'd balked. But then, about a week after they got the TV, Dave amused Felicia by admitting with a grin that he didn't know how they "ever lived without it."

"Hey, I am in ministry, not business. What I am doing is a calling from God and affects souls, Felicia. What you are doing affects—"

He had gone too far. She went in for the kill. "Nobody? Is that what you want to say, Dave?"

"No, but I don't understand why you can't be more involved in church ministry like—" Dave stopped short.

"You mean like Nancy Borden?" Felicia burst out. "Is that who you were going to say, Dave? Your girlfriend, Nancy Borden?"

Dave stared openmouthed at her with such a mixture of surprise and hurt that Felicia knew she had now gone over the top. But there was no turning back now.

"My what?" he asked in a strangled voice.

"You can call her whatever you want, but I know what's going on."

Dave's face turned from sour to amused. "Okay, I'll bite. What's going on?"

Felicia was so angry she felt like acid was burning the inside of her mouth. "Don't try to play it off, Dave. I know you two have something going on, and I wish you'd just come clean with me so we can get on with our lives. But you need to know that I will fight tooth and nail for custody of—"

"Whoa, stop." He held up his hand. "What are you talking about? Custody? Felicia, *there is no affair going on.* Why would you think I'd do something like that?"

Felicia told him the basis for her suspicions—the note, the meetings, the roses.

Dave laughed. "I think you've been watching too many of those Lifetime movies. First of all, you need to understand that Nancy Borden is a lonely lady. She lost her husband three years ago, so she throws herself into taking care of everybody, not just me. She was overinvolved in the planning of that VBS—to the point where I almost asked her to step down as director."

Now Felicia was the one openmouthed.

He motioned for Felicia to join him over on the sofa. They sat down, but Felicia was careful not to touch Dave. She didn't want him to think he was off the hook quite yet.

"Now, about the note. At one of our VBS meetings, she was complaining about some shoulder pain from working too long in her garden. So I gave her that tube of Mentholatum that you bought me when I strained my calf playing basketball with the men's group. So even though the note made it sound that way, I *didn't* rub her shoulders—I gave her a tube of rub!"

Relief flooded over Felicia, but she needed to hear more.

"And then the flowers. Kay Jennings volunteered at the last minute to oversee all the crafts for the VBS because you know Janet Wright had to go for her hip replacement. So Nancy offered to cut and arrange roses from her garden to give to Kay as a thank-you."

Felicia's relief was turning to embarrassment.

"I can't speak for why Nancy threw away your soup or why she seems to, as you say, supersede you everywhere in the church. But I'm guessing it's unintentional. Like I said, she was a completely at-home wife and mother whose husband is now dead and whose kids are grown and moved away. She has a need to be, well, needed."

Felicia tucked one leg underneath her on the sofa, then clasped Dave's hand. She still wasn't comfortable with Nancy's intentions—those stories from the seminary wives haunted her—but she was overjoyed to know that Dave wasn't pursuing anything.

Yet that didn't make up for what she perceived as Dave's view of inadequacy in her.

"I thought for sure you were having an affair because Nancy represents everything you want—and I'm not any of that," Felicia said quietly as she ran her free fingers over Dave's hand. "And I know lonely women can fall for their pastor because he's such a great spiritual leader and all."

Dave pulled his hand away and used the tips of his fingers to lift Felicia's face. He gazed tenderly into her eyes. "*Mi amor*, I don't want you to be like Nancy. God knows I was about bored to death working with her and that VBS committee. I was so glad when it was finally over last week. Those women have nothing to talk about except what they're making for dinner and the latest episode of *Oprah*! I like a woman who can talk stocks and sports with me—and one who knows how to wear a red dress when she goes on a date with her husband to a fancy-schmancy restaurant in the big city."

They both chuckled.

He reclasped her hand. "But I do need your involvement at church. It seems like you want nothing to do with the ministry, and I want the affirmation and closeness that comes with a shared ministry."

Felicia was quiet as she considered Dave's words. "You know, earlier this year I was at that pastors' wives tea where I met . . . uh . . . anyway, the speaker said that being a pastor's wife is a calling. But you're right in what you said earlier. I didn't sense the calling, and I didn't sign on to being a pastor's wife. I'm not one of those women"—Felicia saw Mimi's face—"who grows up preparing to be a pastor's wife. Not that there is anything wrong with that. It's just not the core of who I am. My number one call is to be a disciple for Christ, and my number two call is to be your wife and Nicholas's mother. And I know I haven't been that great at it, but I'm trying."

"And your number three?"

Felicia thought, then laughed. "Housekeeper?" she asked meekly, batting her eyes.

Dave snorted. "Seriously. I think we have that covered for now with Becky anyway."

Felicia jumped around to face Dave. "Oh, speaking of Becky, the weirdest thing happened the other day."

"What, did she drop by with some latkes or something?"

Felicia laughed. "No, silly. I called her to make sure we were still on for tomorrow morning, and her husband answered."

"So?"

"*Sooo* . . . this is how he answered." Felicia dropped her voice to a man's tone. "'Hello, Rabbi Eli . . . I mean, Cohen residence.'"

Dave looked unimpressed. "He's a rabbi. Big deal. You knew she was Jewish."

"Yes, but she told me her husband worked at the tool and die plant over in Cheeksville. How could he do both? And why would they be living in Red River if he's a rabbi—the closest synagogue I know of is in Cincinnati, isn't it?"

"Yep. Huh." Dave reached down and fixed his sagging left sock.

Felicia was disappointed that Dave didn't recognize the possible conspiracy. Then again, her perceived "sinister plots" weren't proving to hold much water these days. "Maybe you could invite him to that pastors' breakfast thingy? That way if he accepts we'll know the truth, but if he doesn't—"

Dave threw his hands in the air, shook his head, and laughed. "You are *quite* the businesswoman, *mi amor*—persuasive as all get out!"

"I got you to marry me, didn't I?" Felicia asked with a twinkle in her eye, then she turned serious. "You know, I have to say I *do* have a calling to be a businesswoman. But that doesn't mean I can't be more involved in church too. Besides, I have a couple of surprises for you."

Felicia filled Dave in on her new Tuesday-night Bible study and on the comedy night at Brew-Ha-Ha that she'd arranged with the singles' pastor.

"Wow." Dave looked stunned. He wrapped his arms around Felicia as he kissed the top of her head. "I owe you an apology. I've been way too hard on you. I keep thinking about everything I have to do to get this church motivated again, but I forget that you are a fish out of water here. LA is a long way away, and you've given up an awful lot to follow me toward my calling."

"Eh, no problem," Felicia said. And this time she meant it. It felt good to snuggle. It had been weeks since they'd been close like this. "Home is where you and Nicholas are. Of course, it would be nice if that home had warm winters and good malls—"

Dave play-swatted her on the arm. "Once we get this church up to a thousand on Sunday mornings, I'll start applying to Hawaii pastorates only, okay?"

"Mmmm, and San Diego would be okay too."

Their beach dreams were interrupted by the ringing phone. Felicia popped up to get it, noticing yet another small run in the foot of her hose as she marched to the kitchen wall and grabbed the receiver.

"Hello?"

"Oh, hi, Felicia. This is Melinda. Jake's mom?"

"Hi, Melinda. Is Nicholas ready to come home now?"

"No, but I need you to come get him."

"Is there something wrong?"

"Well, yes. I just caught him biting Jake. And when I tried to calm him down, he bit me!"

Felicia turned toward Dave. His head was back against the couch, obviously still dreaming about churches near palm trees and ocean breezes. "We'll be right there."

Hearing Felicia's tone, Dave looked up with concern.

"It's Nicholas. He's biting again."

"I thought we had that licked. So to speak."

"As did I. And at the day-care director's house, of all places! What are we going to do?"

Dave jumped up and grabbed his car keys. "We could yank out his teeth, I guess."

Felicia laughed. She wasn't sure what to do about Nicholas, but she sensed a confidence between her and Dave that she hadn't felt in a long time.

Starting toward the door where Dave was waiting, Felicia stopped to remove her snagged pantyhose. She placed them on the counter next to a bottle of clear nail polish, making a quick mental note to repair them later.

Dave raised his eyebrows. "Why don't you just throw them away and use a new pair tomorrow?"

Felicia slipped on her sandals. "Because sometimes it's better to patch a snag than start over," she said, grabbing his hand and giving it a squeeze as she started out the door.

CHAPTER 40

Jennifer

Monday, August 28
7:14 p.m.

Jennifer was sorting through a box of baby clothes and toys when the door-bell of the women's shelter rang out. Stella, the shelter's director, walked by the front room and motioned Jennifer to follow her to the door.

Stella looked out the window to see if the woman outside was alone. When she said she was, Stella unbolted the door. The staff called the shelter The Fortress because of its security, but everyone knew that the extra measures were necessary to deter angry boyfriends and husbands whose battered girlfriends and wives were inside. In fact, the building had no sign announcing it—all clients were referred by other agencies, and volunteers had to sign an agreement not to identify the building's location to anyone.

As Stella held open the door, a haggard brunette walked in. At first she appeared to be in her thirties, but when the woman took off her scarf—revealing sores and spots on her head and neck—Jennifer realized she couldn't have been much more than twenty-five.

"Hi, I'm Stella, and this is Jennifer. And you are?"

"Jess. Jessica, actually. Jessica Graham," she said in a near whisper that revealed a Kentucky accent. Even though it was a warm night, her body was shaking as if she were chilled. "The women's health center downtown said I should come here."

Stella motioned to a side office, and Jessica headed that direction. Stella started to walk behind her, then stopped and turned back to Jennifer. "Why don't you join us, Jennifer, so you can reacquaint yourself with the intake process?"

Jennifer dutifully followed the two women into the office, which used to be a bedroom. The shelter was a converted two-level house with a bottom floor that was used for offices. The top floor had a TV room, four bedrooms, and two bathrooms to house women until longer-term accommodations could be found for them. Jennifer had spent two weeks in room 2 when she was a client.

As the women sat down around a table, Stella handed Jessica a bottle of water from a box on the floor. "Are you hungry?"

Jessica shook her head.

After taking down some basic information, Stella asked Jessica why she was at the shelter.

"My husband. He's . . . he's hittin' me. And I can't . . . can't take it no more. Especially now."

"Have you contacted the police at any point?"

That's when Jessica looked at them for the first time. As Jennifer peered into the young woman's watery dark eyes, she remembered how horrible she had felt—helpless and beaten down—when she'd first arrived at the shelter thirteen years ago.

"The police? Huh, that's funny," Jessica said, then looked back down.

Stella glanced at Jennifer, then back at Jessica. Stella's cool yet persistent manner made her an effective director for the shelter. Jennifer made a mental note to try to emulate Stella when she started doing intakes again. Jennifer knew she had a tendency to get too emotionally involved with the women.

"Jessica, the first step in getting"—Stella consulted the sheet she had filled out—"Ron away from you is to contact the police and place a restraining order against him. Do you want us to help you do that?"

Jessica looked up again. This time Jennifer saw anger in the young woman's eyes. "Yeah, well, when you go callin' down there, be sure and ask for Sergeant Graham." She shook her head.

"Sergeant . . . Graham?" Stella asked. "Is that a relative or something?"

"No, that's Ronny," Jessica said. Her shoulders started to heave as she sobbed. "He's a cop."

8:06 p.m.

While Stella called the shelter's liaison at the police department—a woman named Stephanie who had become a police officer after surviving a near-fatal attack from her ex-husband—Jennifer showed Jessica around the shelter.

"Here is our chapel, in case you want to pray or have someone pray with you," she said, holding back a door to the house's former dining room so Jessica could see in.

"Will y'all make me do some kind of religious thing to stay here?" Jessica asked in her Southern twang.

"If you mean, do you have to attend church, we would like for you to. But you don't have to in order to stay here." Jennifer remembered how relieved she had been to hear that when she was taken into the shelter.

"Good," Jessica breathed.

The two climbed the carpeted stairs to the second floor. A pregnant woman, her hair in braids, waved at Jennifer as she darted into the bathroom.

"Will she get to stay here until her baby is borned?" Jessica asked.

I hope not, Jennifer thought. Every time she saw Melissa, the pregnant woman, she felt a pang of anger because she knew this was yet another child—making a total of four—that Melissa would not be able to provide for. Jennifer had fantasized about being at the baby's delivery and snatching it away for her own.

Jennifer tried to sound cheerful, despite her pain. "We are working on getting her situated somewhere else before the baby is born. Let's go down there to room 2 and get you settled."

When they got to the door, Jessica waited for Jennifer to open it. "Go ahead, Jessica. Open the door to your new life." Jennifer knew it sounded corny, but she wanted to be encouraging. She remembered how overwhelmed and scared she'd felt when she was faced with the opening of that same door.

Jessica turned the knob, opened the door, and surveyed the pale yellow and white room. "Wow," she said with big eyes. "This is really nice."

"Yes, it is, isn't it?" Jennifer was pleased that Jessica seemed enamored with the space.

She had talked Sam into allowing her to spend the money on redecorating it—the room she had lived in those years ago—as part of her new commitment to the shelter. Father Scott had been right about his instruction for Jennifer to work with the women and their children at the shelter. Jennifer still wasn't pregnant, but volunteering at the center had reassured her that she had a nurturing instinct. And that instinct and love overshadowed any influence of her mother's poor parenting. If she did ever have a baby, she wouldn't be destined to repeat the same patterns as her mother.

And she knew Sam would be a great father. Gentle. Loving. Caring. Protective. Present. All the things her own father . . . and later her stepfather . . . were not.

Jennifer sat on the bed and patted the spot next to her. "Jessica, have a seat. Let's talk about what you need to get on your feet again. Did you bring any clothes with you? How about—"

"It feels so good for someone to finally know," Jessica interrupted, seemingly oblivious to Jennifer's questions. Her eyes stared off into space. "I never could tell no one. I mean, all our friends are Ronny's cop buddies and their wives or girlfriends. I couldn't trust any of 'em. And who was going to believe *me* anyway?"

Jennifer stopped and thought about what Jessica said. She'd never considered the similarity between being a pastor's wife and a cop's wife, but it was there. "How have you dealt with the loneliness and having no one you could open up to?" she asked, secretly hoping to find some insight for her own situation.

"I, well, I met up with someone else."

Oh, here we go, Jennifer thought. *Do these women always have to be sleeping around and . . .*

Jennifer stopped her own internal diatribe as she remembered that her situation hadn't been much better when she'd arrived at the shelter. *But at least I wasn't having an affair on my husband!* she argued. Of course, she was living with someone outside of marriage, but that wasn't as bad. Was it?

"So, this 'someone else,' does he know what Ron did to you?" Jennifer asked, trying to hide her cynicism.

"No. I kept on making excuses about the bruises. He's a cop too," Jessica said matter-of-factly, then lifted her hand to a red scab on her cheek. "I think he was just putting up with me to get me in bed, though. He probably didn't care if Ronny beat me or not."

Some women might have wondered why Jessica would stay with a bully husband and an uncaring boyfriend, but Jennifer understood. She lightly brushed a few strands of hair back from Jessica's eyes.

"We get ourselves into some pretty nasty messes, don't we?" Jennifer said. "You know, by the time I got here, my boyfriend had almost knocked out my hearing in my left ear from hitting me against the wall so many times."

"That's why I left when I did," Jessica said, rubbing her abdomen. "I knew Ronny was going to kill this baby, and maybe me too."

Oh, great. Another prego I'm going to have to endure around here. Can't we just minister to battered menopausal women?

Jennifer pasted on her pastor's-wife smile. "Oh, so you're pregnant then?"

Jessica nodded as Stella walked into the room. "Okay, Jessica. Tomorrow morning Sergeant Steph will be over to talk with you about the restraining order. And don't worry. I told her about your husband, and she promised to make this confidential."

Jennifer popped up off the bed. "I'm going to run down and see if we have any clothes that Jessica might like until she has a chance to get her own."

She slid down the hall, happy to escape any further talk about Jessica's baby. As she bounded down the stairs, she heard the doorbell ring. Worried that it might be Jessica's husband, she peeked out the side window before going to the door.

But what she saw was just the back of a lady as she darted on yellow high heels to her car, jumped in, and drove away quickly.

Jennifer stood watching the taillights of the woman's car fade in the distance. And she wondered: *Why on earth was Kitty Katt here?*

Lulu's Café

Tuesday, August 29

12:20 p.m.

"You told him that?" Jennifer's mouth was agape.

"Yes, I did," Lisa said, feeling freer than she had in a long time. "I thought he was going to pass out when I dropped that bombshell on him."

"But then you clarified it, right?" Mimi asked, concern on her face. "You told him you meant you didn't want to be married the way the relationship was going."

Lisa nodded. "Yeah." She grinned like a Cheshire cat. "But not for a while. I let him sweat bullets first."

"That's my girl!" Felicia clapped her manicured hand down on the table.

"And did he sweat bullets?" Jennifer asked.

"Well, he tried to blow it off, like he's done for the past three years," said Lisa. "All the excuses about how he's a senior pastor now and . . . you know the routine. But something must have gotten through to him because he said he didn't want to lose me." She paused. "We'll see if he means what he says long-term. But it's a start . . . and it's been more than two weeks since then."

Lisa went on to explain that she laid it all on the line—just like Mimi had told Felicia to do with Dave. "I told him the truth. That I love him. That I want to support him and God's call on his life . . . *our* life together. But he's become so consumed with being Super Senior Pastor, that he's neglected the most holy of human relationships—our marriage. How can you minister and build God's kingdom if you're not ministering and building God's kingdom at home? I told him that, as a pastor, he's expendable. He could leave the church tomorrow, and God would find someone else to fill his role. But nobody else can or should fill his role as my husband and the father of our children. Only he can be my husband. And if he isn't, that void may cause me to sin by looking for someone or something else to fill it—something not God-honoring.

"I realized something else while I was talking to him," Lisa continued. "I think part of God's design for marriage is to serve each other—and sometimes serving means telling the cold, hard truth instead of letting the status quo go on."

"Serving in that way is a huge risk," Felicia agreed. "I found out the hard way that I wanted to please my husband, but not necessarily serve him. It was easier for me to make chicken enchiladas, his favorite dish, or massage his feet, which I knew he'd enjoy and appreciate, than to confront him about Nancy Borden."

"But did you?" Mimi piped in.

"I did. But not right away," admitted Felicia. "I was all gung-ho when we talked about it last time we met. But somewhere between here and Red River, I lost all my confidence again." She hung her head. "Actually, I didn't say anything to him until a few days ago. I think I only did it then because

I flew off the handle and started spouting off all sorts of stuff to him. Oh, and I knew I'd have to answer to you guys!"

Lisa couldn't take it anymore. "Well, is he having an affair or not?"

Felicia broke out into a huge grin. "No ma'am, he is not. He's not the sharpest tool in the shed when it comes to appropriate relationships with female church members. I think he's finally figured out that one—not from my persuasive skills, but from the soapy sponge I was waving at him."

Lisa nearly choked on a swig of tea.

"But nothing physical ever happened," Felicia explained. "And there wasn't an emotional affair either, thank God. He promised to back off from spending so much time with Nancy. And he swore he'd never again be alone with a woman." She grinned. "Unless it's one *mamacita*—hot mama— which, of course, would be me."

Lisa joined the other women as they cackled. She couldn't believe how long it had been since they'd last been together. Almost a month. After their spontaneous Saturday get-together and all the bombs that had been dropped then, they'd decided to skip the following Tuesday's lunch so they could spend that hour doing some serious praying for their situations.

But then their next meeting, last Tuesday, had to be canceled, since she had a migraine and Felicia had come down with the flu. It felt good to be together again. Lisa hadn't realized how much she depended on these women until they weren't together. *Absence really does make the heart grow fonder, I guess,* she thought as she watched them eating and laughing and chatting.

"Well, not to change the subject, but I am," Jennifer said brightly, cutting into Lisa's thoughts. "A lot has happened since the last time we were together."

Jennifer told them about her last conversation with Father Scott and how he said he didn't want to see her anymore. She said she was pretty upset by his announcement, but after calming down and really thinking about his words, she was grateful he'd taken that stance with her.

"You just talked about serving our spouses." She looked at Lisa, then at Felicia. "But I think that's a concept for all relationships. Father Scott took a huge risk in serving me by telling me the truth." Then she told them that she'd started volunteering at the shelter.

"Oh!" She raised her hand. "And I almost forgot about the juicy part. Last night, while I was at the shelter, none other than our own beloved Kitty showed up—snuck up, really—and dropped off a box. And here's the weird part. She did it at night, and she rang the doorbell, then rushed back to her car, as though she didn't want anyone to know. When I opened the box, it was filled with maternity clothes and an unsigned note that said,

I know these aren't the latest style,
but I thought they might work for someone.

I sorted through the box. The clothes aren't from the eighties, when Kitty had her kids—they're seventies style."

"That seems out of character for Kitty." Lisa flicked her long hair over her shoulder.

"But also, that shelter is strictly secret. Only trained volunteers and city social workers know where it is," Jennifer said. "So how did she? Unless she volunteered there—which seems highly unlikely. Plus, why be secretive about dropping off a box of clothes?"

"I'm surprised she would do anything secretive—we know how she loves publicity!" Felicia offered.

"That reminds me," Mimi chimed in, "a month or so ago, while I was volunteering at the food pantry, a woman who works there told me that Kitty stopped by and donated money for a specific person—a younger man. I wonder what the connection is. Or if there is a connection."

"What is she hiding?" Jennifer held a chicken finger in the air. "An affair with a poor man on food stamps?" She munched down.

"Hardly her type, don't you think?" Felicia said with a frown.

The PWs all munched quietly for a minute. Lisa tried to imagine what Kitty was up to. *All these loose ends . . .*

"I have some connections in Cincinnati," Felicia finally said. "What if I did a little snooping on the Grand Poobah of snoops?"

Felicia's suggestion made Lisa uneasy. She didn't want to think she was gossiping about Kitty. And even though Kitty's behavior as of late had been highly suspect, she still wasn't sure if it was their business. "I don't know . . ."

"Come on, Lisa," Jennifer prodded. "After all the cruel things she's said to or about you and your husband in the past, don't you want to dig in a bit to find out how to skin the cat?"

"But that's not our right," Lisa defended. "God wouldn't honor or bless us for doing something hurtful to her—even if she deserves it."

"It's not as if we're going to blackmail her or anything," said Felicia. "I just want to know what the skeleton in her closet is. She acts as though she doesn't have one. But I can guarantee you she does." She licked her lips, as though in anticipation of a great challenge. "And I mean to find out."

Lisa could almost hear them whispering, *Here Kitty, Kitty, Kitty . . .*

Jennifer

Friday, September 1
7:46 p.m.

Jennifer opened the medicine cabinet and popped a few ibuprofen. She had cramps. And they were especially severe this time.

Sam was sitting in the living room, looking back and forth from the Reds game on TV to his sermon notes.

"I've got cramps," Jennifer said as she stood in the archway between the hall and the living room, her hands on her hips as she waited for a response from Sam.

"Did you eat something bad?" Sam asked absentmindedly. Her continued silence forced him to glance up and acknowledge her. The expression on her face must have helped him click on what she'd meant.

"Well," he said with a slight smile, "I guess I don't have to scheme about how to get you in the mood the next few nights."

Jennifer let her hands fall off her waist as she walked toward him. "Sam!

I can't believe how selfish you are! Dr. O'Boyle said this medicine would work within three months, if it was going to. Obviously it hasn't, and while I'm trying to deal with it, you're just thinking that you'll have to miss sex for a few days?"

Sam removed his glasses. "And this from the lady who is all about sex every month during those few 'precious' days? I'm tired of feeling like a sperm donor for you. Is that all making love is to you, Jen—just a way to make a baby?"

Jennifer stood in front of him and crossed her arms over her chest. "I can't believe how unsupportive you are. For all we know, it's *you* who's the problem, not me."

"It's not me, all right?" Sam was almost yelling, which caused Jennifer to take a step backward.

Sam shook his head and jumped off the couch. Snatching his keys off a hook on the wall, he muttered, "I'm outta here," and burst through the front door. The screeching of his tires on the driveway made Jennifer's head swim. It was a scene she'd seen played out time and again growing up with her out-of-control mother and relentless stepfather.

A spark of desperation reminded Jennifer that a bottle of red wine was in their bedroom closet—a Christmas gift a few years back from a neighbor who didn't realize they weren't drinkers. Jennifer had been meaning to cook with it but kept forgetting.

Maybe a few drinks would help, she thought as she stood frozen in the living room, with TV commercials blaring between innings. Then she realized that, as adept as she'd become at opening beer bottles in her pre-Christian days, she'd never opened a wine bottle and didn't know how. Besides, there was no way she was going back to her drinking days. No matter how bad things got.

Jennifer threw herself on the couch. *Is this it? Is my marriage over? Maybe that's why God hasn't given me a baby. He knows I wouldn't be able to hold my marriage together.*

She remembered what Father Scott had told her several weeks ago—about how she needed to stop focusing on having a baby. But that wasn't as easy to do as volunteering for the women's shelter or praying for others. She couldn't just turn off her deepest desire.

The ringing phone interrupted her thoughts. "God help anyone calling here right now," she said aloud as she reached for the phone. "Hello." Her voice wasn't exactly hospitable.

"It's me."

Jennifer recognized Sam's voice over his crackling cell phone. A businessman in the church had given Sam his used phone when he got a new one, but it never seemed to connect correctly. Jennifer figured that's probably why the guy dumped it on Sam to begin with.

"Where are you?"

"I'm sitting in the Kmart parking lot down the street."

"Oh."

"Jen, I had to get out where I could breathe . . . and think."

"Have I made it so you can't even breathe?"

"No, it just seems like you walk around with this sandwich board that says, 'I want a baby,' and that's pretty much all you are about these days. I'm tired of it, Jen."

Jennifer sniffled. "Me too. I'm so sick of dealing with this, Sam. It's just that . . . hello? Are you there?"

His phone had cut off.

Jennifer clicked off the phone just in time for it to ring again.

"Hello?"

"Sorry about that. This phone stinks, doesn't it?"

They both chuckled, glad for the comic relief.

"Sam, can you come home so we can talk? This phone thing is weird."

"Yeah, but there is something I need to tell you, and I think it would be easier if I do it now."

A huge lump formed in her throat. Was he leaving her? After all, she hadn't been much of a pastor's wife lately . . . or a husband's wife, for that matter.

"Okay, shoot." She had been working on acquiring Stella's calm demeanor.

"There's a reason I've been telling you I don't need to go to the doctor for that sperm test."

"I know. The porn thing."

"No, that was just an excuse." Sam took a deep breath. "I know my sperm are fine because—"

Silence.

"Sam? Are you there?"

Not again!

Jennifer clicked the phone off. It rang so quickly that she didn't bother with "hello." She got right to the point. "Okay, Sam, I got to where you said 'I know my sperm are fine because' before I lost you."

A man cleared his voice, then asked, "Mrs. Shores?"

Oh no! "Uh, yes, hello?"

"This is Allen Simmons. We met on Sunday? Pastor Sam asked me to call if I could get us a tee time tomorrow."

A hot wave of embarrassment ran up Jennifer's neck. Had he heard? How could he not have? "Sure, uh, Allen. I'll be happy to let him know. Have a nice eve—"

"I didn't tell you what time yet."

"Right. Sorry, I just—"

"Yes, I realize I must have interrupted something."

Jennifer didn't know what to say to end the uncomfortable silence.

Fortunately Allen didn't let it go on too long. "If you could just let him know it's seven a.m. at Running Pines."

Jennifer offered a quick good-bye and clicked off the phone. She was staring at it, wondering if Sam would call back, when she heard his car pull into the driveway. She picked up the TV remote and turned off the game.

When he walked through the door, Jennifer could see that he had been crying. Strange—the relief that washed over her, knowing that he felt deeply enough about what was happening to be emotional.

"Sam? Are you okay? Your phone dumped out again and I never heard what you said."

He didn't say anything, so she followed him to the couch.

He took another deep breath. "Emily was pregnant when she died."

Jennifer's mouth fell open. Tears formed in her eyes. But instead of jealousy over another pregnancy—as she so commonly felt these days—she was flooded with compassion for Sam. "How come you never told me?"

"I . . . couldn't talk about it. Only her parents and her sister knew. She was about ten weeks along when the accident—"

"Oh, Sam. Oh, sweetie."

Sam buried his head in her neck, and she put her arms around him. She couldn't remember the last time she'd comforted Sam. It seemed as if she was always the needy one these days.

Sam lifted his head up. "I know you think I've been ignoring you when you talk about all of this infertility stuff. But I think I was avoiding it because when I thought about you being pregnant, I got this horrible feeling like—"

"Like you thought I might die too?" Jennifer pulled a tissue from her pocket and tenderly wiped Sam's cheeks.

"I . . . guess so. And then when I was sitting over at the Kmart lot, I got to thinking about how awful this is for you, and how you must feel like a failure."

Hearing the word, Jennifer stiffened, defensive. Then it occurred to her that "failure" was exactly how she felt.

"And I didn't want you to feel that way. If anyone is a failure, it's me for not being honest with you and supporting you the way I should have."

They both sat back on the sofa. Jennifer was winded, like she'd been on a fast walk. Just hearing Sam's explanation healed weeks of hurt and sadness.

"You might not believe this," she said, "but I'm becoming okay, I think, with not having a baby."

"You're right—I don't believe it," Sam said lovingly as he hugged her.

He *was* right, and she knew it. But something had changed in her. The teeter-tottering of suffering and survival in her life had made her stronger. For the first time, she sensed that as much as she wanted a baby, she wanted God's approval and Sam's love first.

"You know, there are other ways to have a baby," she said finally.

Sam kissed her on the cheek. "I will do whatever you want, sweets. Why don't you call that Dr. Leprechaun and see what he suggests?"

Jennifer giggled. But as she thought about phoning Dr. O'Boyle, she remembered Allen's message for Sam.

"Oh, before I forget, Allen Simmons called and said you have a tee time tomorrow."

"Great!"

"Yeah, well, you need to hear the rest of it first." Jennifer filled him in on what Allen had heard.

Sam guffawed with laughter. "Well, I guess I won't have to worry about embarrassing myself over my golf game tomorrow!"

43

Lisa

Saturday, September 9
1:30 p.m.

Lisa was reading the latest John Grisham novel when the doorbell rang. She glanced at the clock on the wall. *1:30.*

Who in the world could that be? she wondered as she creased the corner of the page she was reading.

She checked her reflection in the hall mirror on her way to the door. Her hair was shoved up in a ponytail, but large strands at the front had fallen out. She was wearing no makeup, her grubby cleaning jeans, and the I ♥ New York T-shirt she'd purchased as a souvenir when she and Joel went there ten years ago.

She tried to fix her hair quickly and pinched her cheeks to give them a little color, but realized it was hopeless. She hoped it was nobody from the church—or Publisher's Clearing House. Callie kept entering those contests under Lisa's name, swearing that the Bartons were going to be the next big winners.

She hesitantly opened the door after the doorbell chimed again. There, on the other side, stood someone behind a huge bouquet of flowers. Then the flowers dropped just enough to reveal the person's face.

"Joel?"

Joel handed her the flowers, then lifted his index finger to say, "Hold on," while he ran back to his car. He reached into the backseat and pulled out two life-sized cutouts. One was of Joel, standing with his arms outstretched, as if asking for a hug. The other was of Lisa, her arms folded and smiling wryly.

Lisa threw back her head and laughed. "Where did you get those?" she asked as he carried them up the walk to the porch and set them down, so they both faced her.

"I grabbed a few of our old photos and took them to Walgreens to their photo department." He seemed pleased with his surprise. "I made these to remind us of who we used to be . . . and who I still want us to be."

This was the old Joel she'd fallen in love with way back in youth group. The one who'd wooed her all the way through high school and even while he was away at Bible college. She smiled at him, wanting to believe he'd changed, but suspicious and afraid to get her hopes up.

Joel ran back to the car one more time and extricated a huge banner from the trunk. The sign was attached to two wooden stakes, one at each end. He walked across the lawn and stuck one of the stakes into the ground, then carried the other end past the front of the house to the other side, where he again pushed down the stake. He stood to the side while Lisa read the words:

I'm sorry for being a jerk. I love you more than anything.

Lisa crossed her arms, mimicking the life-size cutout next to her. "Really?"

"Really," Joel said, walking up the steps onto the porch. "Okay, well maybe not more than double-fudge brownie ice cream. But almost. Definitely not more than Bengals games."

Lisa laughed again.

Joel knelt down and groaned. "I'm getting too old for this," he complained laughingly. "I need you. I love you. I was wrong and had my priorities messed up. Will you forgive me?"

She patted her foot next to his knees and wrinkled her brow. A mischievous grin stretched across her face. "I'm not really sure about this. My twin and I will have to give it some serious thought."

"Well, seriously think about *this*." Joel jumped up, grabbed Lisa in his arms, and kissed her passionately.

A passing car honked, and Lisa felt him start to pull away.

"Look, it's the Abramsons!" He pointed and waved.

"Hey, Pastor, what are you two lovebirds doing?" Ron Abramson yelled as he slowed in front of their house.

Lisa expected Joel to forget she was there, as usual, and rush to talk church business with Ron.

Instead, he drew her closer. "I'm doing what any husband would be doing to a wife this beautiful," he called. Then he leaned in and kissed her again.

Lulu's Café

Tuesday, September 12

11:55 a.m.

Lisa opened the door wide to Lulu's and dragged in the life-size version of herself, being extra careful not to hit or bump her "self" on the door sides. As soon as she got in, she stood her twin on its feet and straightened her beige gauzy blouse and maroon skirt.

"What in the world are you doing?" Gracie asked as she stood behind the counter, getting ready to pass an order to the cook in the back.

Lisa sighed contentedly and fluttered her eyelids like a flirt. "I've decided to clone myself, Gracie. Pretty lovely, huh?"

Gracie rolled her eyes. "You're a stiff!"

Lisa burst out laughing and wound her way toward the back of the brightly lit café. Everything looked and felt wonderful to Lisa today. She was a woman in love. Her husband had surprised her this morning with breakfast in bed and a foot massage. Then, since the kids were in school, she and Joel had sneaked into Ricky's bedroom and played The Legend of Zelda on his television. They had laughed and kissed and enjoyed each other like they used to. Lisa had even taken him into her closet and showed him the nurse uniform again. Yes, it had been a wonderful morning. And she couldn't wait to tell the girls.

She looked out the front window of the restaurant to make sure none of them had arrived yet. Then she slid into the far seat and angled "herself" next to her.

"Did you want two iced teas today? One for you and one for yourself?" Gracie yelled toward the table and laughed. Several of the other customers—the ones who'd been watching Lisa's spectacle—laughed too as they glanced toward Lisa and her alter ego.

"Just the one for me," Lisa answered loudly. "My twin's trying to cut back on the caffeine."

Just then Lisa caught sight of Mimi's green minivan pulling into a parking space in front of the restaurant. Lisa double-checked her cutout's position, slightly readjusting it. Then she picked up her napkin, placed it on her lap, and sat straight up, trying to act as casual as possible.

As soon as Mimi stepped through the door, she did a double take. Then she squinted her eyes in surprise. Lisa gave a little wave in greeting and watched Mimi break into a wide grin.

Mimi got to the table and spoke directly to the cutout. "Hey, Lisa. Who's your friend?" Then she glanced at Lisa. "Hi, I'm Mimi. You must be new in these parts."

"Whoa-*hoh*!" Jennifer's voice rang out through the café. "That's a looker!" She strode over to the table and squeezed in next to Mimi, across from the cutout. "I didn't realize we were now allowing visitors to our lunches." She held up her hand. "Don't tell me. I gotta see Felicia's response first." She glanced down at her wrist. "Speaking of, she better hurry. I'm not sure how long I can hold out staring at the Doublemint twins."

A minute later Felicia entered the café and stood just beyond the doorway while she removed her sunglasses and waved at Gracie. She looked splendid in her violet jacket, patterned scarf, and ebony slacks.

Gracie waved back and nodded toward the back booth. "There's a pastor's wife back there who's lost her mind," she called.

Several of the customers laughed again.

Felicia turned toward the back and the two Lisas. She wore an odd expression, as though she was trying to figure out what to make of the sight. But when she drew closer, her face brightened. "Excuse me," she said to the cutout, "but I believe you're in *my* spot." She glanced over at Lisa. "Makeup?" she said, sounding impressed. "I like the eye shadow and lipstick. Very good color choices for you."

Lisa beamed and flipped her hair back. Then she started to push the cardboard duplicate from the booth. Felicia grabbed the side closest to her and helped lift it into the booth behind theirs.

"Okay, spill," commanded Jennifer. "This is too good."

Lisa couldn't keep quiet anymore. "Joel made this for me! And he made one of himself too. I can't believe the change I've seen in him."

"I don't get it," Mimi said. "Why would he make a life-size cutout of you and him?"

Lisa felt like a schoolgirl gushing over her new boyfriend as she told them about how he had arrived home that past Saturday with the banner and cutouts and flowers. "My heart was doing backflips over seeing the old Joel—the one I fell in love with. But I was a bit skeptical that this was just an act and he'd go right back to ignoring me. But he hasn't. We've started praying together again in the mornings and going for walks. He's asked me to keep him accountable about his time spent at the church. And he's started telling me he loves me. Every day."

She paused to catch her breath. "I know we still have a ways to go—

especially to make up for the last three years. And there are still moments when he doesn't get things right. But he's *trying*, and that's what's so great to see."

"That's great!" Jennifer exclaimed.

Felicia clapped her hands. "Good girl, you held out."

"Lisa, I'm so happy for you," Mimi said and teared up. She fanned herself and half laughed. "I'm so hormonal!"

Gracie arrived with a tray of drinks. "Do you women make a habit of crying?" she asked as soon as she looked at Mimi. "I've never seen women gush as much as you girls." She shook her head again. "I took the liberty of guessing your drinks." She passed the 7UP to Mimi. Jennifer got the milk, Felicia the Diet Coke, and Lisa an iced tea. "I would have brought one for your friend," she motioned behind them with her head, "but she looked like she needed something stronger to loosen her up." She chuckled at her own joke.

Jennifer groaned.

"Get it?" Gracie said. "Loosen her up? She's a stiff."

"Yeah, we got it." Felicia shook her head. "You need to keep your day job, Gracie."

She rolled her eyes again and walked away.

The women went back to discussing Joel's transformation until they'd exhausted that topic, then moved on to Mimi.

"How's the pregnancy coming along?" Lisa asked.

Mimi nodded. "Well, the nausea is gone, but now I'm tired all the time. So I've had to let some things go in the house."

Lisa, Jennifer, and Felicia gasped together in mock shock.

"I know, I know." Mimi laughed. "Mark promised he'd help more around the house—we'll see how long that lasts. And the good-for-nothing slobs I call children have been threatened that they'll have to sleep on the back porch if they don't keep their rooms clean.

"But the biggest surprise is that I'd forgotten how emotional I get during my pregnancies. My hormones go all over the place. Last night I cried at an insurance commercial! Then during the baseball game, I started to cry again when one of the players hit a grand slam. Mark and the kids were on their feet cheering the Reds, and I just sat there, crying and clapping. MJ took one look at me, groaned, and said, 'Mom, get ahold of yourself. It's embarrassing.'"

She laughed. "But I've felt the baby move now, which awes me that I'm creating life. Mark came home the other day, and I asked him, 'What did you do today?' After he finished telling me, he repeated the question to me. I told him, 'Oh, I made a baby today.'"

She *aahed* quietly. "This baby has made my whole life out of control. No . . . my life was out of control *before* then. But somehow this baby has helped me refocus on what my priorities *should* be." She looked next to her at Jennifer, then across at Lisa and Felicia, and her eyes filled again. "Relationships. Family. Friends. And for the first time—with my life falling to pieces around me!—I've started to feel at peace. It's really wonderful."

"Mimi." Jennifer touched Mimi's arm. "I want you to know that seeing you pregnant when that's all I've ever wanted has been such a struggle for me."

Mimi nodded, as if understanding Jennifer's confession.

"And I want you to know that *I* know I've been selfish, wallowing in my self-pity," Jennifer admitted. "Shame on me that I haven't been supportive to you. But I really am going to be there for you. And I really am so glad that you're on the road to finding peace. I'm so sor—"

Mimi cut her off. "Don't you say another word. All's forgiven and forgotten. Don't worry about it again. We're friends—in the great, easy times, and in the tough ones. We need each other."

Jennifer nodded and threw her arms around Mimi.

Gracie had started to walk to the table to take their order but halted, evidently noticing Jennifer and Mimi's embrace. She waved her hand at them and muttered to no one in particular, "Think they're here to camp. I should just make up an order for them and put it in. They probably wouldn't even notice . . ."

Good old Gracie, Lisa thought and grinned. Then she turned her attention back to her friends seated across from her.

"I also have an announcement to make," Jennifer said, breaking her embrace and scooting around to face Lisa and Felicia. Lisa could hear a collective intake of breath from Mimi and Felicia, as if waiting to hear that Jennifer was pregnant.

Jennifer shook her head. "No, it's not that. So you can breathe again. But it may be something better. I'm talking to God again. *Really* talking to him."

"Thank you, Jesus," Lisa said, genuinely thrilled to hear Jennifer's words. "I've been praying for you to find your way."

"Well, I still have a long way to go. But I'm taking baby steps. So to speak!"

"What finally did it for you?" asked Felicia.

"The oddest thing, actually." She leaned back a bit. "Emily."

"Sam's first wife?" Mimi asked.

"Sam's first wife," Jennifer agreed.

"Wait," Lisa said. "I'm confused. How did a dead woman who used to be married to your husband draw you back to God?"

Jennifer explained that Friday before last, when she'd started her period again, she'd snapped and gotten into an argument with Sam about how he didn't seem to care that she wasn't pregnant. "I knew I was overreacting, but I couldn't stop myself," Jennifer admitted. "I needed to know he was hurting like I was. Well, I said some pretty nasty things to him, and he walked out. When he came back awhile later, we'd both calmed down enough to talk. For the first time, he told me about Emily. That she was pregnant when she died."

Mimi gasped and brought her hand to her mouth.

"He said he was afraid to get his hopes up about having kids because he was afraid if I got pregnant something would happen to me too."

Jennifer started to play with the ring of water around her glass. "My nurturing instinct kicked in, and I realized how much I love my husband, and what he's already gone through."

"He was afraid of losing you," Lisa said sympathetically. "See? I told you he loves you."

Jennifer cocked her head to one side and smiled. "Yes, he does."

"And God?" Lisa probed.

"Somewhere during that time—when I was holding Sam in my arms as we talked about his past—I realized God loves me too. Something seeped into my soul . . . a whispering that said, *I will never leave you. I know your name. I have it written on my palm. I love you . . .*'"

Jennifer pressed her lips together and blinked hard up at the ceiling. "*I love you.*" She looked back down and stared at Lisa. "What kind of God would let me question him and be angry with him and totally ignore him, then tell me he loves me? How could I not run back to him?"

"He loves our 'who,' not our 'do,'" Lisa answered. "He loves *who* we are and *who* we're made to be in Christ. Our *do* doesn't affect how he feels and thinks about us."

"I like that," Mimi said.

"So do I," agreed Felicia.

"Have you told Pastor Scott of your renewed faith?" Mimi asked.

Jennifer shook her head. "Not yet. I was thinking of asking Sam to take off a Sunday and join me at Mass. I don't know what exactly they do in that church during Mass, but that place was really the beginning of my faith journey back to God. And I want Sam to share it."

"Well," Mimi said, "I suppose if God can show himself through birding and pottery, he can use a Catholic to help a Protestant!"

"So what about you?" Lisa faced Felicia. "What's going on with you?"

Felicia looked around the restaurant, then pointed at herself and said in a Brooklyn accent, "You talking to me?"

The women cackled.

Lisa jabbed Felicia's elbow. "Watch it. Or I'll sic my twin back there on you."

"Okay! Okay!" Felicia lifted her hands above her head, covering her face in mock self-defense. "Things are good," she said happily, but more seriously. "Dave loved the Brew-Ha-Ha idea for the singles outreach."

"Yes!" Jennifer put two thumbs up.

"And the Brew-Ha-Ha owner, Jim, seems open to hearing about God. He found out I'm a pastor's wife and told me, 'Any pastor's wife who's willing to help a guy whose bar is in trouble for manslaughter must be okay,'" she said, imitating the owner in a deep voice and slight Southern accent. "I asked him if I could talk to him about God sometime. He shrugged and said . . ."

Felicia donned the deep voice again. "'Well, I have to be here for the singles thing, now don't I? So I guess I'll have to hear enough about him then.' Hey, it's better than him saying a straight no!"

The best thing, though, Felicia said, was that Dave was beginning to understand her. Her need for individuality and her calling to professional life out in the world. But that didn't mean she didn't want to be involved in his ministry too. "I promised I'd try my best to support him, and he promised the same to me. Now if I can just be as successful in my child-rearing efforts as I am with my career."

The women chuckled.

"I'm telling you," Mimi said, "try that mouth spray. Just make sure you get it in the kid's mouth *before* he bites you!"

"That'd be the day." Felicia smiled. "Nicholas knows I'd string him up. Anyway," she continued, mildly wincing, "the other day Dave handed me a brochure for a pastors' wives' retreat next March—"

Lisa, Jennifer, and Mimi nodded and groaned in unison. "Kitty Katt."

"Leave it to Kitty to plan and advertise six months in advance," Lisa said incredulously. "I guess so we don't have any excuse to say no."

"So you received it too." Felicia's tone indicated more of a statement than a question.

"My husband thinks that because he enjoys getting together with the other pastors," Jennifer said, "I would enjoy getting together with the other pastors' wives."

"Well, you do," said Mimi slyly. "Every other Tuesday, forty miles from Red River."

"Look," Lisa added, feeling the need to explain why she didn't want to go to the other pastors' wives' functions, "there's this level of stuff that we can't admit to one another because we're all in competition in some way. Or is that just my feeling?"

The others all *mmm-hmmmed* in agreement.

Felicia jumped in. "So I have to ask. Honesty time. Has anybody told their husbands about our meetings here?"

Lisa held up her hand. "They're secret lunches. Why call them 'secret' if anyone else knows?"

"Think about it," Mimi said. "I can just see my husband blurting out to Norm Katt about my coming here to get together with pastors' wives, and Norm telling Kitty. That's all we'd need—her to show up and take over. This isn't a dog-and-pony show, you know."

The words had barely passed Mimi's lips when who but Kitty Katt herself entered the café . . . with the younger man they'd seen in the second-story window from across the street.

CHAPTER

45

Lulu's Café

Tuesday, September 12

12:41 p.m.

"You have to be kidding me." Felicia inclined her head toward the front of the café.

The others turned and gaped. "Of all the timing," Jennifer muttered.

"Speaking of dog-and-pony show," Mimi's words almost tripped over Jennifer's.

Kitty Katt stood in the entryway of Lulu's, dressed in a black suede jacket with fringe that matched the color of her hair, slightly off-black pants, and those yellow pumps.

Felicia glanced at the pumps and remembered what Mimi had said once at an earlier lunch. *She looks like she's wearing bananas on her feet.* It had seemed funny at the time, but that was before Felicia watched her standing there in broad daylight, cuddling up to a man *who was not her husband.*

"I don't believe what I'm seeing," whispered Lisa. "Being a pastor's wife is Kitty's entire life and existence. I can't imagine that she'd give that up. And especially not for the likes of him."

Felicia looked at the man. He was taller than Kitty, about five foot eleven, with dark hair and stubble across his face and neck. He appeared to be in his midthirties, Felicia figured. His clothes spoke of good quality but were wrinkled and dirty.

Felicia started to think quickly. She knew the girls couldn't hide. It was only a matter of seconds before Kitty recognized them. Thinking of Nancy Borden and how Felicia had felt when she thought Dave was having an affair made Felicia decide to do something rash. She hoped the others would understand.

Felicia scooted out from the booth before anybody could stop her and started walking toward the front of the café. Behind her she heard Lisa whisper, "Felicia, no!" Felicia straightened her back and walked purposefully to Kitty.

Kitty noticed her and swallowed hard. Then, apparently, she regained her composure. She jutted out her chin and stiffened her back a bit. Then she flashed a toothy grin.

Even caught in her sin, she tries to maintain control! Felicia thought, incredulous.

"Kitty," Felicia said as she stepped directly in front of her, "what a pleasant surprise to see you here. Of course, you know some of my friends." She gestured toward the booth in the back. Then she pivoted back to study the man's hardened face. "I'm Felicia Lopez-Morrison." She extended her hand. "And you are?"

"This is Seth," Kitty interjected. "A friend."

The man sneered as he stepped backward toward the door. "I'm taking off," he said in a raspy, hardened voice that matched his looks. "You can hang out with your friends."

"Seth, wait," Kitty called after him as he walked out the door, turned left, and soon disappeared from sight.

Kitty turned back to face Felicia and pursed her ruby red lips in a tight-lipped smile. "Well, well," she said nastily. "What a true gift running into you has been." Then she turned on her heel as if to leave.

Oh no, you don't. Felicia grabbed Kitty's arm. "Come join us for lunch, Kitty. I insist."

Felicia knew she may have had trouble confronting Dave about his indiscretions, but she had no problem talking about this woman's.

"I really don't think—" Kitty broke off when Felicia propelled her toward the booth in the back.

The inquisition was about to begin. Felicia watched Jennifer jump out of her seat and grab a chair from a nearby table, which she sat in. Felicia inwardly cheered her. *Good girl. Put Kitty in the booth next to Mimi, where she won't be able to escape.*

When they arrived at the booth, Kitty dug in her heels. "I'd rather stand, thank you. I won't be staying long."

"Actually, Kitty," Jennifer retorted, "there are some things that need to be cleared up. So we'd prefer you stick around and do that. Unless . . ." Jennifer looked down at her fingernails and picked at one. ". . . you'd rather we have a chat with your husband."

Kitty pursed her lips again. "You're making a big mistake by threatening me, Jennifer. And besides"—she lifted her chin—"what would you say? You don't know anything."

"We know you were standing arm in arm with a man who isn't Norm," Felicia said, still holding Kitty's arm.

"Your word against mine." Kitty tried to break the grip, but Felicia pushed her into the seat.

Mimi joined in. "We also know that you dropped off a thousand dollars at the food pantry for a man we can only assume was the one who just left."

"And," Lisa said as Kitty opened her mouth, "what exactly was the conversation you were having when I saw you in the post office?"

"I have no idea what you're talking about. I never saw you in the post office."

"Hmmm," Lisa answered. "I seem to recall the words, 'Loving you until the day I die, no matter what you do.'"

"I was talking to my husband."

A snort passed from Mimi.

"Fess up," Jennifer said. "We know you're having an affair."

Kitty looked genuinely shocked and appalled. "I would *never* cheat on my husband!"

Felicia stared at Kitty from across the table. "Wow, this gives us some great conversation material at the next pastors' wives' tea."

"You have no idea with whom you're dealing," Kitty said determinedly, but Felicia thought she heard a slight hesitation in the woman's voice.

"Nor do you," Felicia shot back, ready to meet the challenge. *I work at a top PR firm*, she thought. *I've handled worse than you.*

Kitty sat back and closed her mouth. The women continued to throw comments and accusations toward her, but nothing worked. Kitty Katt simply wasn't talking . . .

1:19 p.m.

"We've got all day, you know," Mimi said. "We can stay here until Sunday morning if we need to."

Kitty was seemingly unfazed by their entire courtroom drama.

Then Felicia felt someone squeeze her arm. It was Lisa. When Felicia's eyes met hers, Lisa shook her head just slightly. "This isn't right."

"What?" Felicia mouthed the words and watched Lisa shake her head again.

The next time Lisa spoke, she did so with a quiet compassion. "Kitty," she started, "before you arrived, we were being honest about some of our fears and failures." She paused. "My husband and I have been struggling for more than three years, and I was on the verge of leaving him. Felicia loves her job but feels threatened because of the church's expectations of what a pastor's wife should and shouldn't be."

What is she doing? Felicia thought, angered that Lisa was telling all their secrets. *All this time we've been vulnerable—so Lisa could blurt everything about our lives to the queen of arrogance?*

"Mimi's pregnant and doesn't know how she's going to manage accomplishing everything that's on her plate," she continued.

Felicia saw Mimi swallow hard, then cough.

"And Jennifer has been dealing with anger toward God because he hasn't given her a baby." Jennifer shot Lisa a harsh look before focusing on her lap.

But then Felicia caught something that surprised her. She saw Kitty break just a bit as she shuddered slightly and glanced at Jennifer. *What is Kitty thinking?* Felicia wondered.

"The truth is, Kitty," Lisa said softly, "we've all been struggling with some painful issues and trying to figure out where we fit in and where God fits in in all this. This is probably difficult for you to understand, but sometimes we all wonder if God loves us or if he's forgotten about us. Sometimes his silence is deafening to us. Or at least to me. And we've felt as if there's not another soul we can confess these things to—except each other."

Once again Gracie started to come over to their table, but Felicia shook her head. She hoped Gracie would understand. Fortunately Gracie caught the meaning and backed away quietly.

Time seemed to stand still, as if it, too, was wondering if Lisa's plan, whatever it was, was going to work.

Maybe she's hoping Kitty will be killed with kindness rather than accusations.

Just as the thought passed through Felicia's mind, she noticed Kitty begin to wilt. Then the woman dropped her head in her hands. Her shoulders began to shake and heave violently but silently.

At a loss for what to do, Felicia looked around at her friends. They all just sat there awkwardly, as though none of them had expected this outburst to occur. While Felicia wasn't sure what she had expected to happen, she was pretty sure she didn't imagine Kitty would droop into a sobbing, silent mess.

After several minutes Lisa leaned over and touched Kitty's head. "We all understand how difficult ministry marriages can be. We carry such weighty expectations—from other people, from our own families, and even from ourselves. And they're impossible expectations to meet. But I'm sure if you talked to Norm and told him—"

Kitty looked up. Her perfect hair was smashed in the front and falling in disarray at the sides. Her mascara was smudged to the point she looked like Tammy Faye caught in a rainstorm. Her lipstick was now smeared outside her lip lines. And the tears had stained her cheeks and drawn wide streaks down her face.

"That man you saw me with—apparently several times—is *not* a lover," Kitty insisted. "I would *never* cheat on my husband." The way she said it convinced Felicia that Kitty had to be telling the truth. She knew Kitty would not allow herself to look that way or to lose control like this. Not even over an affair. *It just wasn't Kitty's style,* Felicia assured herself.

"Kitty, I believe you," Lisa said compassionately. "You have to admit, though, your actions seem rather suspicious."

"No," Kitty said weakly. "You just don't know."

"Try us." Mimi finally spoke up.

Kitty considered Mimi, as though she were seeing her for the first time. "That boy—that man—is . . . my son."

1:29 p.m.

Felicia's mouth dropped. Mimi squinted again as though she didn't hear correctly.

"When I was sixteen," Kitty began to explain, "I got into some trouble. I was a pretty wild child. Very rebellious. My 'boyfriend' was older and married. When I got pregnant, I had these grand ideas that he'd leave his wife and run away with me. But of course that never happened. And when my parents found out, they kicked me out of the house. I had no place to go."

"Until you found the women's shelter," Jennifer volunteered. At Kitty's look, Jennifer explained that she was working there the night Kitty dropped off the clothes.

"I held on to them for all these years because they were my connection to my son. But when he reentered my life, I no longer needed the clothes. I wanted them to go to somebody who did."

Jennifer nodded.

"So you had the baby and gave him up for adoption?" Lisa offered.

Kitty stared absently toward the wall. "Once Seth was born and I placed him for adoption, I went back home and tried to pretend nothing had ever happened. It seemed like it should be easy enough, since that's what my parents did. But I could never shake what I'd done."

"You were young," Mimi consoled her. "You had nobody to turn to. And you did a very brave thing by giving the child a chance to have a loving family instead of aborting him."

"No," Kitty answered. "I found out later his wasn't such a loving family. He ended up in foster home after foster home. Now he has an alcohol problem and can't keep a steady job. I've been trying to give him money and talk to him about God, but he keeps pushing me away. I've never talked about this. Not even to Norman." She put her head in her hand.

"When Seth came back into my life, I didn't know what to do. My motherly instincts kicked in, and I wanted to love him and take care of him—which he wasn't interested in and still isn't." She gulped back a sob. "But the other part of me didn't want him around to ruin what I'd worked so hard to achieve. Isn't that terrible?" She sobbed outwardly now. "I can never forgive myself for what I've done. How can God forgive me? And who would accept a pastor's wife with my past?"

At those words, Jennifer chuckled. "We would. We're in the ministry. We're not perfect!"

"Don't you think you've been forgiven for what you've done?" Lisa asked.

"That's right," Mimi interjected. "God loves the *who* and not the *do*." She looked proudly at Lisa, who nodded her approval.

"Kitty," Felicia spoke up, "your secret's safe with us. But one thing you need to do is accept God's forgiveness, and then forgive yourself. And if others struggle with your past, they'll answer to God. He's crazy about you."

Kitty smiled weakly at Felicia. "You're right. I know that in my heart."

"I've realized something," Mimi said. "I think all of us, in some way, are desperate for something. Maybe that desperation is what keeps pushing us back to God."

"I think so," Jennifer added. "God allows us to become desperate, because in those moments, if we stay open to him, that's when we really seek him and find him."

"Can we pray for you?" Lisa asked Kitty.

Kitty looked surprised. "Nobody's ever prayed for me before."

"We'd consider it an honor." Lisa bowed her head and prayed one of the most beautiful prayers Felicia had ever heard. It felt as though God was whispering in Lisa's ear exactly what she needed to say. She talked about Kitty's desperation for forgiveness and learning to accept what Christ had paid the price for her to have.

When Lisa finally said, "Amen," Kitty smiled. The first genuine smile Felicia had ever seen from the usually unflappable Katherine Fleming Katt.

Then Kitty looked at Felicia questioningly, as though to ask, *May I get up now?*

Felicia waved her arm to say, *Be my guest.*

Kitty stood and straightened her outfit. "I should go fix myself. Excuse me."

She took two steps toward the ladies' room on the other side of the café before she pivoted on her yellow trademark pumps. "I'd appreciate it if you don't tell anyone about Seth until I'm ready."

The women at the table nodded.

"And I promise not to tell anyone about your meetings here every other week. Of course, I understand why you meet." A tight smile now lurked around the corners of Kitty's mouth. "You smaller church pastors and wives *should* stick together. You feel incompetent when you're meeting with people like my husband and me, who minister over large congregations. The competition is so much less intimidating when you're in the same league."

She swiveled back toward the ladies' room as all the PWs stared, incredulous, at each other. Then, once again, she turned toward them. "Oh, and another thing. Just so we're clear. I am *not* desperate. I have everything quite under control."

And with those final words, Kitty Katt patted her smashed hair and walked away.

"Can you *believe* her?" Felicia said, steaming. "After what just happened? After that beautiful prayer? After all our sympathy?"

Mimi giggled. "And all is back to normal in Red River."

"You know, though, there is one thing we can learn from Kitty," Lisa said.

"Excuse me?" Felicia couldn't believe Lisa would suggest such a thing after what had just happened.

"Think about it. She has this burden she's been carrying around, eating her up inside—and she has no one to share it with—not even her husband."

Jennifer rolled her eyes. "What are we supposed to learn from *that*? Sounds kind of familiar to me."

"Exactly! Except for this group." Lisa pointed toward Jennifer. "We have each other, but she shuts people out. There are thousands of PWs who have no one to talk to, to be real with. But somehow, we found one another."

Felicia looked at her friends. Lisa was right. The PWs griped about their husbands, their kids, and their churches, but they all knew they were just blowing off steam. Even in their most desperate moments, they could still appreciate all the good things about being pastors' wives. Witnessing changed lives. Helping others grow in their faith. Watching God's love permeate people and knowing it makes an eternal difference.

"So should we thank her for this 'learning' experience by sending her an invite for our next lunch?" Mimi offered facetiously.

Felicia launched a sugar packet in Mimi's direction while Lisa and Jennifer groaned and laughed.

Jennifer grabbed her half-empty glass and held it up, then motioned for the others to do the same.

Felicia, Lisa, and Mimi followed.

"Ladies," Jennifer announced, "a toast. Here's to true friendship, happy endings . . . and most of all, to desperation. It's *all* good."

About the Authors

Ginger Kolbaba is editor of *Marriage Partnership* magazine, a publication of Christianity Today International, and author of numerous books, including *Surprised by Remarriage: A Guide to the Happily* Even *After* (Revell). She lives with her husband, Scott, in the Chicago suburbs. Visit Ginger at www.gingerkolbaba.com

Christy Scannell is a freelance writer and editor. She and her husband, Rich, a newspaper editor, live in Southern California. Visit Christy at www.christyscannell.com

CHECK OUT MORE GREAT FICTION FROM
HOWARD BOOKS!

He was a young widower who feared he might never recover from the pain of losing his wife to cancer. She thought she was satisfied with her solo lifestyle until she discovered a romantic mystery. When their worlds intersect in the pages of a secondhand paperback, their lives will never be the same.

ISBN: 1-58229-578-6 • $12.99

Stephy is just trying to make it as an empty-nest mom until she finds her hands full when she becomes a production assistant for a reality television show. Her challenges mount until a series of God-directed events bring a real reality check to the mayhem around her.

ISBN: 1-58229-487-9 • $12.99

As if the jolt of becoming a single mom isn't enough, Natalie Coombs is facing new stresses as the director of the crisis pregnancy center. Natalie crosses professional boundaries and puts her personal safety at risk to put old wrongs to right.

ISBN: 1-58229-433-X • $12.99

COMING SOON...

SECRETS FROM LULU'S CAFE
SERIES

A Matter of Wife and Death

It's a new year—and a new set of problems and praises—for the pastors' wives of Red River, Ohio. Mimi's baby was born on the most hectic night of the Christmas season, and that was just the beginning of his disturbing presence in the Plaisance family. Even more unsettling is Mimi's attraction to her kids' school principal.

Meanwhile, the jets in Felicia's mind are just starting to land smoothly when her boss wants her to hop on one—and move away from Red River, leaving her struggling pastor-husband and biting young son behind. Can she save her job and her family?

Lisa is fighting her own battles in the Barton household, where teen daughter Callie has decided being a PK is not OK, so she's refusing to go to church. Lisa secretly wishes she could join her and not have to deal with the faction that is trying to split their congregation.

As for Jennifer, she's still trying to get pregnant, but time is running out, as are her options. How far is too far in trying to achieve new life?

And then there's Kitty, who continues to try to burrow her way into the PWs' lives. She finally guilts them into attending the regional pastors' wives retreat, yet the event turns out to be anything but a safe haven. When one pastor's wife does not return home, all are forced to reevaluate their callings and their lives.

How will the PWs cope with these latest challenges to their marriages, families, and churches? Find out in *A Matter of Wife and Death*, the second installment in the Secrets from Lulu's Café series by Ginger Kolbaba and Christy Scannell.

HOWARD
Fiction
A DIVISION OF SIMON & SCHUSTER